HARD PURSUIT

BARRIE TAYLOR

Black Rose Writing | Texas

ISBN: 978-1-68513-430-3
PUBLISHED BY BLACK ROSE WRITING
www.blackrosewriting.com

Printed in the United States of America
Suggested Retail Price (SRP) $21.95

Hard Pursuit is printed in Minion Pro

*As a planet-friendly publisher, Black Rose Writing does its best to eliminate unnecessary waste to reduce paper usage and energy costs, while never compromising the reading experience. As a result, the final word count vs. page count may not meet common expectations.

Writing a book was something I wanted to do since I was a kid, but to take something like this on you need life experience and knowledge. As time and life rolled on, both of those things came my way, as they do with everybody. I had the ideas swirling around in my head for months before I decided finally, to put pen to paper, literally. I like to write my first draft long hand.

I should start by thanking Karen and the rest of my family for putting up with me parking myself on the settee for hours on end while I put this story together. Thanks to Reagan Rothe and all those at Black Rose Writing for taking a chance on a first timer, without these guys, the book you now have in your hands would not exist. I'd also like to mention Sharon and Kevin, who as review readers, took the time to give me pointers. Thanks for your help.

My parents both loved to read and the bug bit very early. Growing up in a military household quickly got me an appreciation and respect for those who serve or have served, so this book is dedicated to all those at home, abroad, on the sea, on the land or in the air past, present and future.

Thank you, and I hope you enjoy.

HARD PURSUIT

ONE

Seated in the front seat of his Panavia Tornado GR4. Flt Lt James McCleland had his eyes fixed forward, staring to see anything as the aircraft skimmed over the wide expanse of the Afghan desert. His mission saw him as part of a three ship formation sent to bomb a factory suspected of producing chemical weapons.

Flying north from Camp Bastion, the three Tornadoes were part of a wider offensive launched that day to knock out installations suspected of furthering the Taliban's ability to make war.

Teamed with his navigator, Steve Peters the two had become a good unit, thinking and acting in tandem. Called up for service in the War on Terror, something that no-one particularly wanted to be involved with, they found themselves posted and quickly given this mission. Now they were here, hammering across the desert at 600 knots, armed with bombs, missiles and a fierce determination to succeed.

"Target ahead," the microphone distorted voice of Peters came through the bone dome. A quick look at the avionics told Jim that he was on the right track and the altitude was good. The gray shape of a concrete and glass building came into view, a large rectangular monstrosity that stuck out like a sore thumb against the reds and browns and beige of the surrounding desert. Jim flicked the arming button on his flight stick.

"Armed," he reported back. The Tornado gained ground on the target incredibly quickly. Jim pulled the nose up just a little and pressed his fire control button. Four bombs fell away, heading in the same direction of the aircraft as the forward throw guided them to the target. Straight and true, the bombs hit and detonated. A large cloud of dust and flame launched skywards as the factory disintegrated under the combined power of the Tornado's bombs. Jim put the aircraft down to the deck again, banked around and headed for home.

Then an urgent beeping in his headset alerted him to sudden danger.

"Incoming fire!" Peters shouted from the back seat.

"Deploy flares." Jim tried to remain as calm as he could as he slalomed the Tornado from side to side.

He knew that the incoming weapon was probably a heat-seeking missile, designed to home in on the big bomber's unmistakable heat signature generated by the RB199 engines. The flares blasted away and fell aft, but the warning alarm kept sounding.

"Chaff didn't work," was the comment from the back seat.

The Tornado was rocked by an explosion and the flight controls immediately went dead in Jim's hands.

With no directional or stability control, they were a dead duck and there was no response from the engines either. A trail of smoke billowed from the rear of the aircraft, and the acrid smell of burned metal and plastic filled the cockpit.

"I think it's time to leave. Bail out," Jim said with remarkable calm as he pulled the handle marked eject. He was suddenly aware of the sky rushing past his face as the powerful launch cartridge rocketed him and Peters away from the burning Tornado, which promptly nosedived into the ground and exploded in a tremendous fireball. That was the last thing Jim remembered before he blacked out.

Faint sounds and voices grew stronger and the darkness became a dull cloudy color, then his vision returned. His head ached. Jim awoke to a surly looking man. Not Arabic as he had expected but Caucasian.

What the hell was this? The room was cold and dark with hardly any light except for a single electric light bulb.

"J. McCleland, I assume?" the man said, leering at Jim.

"Yeah. That'd be me."

The man paced around in front of him. Jim realized that a couple of other guys were holding his arms.

"You and your friends destroyed my property. You interfered with my business. That makes me... unhappy." The guy had a Russian accent. A Russian in the middle of Afghanistan? Didn't he realize that his own war with this place had finished a couple of decades before? What had they stumbled into here?

"Good, I'm very glad to hear it!" McCleland shot back. Someone grabbed him from behind and pulled him up straight.

"Insolent and bad mannered. Two qualities I never thought were becoming of one of Her Majesty's officers," the man said. "I do not appreciate being spoken to in that manner."

"Well, that's your problem, isn't it? It's your move," was the cool reply. "I somehow don't think that the Russians have any business being in the middle of Afghanistan."

The Russian wheeled around on him. "We have no business? So says the man from a nation which kills people indiscriminately."

"You need to get yourself to an optician. Do I look like one of the Taliban to you?" Jim scoffed.

The guy holding Jim by his right arm moved their hand to his shoulder while grabbing him by his swept back hair. The Russian looked genuinely angry.

"No back talking, Mr. J. McCleland. You have a singular wit, but it will help you here." Krasnov went to a table and picked up a rather unpleasant looking metal object. It had a small, curved blade. "Why did you bomb my building?"

Jim looked at the scalpel. He could either bend to his captor's will, something that did not sit well with him. Or... he could bring his personality to bear. He rolled his eyes. "You want me to answer the question but you don't want me to talk to you. Make up your bloody mind, pal."

He decided on the name-rank-number approach. A punch to the face stopped that. He felt his wrists being tied behind his back. Something he remembered being told as a kid reminded him to stiffen his wrists and hands, which he did. It would give him more room to move should they bind him.

In the dim light, the scalpel blade was waved slowly in front of Jim's eyes.

"You will answer my questions, Mr. McCleland. Yevgeny Krasnov has never failed in his interrogations before." The Russian indicated to his two thugs to give their prisoner a work over.

"If you with hold anything, you will suffer. If you attempt to deceive me, you will suffer. If you forget anything, you will suffer. In any case, you will suffer, and then you will die."

"Is there an option for a chicken tikka masala with that?" Jim was determined to defy his captor, no matter what the cost.

Krasnov loomed large. "I want to know the military strength around your encampment."

Out of the corner of McCleland's left eye he could see one of them reaching for a two by four.

As the guy was turned away his line of sight changed just for a moment.

Now.

Jim kicked out and sent him sprawling, unprepared for the sudden attack, then turned and double fisted the second man with his still bound wrists full in the face. Krasnov went to pull a gun, but

McCleland ran, leaping at full speed into the air and landing a stunning drop kick to the

Russian's broad chest, which caused him to reel backwards.

Grabbing the gun from Krasnov's holster, he fumbled with the trigger against his bound wrists but managed to fire twice, the loud reports echoing through the chamber. The two thugs dropped to the floor. Slipping the bindings from his wrists, he kicked Krasnov in the face, sending the

Russian rolling to the floor.

"Looks like you just got bombed, pal."

McCleland bolted from the dimply lit room, burst through a door and found himself in a darkened corridor. Light dimly pinpointed one end of the corridor off to his left, which he turned and made for. If he was going to get out of this hellhole, it had to be now.

Dampness hung in the air making the walls and floor stink with the odor of stagnant water. No matter.

Jim realized he was still wearing his flight suit and the gun he had appropriated from Krasnov was in his hand. He padded along the corridor.

From behind him, he heard the Russian shouting for him to be stopped. He heard the hammer of feet and gunfire. Forcing himself down and backwards, the flowers of automatic gunfire bloomed towards him. The air ripped with the passing of the rounds that failed to find their targets. He pressed himself against the wall and fired towards the peals of flame. Yelps of pain and the soft thud of falling bodies came. Jim went back and scooped up any firearms he could get his hands on. In the dim light, he noticed he was holding a Ruger .357 revolver which must have come from an American officer that had suffered a similar fate to what he just had.

What were the Russians doing in the middle of the Afghan desert? It made little sense. They had no business being anywhere near here after giving up on their war with the country two decades before.

He shrugged such ideas from his mind. The priority was to get out in one piece. As an officer, it was his duty to effect escape if possible. He took off down the corridor again and took a pop at anything that moved.

Noticing the daylight growing stronger and the accompanying heat begin to fill the dank space,

Jim surged ahead and upon reaching the end of the hallway, there was bugger all except the whole Afghan desert in every direction.

Packing crates were dotted around. Supplies either dropped off or appropriated somehow. He had just seconds to make good his escape or he would surely be executed. He was sure Krasnov was just behind, about to appear with God knows how many of his people all baying for his blood.

Looking around, there was nothing to give away the underground base beyond the smoking remains of the building that he had bombed.

A truck parked nearby was being unloaded. Jim checked his ammo and the revolver's rounds were replaced. Keeping low and moving through the wooden boxes dotted around, Jim made his way towards the ancient vehicle which had clearly seen better days before popping up, his revolver ready just a few yards from his potential method of escape. At his approach the man unloading the vehicle dropped the box that he was carrying and began to pull his sidearm. Jim gunned him down without hesitation and then took care of the driver in the same way.

Hopping into the driver's seat, he started up and began to pull away. Another truck that was either being loaded or unloaded was at hand. The shawled features of the workers began running towards him, guns ready. In the mirror, he saw Krasnov emerge from the mouth of the tunnel, who began frantically waving, indicating for Jim to be stopped. The other truck started, probably aiming to ram him but wasting no time, McCleland aimed at the fuel tank, and fired his two remaining rounds.

Fortune remained on his side. The opposing vehicle was utterly consumed by a fireball, sending flaming debris in all directions and ending Krasnov's efforts to recapture him. Dropping the truck into a higher gear, Jim drove off into the barmy evening, heading for as best as he could work out based on the sun in the sky was, home. The situation would certainly make for an interesting mission report, until he realized Steve would not be there to co-sign it. That stung Jim deeply.

Steve was a good guy and now he was gone. He slammed the steering wheel with his fist. He could not afford to get sidetracked now.

He planted his foot down hard. He needed to get as much distance between him and the Russians as he could. Who knows what they had stashed around here to deal with would be escapees?

Arriving at a rough road, he swung the wheel and headed towards the direction of the setting sun.

TWO

Six months later

Air Vice Marshal John "Black Jack" Cartwright had never seen so much gold braid. He knew that the Air Marshal had been held in high regard, but he was surprised by such a turnout. St. Clement Danes Church was scene of something akin to a state funeral. The quaint building surrounded by more impressive looking monoliths built to promote big business seemed out of place in this part of London.

The blaring horns and smell of unburned fuel in the stop start traffic permeated the air, and combined with the steady rain, it made for an unwelcome atmosphere.

But it didn't stop several hundred mourners from turning out, including the man's widow and grown children. The Air Marshal had died in suspicious circumstances of which the official investigation had found nothing, but in the halls of the air staff, the furor was immense.

He had bought a narrow boat to enjoy his retirement, intending to explore the nation's canals and on the very next day, the handsome, and brand new, vessel had exploded at its moorings. The former Victor tanker pilot and decorated veteran had apparently gone down with his ship.

"But, he can't die! He was supposed to outlive all of us!" was the general protest.

Indeed, the Air Marshal had a seemingly endless supply of energy even in his later years. To have simply disappeared and been declared dead was unthinkable. Cartwright took his seat near the back of the church. He had only had cursory contact with the man, but not turning out to pay respects would be frowned upon.

"We're gathered here today to remember the life of Air Marshal Rod Norman Berry. He was a man of enormous courage and dedication. He served the Royal Air Force…"

The speech went on. Cartwright knew the details and had no real desire to listen to a blow by blow account of his former CO's life and career. He knew what he wanted to know. Berry was a loyal and proud man who left no stone unturned in his pursuit of keeping the skies over Britain safe. He had been a hard taskmaster but never less than a fair man.

The reading ended and Cartwright turned his thoughts inwards. There must be something more to the man's mysterious and timely demise. It seemed rather too convenient for such a thing to happen just after Berry's retirement.

Cartwright's eye was caught by a familiar face. Air Chief Marshal George Simpson. The subordinate nodded to the superior. The service came to a close and the mourners filed out, Cartwright among them.

He found a quiet bench within the church grounds and sat down. It had been a strange day.

As the crowd filed out of the church, the hug of people would make a perfect cover for someone with suspicious motives, Black Jack thought. Movement caught his eye. Off to his left an officer wearing Royal Navy commander's stripes doubled over, favoring his leg. Suspicious, Cartwright went to him as the man began choking, foaming at the mouth. A heart attack did not strike so suddenly. Poison most certainly did.

"Take care of him!" Cartwright commanded.

Searching about him in an attempt to spot the attacker, the pointless endeavor ran concurrently with a jacket being placed over the now dead navy officer's form. A flurry in the crowd got Cartwright on his feet and in pursuit. He cursed the fates, wishing that he was armed, but the regulations being as they were, he had to do this as is.

Heading up the street towards Aldwych, Cartwright saw on the other side of the street a figure moving along, not running but certainly walking faster than usual. Without a radio, he couldn't call in police backup, but the wail of sirens approaching gave him some hope. Crossing the street, Black Jack kept the miscreant in sight. If whoever it was got to an underground station, then any hope of apprehending him would be lost.

"Hey!" he shouted.

Whoever it was heard the hail and jogged along the road, indeed making for Temple tube station.

A police car tore around the corner from the opposite direction and headed towards them. The white car with its distinctive fluorescent yellow markings raced along the road, despite Cartwright's attempts to get the attention of the driver.

No wonder the crime rate is so high if they don't pay any bloody attention, he thought grimly.

The fleeing form of the assailant had made it to the gray art deco frontage of the underground station and headed in to the main entrance, making for the escalator which would surely take whoever it was down to the platforms. With little other choice, Cartwright bounded down the metal steps of the traveling staircase in his efforts to keep up.

He reached the platform just as a train was leaving, and through the windows, he could make out the dark jacket and hat of the man who had caused the commotion.

His anger rising, Cartwright made his way back up to street level, not relishing the report he was going to give.

"The navy officer who bought it was Commander Phelps of the *Valiant*. Our colleagues at the Navy are... not happy, Jack." Air Marshal Simpson leaned forward, clasping his hands across the highly polished table. His office surrounding them was comfortable, if functional. A vast portrait of a Canberra adorned the wall on one side of the room.

The sunlight bathed the room in golden shards which were admitted through the window behind Simpson's desk.

He rose at the address, thinking that this was an official order. "Sir."

Simpson gestured for him to retake the seat and he sat down opposite his friend. "Funny business, isn't it?"

"Yeah," Cartwright agreed. "The game of life rolls on."

"I wasn't talking about that, Jack. I mean the Air Marshal and the commander going west." For two officers of such caliber to die in suspicious circumstances caused more than a little concern.

"I'll agree, something doesn't add up."

A folder was opened and placed in front of the Air Vice Marshal. Simpson pointed to the particulars of the report. "The autopsy revealed ricin. If you remember the Bulgarian guy who died in similar circumstances?"

That changed everything. This was no longer a suspicious incident, more an outright murder.

Black Jack nodded. "I do. Wasn't he tagged with an umbrella or something like that? The Russians denied the whole thing."

"Right," Simpson confirmed. "They did the same with the guy they irradiated right here on our doorstep too."

The case of Aleksandr Litvinenko had frustrated the police and security services recently. It had certainly left a lot of unanswered questions tied up in bureaucracy and red tape.

"Any connection between those, the funeral and the officer who was killed?"

"Beyond that they were both military officers? None at all."

On the surface, there was no angle to work from and no apparent way in to this case. However, Cartwright's intuition was telling him that a much bigger game was being played than simple coincidental murder of unrelated people.

"If someone is targeting the British military then it's up to us to find it and stop it. Someone was killed at an RAF state funeral, which makes this our responsibility."

"What are your orders, sir?" Cartwright asked.

The two men looked at each other. "I want you to take a look in to this. You have experience air side and in intelligence which makes you a good choice for a job of this nature. Something is going on, and we want to know what. I don't mind what methods you use, but keep it low profile, if you get my meaning."

"Why me, sir?" Cartwright asked, hoping the question wasn't too impertinent. "Surely this is more of a job for MI6 or Special Branch?"

The other man smiled. "Because you know when something is fishy and when something isn't."

Jack understood the implication of that, alright. "Yes sir."

A scratch of the chin and Simpson continued. "We're an emasculated force, Jack. The whole service and the other military units have been shrunk over the years. We have no real way of defending ourselves effectively anymore. If this is some sort of attack against us, we need to stop it before it goes too far." He looked at Cartwright. "I'm giving you a lot of leeway, Jack, but move quickly."

The gray haired, formidable man was thoughtful. "I'll need a small team of people and not just intelligence guys. I want a good pilot and a top investigator, and not a pair of yes men either. Those people are about as much use as a one-legged man in an arse kicking contest."

Simpson half smiled. "You want a pair of disobedient hell-raisers?"

"You don't send a poodle to hunt down a jackal, you send a wolf," Black Jack replied. "A Red Arrows pilot is no good, they're too well known and the white caps... I need something a bit more heavy hitting than that. And I'll need a place to work from. Somewhere here but not here, if you get my meaning."

Simpson nodded slowly. "I think that can be arranged. Hand pick whoever you like and do this in whatever way you see fit. I can arrange transport, equipment, anything you need."

Cartwright rose. "I'll get right on it."

The head of the RAF regarded the Air Vice Marshal. "Do you have any idea who you want?"

Black Jack knew exactly who he had in mind. He had been putting his feelers out with his findings thus far, but now it was time to lay his cards on the table.

"There's a couple of people I can think of. Working separately they're good, but put them together... it'd be explosive, but we'd get results."

"Nitro and glycerin then?" Simpson pursed his lips. "That goes against the concept of low profile."

But Cartwright didn't look as if he was about to be swayed. "Give me their names and you'll have them."

A folded piece of paper was handed to Simpson, who opened it. Seeing the two names listed, he could already tell that 'low profile' was not in either man's vocabulary.

"What about your plan for how you want to proceed?"

Cartwright was already thinking of a strategy to pursue. This would need careful planning and research. He had a lot of work to do. "I do have an idea. It's risky, but I think it's worth pursuing. And if my suspicions are correct, this is much closer to home than we know."

"What makes you say that?" Simpson asked. "That's a pretty big leap of faith when we don't have a full handle on the facts."

"Call it intuition sir." The AVM's expression was unreadable. "I'll need a few members of my old staff as well. People I can trust."

Simpson steepled his fingers. "Again, tell me who they are and I'll arrange everything. I know of a place that you can use to work from. It's pokey, but if you want to be out of the way, it's ideal."

Cartwright rose from the desk. "Thank you sir."

Air Vice Marshal John Cartwright had joined the RAF in 1973, straight from earning his A- Levels. Fast tracked for pilot duties after officer training, he had become a Vulcan co-captain, then graduated to captain in his own right. Once the Vulcan force had disbanded, he was posted to CO of a Tornado squadron and promoted to Wing Commander.

But life not flying led him to be unfulfilled and a posting to the intelligence branch, essentially to keep Cartwright out of the way had led him to take a hands-on approach to all levels of security.

His plans for a team of this type had been bubbling away in the back of his mind for years.

And now, after this situation had forced their hand, the head of the service had given him carte blanche.

William Clark awoke to darkness.

"Alexa, lights," he said, half asleep. No response, no acknowledgment of his request. If he had been in a higher class hotel or at home he would not have this problem, or he could call a sparky to grumble, but he was on leave. No doubt some lesser light would answer his request.

"This is Mr. Clark in room 558. Requesting service." Still nothing. "Dammit."

He moved to get up, only to find he could not arise from his bed. His ankles were shackled.

"What the hell?" he grumbled.

The bed felt strange. It was harder and more uncomfortable than he had remembered when he fell asleep.

The bed he had barely got used to was soft, cosseting and was specially designed to help the back relax after a hard day. The whole resort was like that; purposely designed to be as comfortable and restful as possible. A whole range of activities were on offer including hiking in the hills behind the resort that he had beamed down to, water sports, tennis, swimming, anything your heart desired. Clark had mentioned to Jim before he left the base that the squadron leader would have found none of those things appealing.

"Why Clarkie?" was the response.

"Because Jim, they're not risky enough for you!"

The team had been returning from their latest mission, and it had been yet another death-defying adventure for the members of Squadron Dark, which the British Broadcasting Corporation would no doubt hype to the heavens of the word got out. Fortunately, it had been shrouded in secrecy. It had certainly been an interesting experience and learning that they would pass close to the Aral Sea, Clarkie had requested a leave of absence. Upon arrival, Clarkie took a cruise around the bay. The water was pale blue and he had been able to make out the different fish and sea creatures under the clear floor of the launch. A very filling meal, in contrast to the food supplements served in the mess hall had filled a spot, and he had retired to bed early. In the morning, he had intended to take a walking tour of the arboretum which offered all kinds of wildflowers from across the region. As someone with green fingers, Haltwhistle would have loved that, Clarkie mused.

Considering what he had just awoken to, all of that was now a moot point.

Suddenly the lights came on and Clarkie found himself unfamiliar with his room. He had expected to see the sumptuous suite he had checked in to a couple of days before with it's bright, airy feel and see the view over the sea.

Instead the room was stone clad with no windows and a heavy metal door. And through that door now walked a Russian officer in the severe uniform that he recognized from the intel pictures he had to study.

Clarkie's lips parted as he recognized his foe.

"Krasnov! Where the hell am I? What are you doing here?"

The fearsome looking Russian had first been encountered in Prague when the British and the Americans had faced off against the old Bolshevik Alliance which had declared war. A secret mission to attempt to sway the Czech city's population to accept western intervention had failed.

The Russians had arrived before anything could be done, and the two sides had literally been about to open fire when the Czech government formally refused any intervention from either side and forced peace on both sides. Krasnov had been especially disappointed that he wouldn't get to go head-to-head against the British especially. He did not have much regard for the Americans, whom he considered uncouth, but the British had more guile and presented a more worthy opponent in his eyes.

Now here he was again. His demeanor and body language was intimidating at the best of times, and the offhand look he gave people was unnerving, especially combined with his shark-like smile.

"Ah, I am glad to see you awake and alert, William," said Krasnov. He moved towards Clark.

"What in blazes is going on here?" Clarkie spat. "Where am I? How did I get here?"

Krasnov cut him off with a wave of his hand and sat down casually across from Clark's bunk.

"All your questions will be answered in time, Wing Commander. But first I have a few questions of my own. If you co-operate, we can go from there."

"I was enjoying my leave but then apparently I'm not on leave anymore." The sarcasm was dripping so heavily from Clarkie that Krasnov could have caught it with a bucket. For his part, the steely Russian merely smiled darkly.

"Shore leave is unfortunately canceled for the foreseeable future. Leave can be re-arranged but first I would like to have little talk."

Clark quickly realized that the old name-rank-number routine would not work in this circumstance, but he duly went through the motions anyway.

"I see that the British method of resisting interrogation is alive and well," Krasnov observed.

"Let me guess. You want lots of nice juicy details from me about something and you're going to torture me unless I talk, something like that?"

Krasnov inclined his head, clearly enjoying the predicament he had placed the British officer in.

"And I'm supposed to be trembling with fear or something? Forget it, nothing is more terrifying than one of Haltwhistle's researched speeches."

"You are correct, Wing Commander Clark. May I call you William?"

Clarkie's jaw set. Over familiarity with people he didn't care for did not sit well with him.

"Do I have a choice?"

"Not really, William." Krasnov rose, and strode around the cell. His imposing 6'1" inch height matched by a broad, thick-set build which filled the uniform admirably. "William John Clark. Wing Commander, Royal Air Force. Graduated Bristol University in May 1998. Joined the Royal Air Force after an unfortunate divorce. No siblings. One daughter. Current assignment, RAF Waddington, Lincolnshire, England as commander of No. 1 Group, Intelligence, Surveillance, Target Acquisition and Reconnaissance better known as ISTAR. Have I missed anything so far?"

"I give you an A for doing your homework," was Clarkie's surly reply. "Is there any point to this?"

Clark did not like people pussyfooting around at the best of times, and he especially didn't like people throwing their weight about.

Now he had this barbarian killer grinning at him and reciting his personal details. He could have cheerfully strangled him repeatedly, if he could have just got his hands on his damned neck. Hell, had he just had that idea pop into his head?

Clarkie, you're supposed to be an officer, he thought to himself.

"As I was saying, I have a few questions," started Krasnov.

"Are you asking me for the secret of the universe? Or the cure to the Common Cold? Because if you are, that's something I know about as much as I know the winning lottery numbers."

Sarcasm was always a good weapon.

"Nothing so deep, William. No. Something much closer to home for you. I want to know the Royal Air Force's strength in the area around Helmand Province, Afghanistan," said Krasnov smoothly.

Clarkie blinked. "I'm a desk jockey, not a field specialist. How would I know anything about that?"

Krasnov merely narrowed his eyes, and his wolfish smile thinned to a grim line.

"You are the head of the unit for the base at which the intelligence reports are gathered. You would sit in on all department briefings.

You would have access to that information," the Russian persisted.

This was all very specific. Krasnov clearly had designs on the Afghanistan sector. A Russian invasion perhaps? The thought made Clarkie's blood run cold. But he was determined to give nothing away.

"Find someone else to annoy with these stupid questions, Ivan."

Krasnov was steadfast. He was determined to get his answers. A good Russian officer never gave up, even in the face of huge obstacles.

And a stubborn British RAF officer could easily be broken. Besides, he had his reputation to think about.

"I do believe you know more than you are letting on, William. It would be in your best interests to answer my questions."

"I don't get told anything like that. Not in detail anyway. Managing people is my line of work.

You should know that," the wing commander growled.

The Russian simply regarded him with a cold look.

"Your skill as a field specialist is well known, even in the Russian Empire." Krasnov replied.

"Surely, William, as one of the British government's most trusted advisors, they would see fit to tell you more than the bare minimum about anything?"

"It depends on the subject."

"The Ministry of Defence's tactical plans and squadron positions, perhaps?"

Clarkie rolled his eyes. How much more of this nonsense was he supposed to put up with?

"Blast your questions, Ivan! You've kidnapped the wrong person. You should have gotten your grubby paws on someone on the front line if you wanted tactical details. As I said, I'm just a humble man manager."

Krasnov simply eyed his prisoner for a moment.

"First of all, my name is not Ivan. I understand that you British pigeonhole foreigners in a vain attempt to give your nonexistent Empire importance, but I find it insulting that you refer to proud Russians, people who serve a country with a rich history as Ivan.

Secondly, my colleagues tell me you were in the Helmand Province some months ago," the big Russian rumbled with contempt.

"It had to do with the shipment of arms and equipment that you and your service so graciously interfered with."

Clarkie's hackles were rising by the second. The memory of being told that hundreds of ammunition boxes that Jim had buried in the desert amid a lot of sweating and swearing came to his mind and he was about to smile, then remembered where he was.

"Oh that? You mean the weapons you were supplying to the locals that your people so helpfully provided? It was a good job we found it otherwise it could have killed thousands of people!" he responded hotly.

Clark recalled the incident vividly. Thanks to those fuzzy little goats that the local tribesmen kept which he had become quite fond of, despite everyone else's disdain for them, the whole of Camp Bastion had been saved.

"Your Flight Lieutenant interfered with our well laid plans. And my good friend Colonel Hantuchov lost one of his best informants in that encounter."

Now it was Clark's turn to be contemptuous.

"You mean that sniveling little spy, Hanson? He was a coward. I thought you Russians believed in honor? Poisoning people doesn't seem very honorable to me!"

Krasnov bristled. Clearly the British man had hit a nerve, much to the prisoner's amusement.

"Taking over countries that are under Russian jurisdiction and claiming them is dishonorable, wing commander!" the Russian general grew even more agitated when Clark chuckled. "You are treading on dangerous ground, Wing Commander!"

"That's a bit rich, coming from someone who tried to start a war, only to be stopped dead in your tracks! You invade countries, bend the local governments to your will and punish anyone who objects. That's not communism, Krasnov. That's fascism!"

Clarkie's heart was beating rapidly. He could feel the blood pounding in his ears, but had said what he wanted to say. If Jim had been here, he would have knocked him back to protect him, but that safety net was not here. So what if the Russian pummeled him? He had got it off his mind. But his captor had suddenly grown calm again.

"William," said Krasnov, his voice icy. "Has anyone ever told you to curb your temper?"

"I thought you Russians pulled out of Afghanistan 25 years ago? Remind me to call Rambo.

He'd love to go back to that country!"

"You have a singular wit, William."

The Group Captain was deep down, horrified about what Krasnov was planning. "I'm sure your superiors would be very interested if you try to go back on a peace treaty signed in good faith."

"My dear William," came the icy reply. "When what I have done and how I have regained our position of power comes to light, I don't foresee any issues from my side."

Clark was about to respond but knew that was exactly what Krasnov wanted. If he showed that he had got under his skin, Clarkie knew he would lose any chance of perhaps talking his way out of this. But he'd be damned if he was going to help these people in any way.

"Take whatever nasty scheme you have up your sleeve and bury it," he said bluntly.

Krasnov looked over his captive like a hunter regarding his prey through a gun sight.

"I have nothing against you personally, William, or even your revered Flight Lieutenant McCleland. To be frank I have a high regard for the Royal Air Force. But from my perspective the Russian Empire's interests are paramount. I will find out what I want to know. I would hate for you to be an empty vessel by the end of it."

For his part, Krasnov grinned and got up. He headed for the door to the cell. He half turned at the doorway.

"I will return later. I hope for your sake that you will be in a more co-operative mood."

"Don't count on it, Ivan," Clark countered, knowing that the insult would sting.

Krasnov merely smiled thinly.

"You are a stubborn man, William Clark. That is a most admirable trait. But I would not wish to have all that marvelous military knowledge, or anything else you have in your mind become useless under our mind-invasion procedures. Not just the knowledge, but the memories, the experiences, the private thoughts. All of those things would be wiped away from you. If I was in your position, I would not want to lose the things that made me unique," there was more than a tinge of threat in Krasnov's voice.

Clarkie sighed loudly and rolled over on his bunk. Krasnov turned on his heel and slammed the cell door behind him. From his bunk, the RAF man heard his captor tell the guard to keep an eye on the prisoner.

The guard watched him for a while through the bars and then returned to staring ahead of him at whatever was holding his interest.

THREE

The gloved fist found its target and its opponent grunted as the blow landed on his chin. A little dazed from the sudden punch, he wasn't ready for another which landed squarely in his sternum.

Reeling from the onslaught, Mark Fogg, the *sifu* of the Ysabel Kung Fu club held up his glove, which his opponent tapped with the fist of his own.

Moving back into fighting stance, the two opponents half bowed and Mark lashed out with a punch which the other man blocked. The Master had guessed this and with his free hand, went for a body punch which his student canceled out with a blow to the solar plexus. It was a glancing strike which had Fogg out of breath for a moment.

"You've got a hell of a punch on you," Mark said. He got up. "And you're fast. But…"

There was always a 'but.' Mark struck out with a low sweep kick which his opponent fell back from and rolled back onto his feet and into fighting stance.

Fogg's sparring partner took off his headgear and gloves, his brow soaked with perspiration and chestnut hair a dank mat stuck to his scalp. His blue eyes under low eyebrows had an impish humour to them, his face with dimples upon his cheeks seemed youthful.

He half bowed with his left hand outstretched and his right balled into a fist, the curled fingers pressed against the left palm.

"But?"

"You don't weigh up what your opponent is doing to counter. You just go in, strike and strike again. Remember to watch his feet and shoulders, or you'll get done over."

"Thanks for the tip."

Mark was sparring with his top student. Fogg's opponent had started as a teenager and kept up the training, finding the coordinated fighting style and inner peace that being able to be proficient in such a physical sport appealing to his senses after having to finish playing rugby.

"Another round?" Fogg asked.

A wet towel was applied to his student's sweat soaked face. He took a swig of water from his bottle and began to put the headgear on again. From his kit bag, his mobile phone began to chime insistently, Fleetwood Mac's *The Chain*.

"Apparently not," he grumbled. He fumbled for his phone and answered it. "Jim McCleland."

The instructions were straightforward and given in a typically clipped manner.

"Yes sir." He began taking his padded head guard off again and packed his gloves. "I'll report with him in two hours."

He threw the phone carelessly into the confines of his sports bag.

"Something up?" the *sifu* asked.

"Yeah. Duty calls. Cheers Mark."

"No problem. See you later. Remember what I said, now."

Taking off his kimono and black sash, Jim packed his bag. He bowed again as he left the *dojo,* giving the same bow and hand salute.

In short order, the big Ford Mustang blazed through the night, its headlights burning into the darkness as it kept up its relentless high speed. It's red paintwork with white racing stripes gleamed under the overhead lights on the dual carriageway as it headed east from the

English midlands towards its destination. Such a machine was a little incongruous on British roads:

American cars, while available were not widely seen so the car's size and throaty sound from its twin exhausts gained it attention wherever it went. Its driver was very proud of his car. He had had to buy it from a specialist dealer, being not readily available in Britain at the time of purchase. He drove it well, a legacy of the advanced and race driving courses he had taken.

Driving was one of his hobbies, and he pursued it like he did with all of his interests, with single minded focus.

Squadron Leader James McCleland changed up through the gears smoothly and quickly as he gunned the Mustang towards his destination. He had the manual transmission option rather than the preferred automatic. He liked it that way, firmly believing that a manual gearbox and clutch setup gave more control over the car. The cosseting bucket seats, trimmed in leather were comfortable yet gave the urge to jump out of them all at the same time. He held both hands on the steering wheel, completely in control of the big car. From the stereo the harsh drumming and fast guitars of Iron Maiden filled the cabin.

As he approached the town, he could see the cathedral on top of the ridge ahead, lit up for the surrounding area to see. On a clear day, he knew that it could be seen from around 30 miles away. He turned off the main road into the housing estate and checked the address he had been given. Finding the house he wanted to stop at, he stopped and hauled his 6'3" burly frame from the confines of the cockpit.

Flight Lieutenant Colin Haltwhistle sat at his desk in his living room, hunched over his laptop.

He was enjoying the video he had found in the back of a drawer that he had forgotten he had.

After finding the thumb drive, he had popped it into his laptop and quickly become engrossed. It was something he had enjoyed as a child, stories his father had read to him and watching it on television during the times he had shared with him. Now Haltwhistle was rediscovering what had excited him. On the screen, images of open wheeled vehicles in close formation held his fascination. The speed, the sensation of danger, the thrill of competition, the smell of burned petrol and rubber. In any case, Colin was just glad for the distraction.

Colin Haltwhistle was in RAF speak a 'white cap', a member of the military police. Originally wanting to be a police detective, he had been bitten by the flying bug after a chance reading of *Reach for the Sky* as a kid. Despite being having a formidable talent for numbers, he disappointed his father by not becoming an accountant. Deciding to change course, he was thrilled to discover that he could combine his twin passions of researching and discovering from clues what the facts were and a life flying around the world.

Sadly for Colin, life as a pilot did not offer itself. He had been chopped from flight training, but he bounced back. Building a reputation as a solid investigator he had gained a commission and continued his work until circumstances a few weeks ago had now thrust him into real action. His young wife Anna had not been too happy with the turn of events but had accepted it as part and parcel Colin's job. She was just hoping that he would come back to her in one piece.

Haltwhistle was not the image of a dashing RAF officer, although he did wear his blues proudly.

A stocky 6'1" with sandy brown hair in a Caesar style, meant he was on the handsome side, Anna certainly thought so. Being an extremely capable investigator had given him the inevitable nickname of Sherlock. He was quickly ruled out of the running for pilot training but had found his niche in the surroundings of the Special Investigation Branch.

He preferred intellectual past times which was at odds with the service's desire for active extra curricular pursuits, but he was a competent man, doing enough physical training to pass the annual examination.

Then he had found the thumb drive while changing, and now Colin was enjoying re-watching what he had discovered. The British Grand Prix of 1988, and he was taken with the driver of the red and white vehicle who wore a bright yellow crash helmet. The race appeared to be being run in pouring rain, a far cry from what passed for Formula One now where at the slightest hint of rain, the safety car was brought out. To a purist who just wanted to see racing, that was just not right. This older style competition was much more intense by comparison.

The doorbell sounded. Colin looked up from his screen. He knew he would be having a visitor, but he had expected the call to come the following morning. Anna answered the door.

"Oh hello, Squadron Leader. Please come in," she recognized McCleland instantly. It was obvious that she had no love for having her peace disrupted.

The two men had met previously, although briefly and had barely been able to say hello to one another. Reputations however, were easier to get to know, and one of the RAF's foremost investigators coupled with a pilot who had earned himself more than a little recognition certainly gave McCleland pause for thought. What could they both be wanted for?

"Don't stand on ceremony, Mrs. Haltwhistle. Just call me Jim," he replied as he stepped into the entrance hall. "Is your man in?"

"Yes, Mr. McCleland. He's in the front room."

"Thanks."

Anna followed him in to the living room. She was typically pretty and in her late 20s, slim and well proportioned. A school teacher, Anna and Colin had married shortly after he had gone to SIB. The living room was decorated with warm pale yellow walls. A built in bookcase was filled with tomes of every description as both Colin and Anna were avid readers. A handful of DVDs, mostly classic westerns and war films and comedy shows such as *The League of Gentlemen*, *Bottom*, *Father Ted* and *Monty Python* and Anna's smattering of romantic movies rounded out the collection. On the shelf below, there were three clear terrariums, which on closer inspection revealed a hairy and rather menacing looking tarantula in each. Colin's interest in exotic pets was barely tolerated by his wife, who had no love for spiders of any kind. What no one knew, was that Haltwhistle kept his sealed written orders amid the arachnids, knowing that most people would have no wish to deal with the creepy crawlies.

"Best not get too far with whatever it is you're watching, Col. We've been summoned."

McCleland skipped pleasantries and got down to business immediately.

"I was hoping it'd be tomorrow, sir?" Colin gave him the briefest of glances, and sipped on a bottle of Mountain Dew.

"Sorry to interrupt your evening. Let's get this show on the road." At Haltwhistle's unspoken question, Jim cut in. "No, I don't know what the full story is, but get your kit together."

Then he noticed the laptop and what Colin had been watching. "Formula One."

Haltwhistle started. "Yeah. Do you watch it?"

McCleland grinned broadly. "My dear old mum enjoyed watching it. She often wished she had been able to go to see it in person. She told me stories of the drivers and cars she had looked up to in her youth." Jim went on. "I never took you to be a car guy. See, while you've been racking your brains over an insoluble problem, you could have shared this with the other guys. You wouldn't be thought of as such a swat."

Haltwhistle thought about that for a moment. "Maybe you're right."

"Don't cut your nose off to spite your face. How did you come across that?"

Colin turned the laptop so Jim could see the screen more clearly.

"I found it on a thumb drive in the back of one of my drawers. I must have put it there and forgot about it."

They stayed for a while longer and watched the race play out. Ayrton Senna won the race and received his laurels, then sprayed the champagne over his fellow drivers and himself.

"That appears to be a waste of good vintage champers," McCleland observed.

"Your mum is not the only one who would have loved to watch this properly," Colin said.

Nostalgia always had a strong effect on him.

He switched the computer off and closed it. "She never got the chance to see a race live."

"Sorry to hear that," Jim said with a touch of regret, knowing how Colin must feel. He looked around and noticed the spiders. "Tarantulas?"

Colin glanced at them. "Yeah. Mexican Red Knee, GBB and Cobalt Blue."

Jim looked at them with interest. "I always fancied getting one, but I don't like spiders."

"They're very easy to care for. Well, those two are," Haltwhistle enthused, pointing to the red and black specimen and the striking blue and green creature. "And they're a good cure for arachnophobia."

"Alright Spiderman, let's start wending our way."

Colin got up from his chair and folded a shirt. Anna came in from the kitchen carrying a teapot and a couple of mugs. Her face fell when she saw what was going on.

"Where are you going?" she asked.

McCleland smiled thinly. He hated to drag the husband away from the wife but duty was duty.

Anna was no fan of Jim's reputed private life and put the teapot down.

"London," was the simple reply. "I'll be in the car."

The petite woman gave McCleland a withering look. She knew of him by reputation and what she had heard was unsavory.

"You had better not get my husband into trouble, Mr. McCleland," Anna warned him. Colin shrank as she jabbed a finger at Jim. "He had better come back without a mark on him."

She may have been small in stature but Haltwhistle's wife was a firecracker in regard to her husband's safety.

Haltwhistle had taken advice from basic training and kept his kit together to up and go at any moment. He hugged Anna tightly.

"Hopefully this won't take long."

"Just take care," she advised him. She looked at his collection of furry friends. "I'll make sure to keep them fed."

"Just one cricket or worm once a week," Colin said to her. "The cobalt blue is very quick, so-"

"I know. I'll handle it," Anna assured him. "Now get gone."

"I love you."

He bundled his holdall into the tight confines of the boot of the Mustang and remembered to get in the right-hand side of the car to take the passenger seat. His demeanor changed once the car door was closed.

"This must have cost a penny or two. Bit flashy, isn't it, sir? Why don't you get a Bimmer or a Merc?"

"Talk about flashy! I wouldn't have one of those if you paid me," McCleland snorted.

"Really? Why not?"

"Because I'm not a pimp or a drug dealer." He looked at Colin. "Don't call me sir, I work for a living. Just call me Jim."

McCleland backed the car on to the street. Haltwhistle's rather more subdued car, a Ford Mondeo slipped into the darkness as the road curved away behind them. Jim pointed the big car in the direction of the A1 which would of course take them to the nation's capital. Once pointed south, the 5.0 V8 sang as the driver opened the car up and sped along the highway, breaking all known speed laws. They both knew that the voucher in the glove box called the 'get out of jail free card' would exempt them from prosecution.

Colin looked over at his new coworker. "A pilot?"

McCleland took a quick glance at him as they rounded a long curve. "Yeah, how'd you guess?"

His jacket covered his wings, and as far as he was aware, they'd not been visible.

"You're right-handed, but the muscles in your left hand are as developed as your other one. That gives away that you use your left hand a great deal, probably on a joy stick based on where you place your hand on the wheel. Your hand-eye co-ordination is above average, so the obvious answer is a pilot." Haltwhistle looked out of the window, waiting for the reply.

"You're not just any snowdrop, are you?" was McCleland's somewhat taken aback comment. "Special Investigation?"

"Yes, sir. You like the flying but not the discipline," Haltwhistle finished. He emptied the contents of his fizzy drink and quickly started another.

How the hell does he know that? flashed through Jim's mind.

As if to answer the unspoken question, the investigator went on. "You don't clean your shoes as well as they could be and your jacket isn't perfectly pressed. Hence, you do the bare minimum to pass the inspection." He smiled. "I looked you over when you arrived at the house."

McCleland gave his passenger a quick look. "You barely noticed me! And you saw all that?"

Colin nodded. By contrast, Haltwhistle's footwear was immaculate and his uniform's folds were Beyond reproach. He clearly took great pride in his presentation.

"I'm just your regular investigator."

"And I'm Mahatma Ghandi!" Jim went over the hows and whys of being called to London.

"Maybe we're due for a debriefing, maybe even a pay rise?"

"I very much doubt that," was the reply from the passenger's seat. They were probably going to be carpeted for whatever lame reason the top brass could think of. McCleland had a way of tuning out superior officers' bollockings so that they just washed over him.

The rest of the team had been granted leave, but more than likely would be recalled if it was for a good old groan-at. It began to rain, but the Mustang's speed didn't drop noticeably. The huge tyres on the slick road caused rooster tails of spray to be thrown up behind the car.

As the miles ticked by the two men bantered back and forth, sharing off color jokes and commenting on the F1 results, the state of the world and getting to know each other. At the mention of the day's football results, Jim pulled a face.

"I never cared for footy. Rugby's more my speed."

"Snap! Leicester Tigers for me." Colin replied, continuing to polish off his drink.

"You git. Your lot beat my team at the weekend!" Jim complained.

Haltwhistle picked up on that immediately. "Gloucester? Tom Walkinshaw owned them. I think his son still does. Got to admire him in racing as well."

"Now you're talking! Yeah Tom owned them until he died." The conversation was picking up given their mutual interests. "That Jaguar he built for Le Mans was gorgeous, and Schumacher was my guy. And he did a good job for Volvo in touring cars."

"I love me some racing," Haltwhistle agreed. He was warming to his new colleague. If they had mutual interests it made things easier. "Yeah, rugby is fun, but racing is number one."

"You won't get an argument from me," Jim said. "Never liked cricket either. Mum loved tennis, but give hours of two people hitting a ball at each other? Pass me the sleeping pills. Talking of sleeping pills, you won't get much kip if you keep downing that stuff. Do you know how much caffeine is in that?"

"Just habit. I haven't seen London since I passed basic training," Colin said, changing the subject.

He had been a young man then and had taken the time to visit a couple of clubs and meet young ladies. But then Anna had walked into his life. It had been an epiphany. He no longer felt the need to window shop.

Conversely, McCleland was vigorously single and seemed proud of his bachelor reputation.

"If we have the time, there's a great pub in Kensington on Edwardes Square," Jim remarked. He liked a good drink to go with the ladies and seemed to know all the good pubs and bars to visit to enjoy both equally.

"I know it! They serve wonderful real ale. The real dark stuff. Very creamy," Colin agreed.

"Then we'll head down there for a drink once all this is over."

Jim smiled as he adjusted himself in the driver's seat. The bucket seat might hold him in place but being stuck in one posture for long time caused the shoulders to get cramp.

"I don't know. All that motor racing has got me thinking of taking in a motor race, but we'll have to see what's on," Colin said.

"That sounds like a plan to me," McCleland grinned, then his face fell. "I don't think your good lady will be too keen."

The glow on the horizon told them that Britain's capital city beckoned. Even at this late hour, the nightlife would be in full swing, and all the shops would be open, selling their ware to all comers. Sadly, those pleasures would have to wait. The summons he had received had said that speed was of the essence and no delay was acceptable.

"Make haste with all due diligence," the man at the other end of the phone had said. That meant just one thing. It boiled down to 'Get your arse over here, now.'

The A1's junction with the M25 appeared ahead, a sure sign for anyone traveling south that their journey was nearly at end.

"I suppose you can take us out of warp drive now," Colin said dryly. He did not feel comfortable unless he was driving.

"Well, I did make it so," Jim shot back.

On the windscreen the raindrops slowed from streaks to being spots. They were just north of Arsenal, and Jim was continuing to run every red light that popped up. The squeal of brakes and yells from other drivers fell on deaf ears as the Mustang continued relentlessly on. The red lights gave way to the roundabouts of Kings Cross and St Pancras district. The seedy dens and back streets of Soho were next as McCleland turned south on to Regent Street heading for Piccadilly Circus. The bright neon lights of the Big Smoke's most famous square mixed somehow well with the dark, rainy weather. The gray brown buildings gave away to the open space of Trafalgar Square, with its lion statues and Admiral Lord Nelson keeping a watching vigil from his column, 164 feet above the city.

The car made its way along Whitehall, passing Horse Guards Parade on the right as the tower of Big Ben and the Houses of

Parliament loomed ahead. Turning over Westminster Bridge, Jim eventually brought the powerful machine to a halt at Waterloo East station. With no real option to park, he pulled up on a double yellow, knowing full well that a traffic warden could take his ticket and bury it as far as Her Majesty felt necessary.

"You don't have to flaunt your dislike for them as blatantly, you know," Colin chided him good naturedly.

"Oh, bollocks to them." Jim climbed out of the car and closed the door.

"They're only trying to do their job."

"Fuck 'em! They're still going to get paid aren't they, even if they can't slap a sticker on my windscreen," Jim said glibly.

The two crossed the rain sodden pavement slabs, glistening from the recent downpour. A large blue door set in a recessed archway lay ahead.

"This is it? I think my car's gonna be up on bricks with the wheels nicked!"

As he had been instructed, Haltwhistle pushed the brick beside the lock to one side and heard the door unlatch. Pushing the wrought iron door open, they stepped down the stone steps that led deep under the station. Lights ahead meant that they had arrived. A wide well-lit open room lined with people at computers. Pieces of equipment in various stages of being worked on were strewn about with technicians checking them. In a corner, maps and photos were pinned to the walls being pored over by a couple of guys examining them closely. It appeared to be all work 24/7 in this place.

In the center of the room, a Russian GAZ 47 jeep was being tinkered with. The bonnet had been removed, as had the wheels and tyres. Colin stopped to watch the mechanics working on it. If he didn't know better, he could swear he made out what appeared to be armor plating being welded into place inside the doors and heavy duty Kevlar applied to the canvas roof of the jeep.

Moreover, the engine seemed to be trimmed with performance parts, aimed at boosting the speed and power output of the vehicle.

"I'd hate to drive that thing," the Flight Lieutenant murmured, a frown crossing his brow.

"Why? It could be fun," said Jim.

"All that extra power in a high axled vehicle? It'd topple over at the slightest corner."

"You need to take the stick out of your arse and live a little, mate," McCleland clapped him on the shoulder cheerfully. So far, Haltwhistle was bookish and a bit too much of a stick in the mud.

A Wing Commander approached them, his blues immaculately presented with its buttons gleaming in the lights overhead.

McCleland recognized him immediately. Casey Matthews. Supposedly he had a no-nonsense attitude but to most people he appeared to have a chip on his shoulder and was used to getting what he wanted by intimidating people. Only young Flying Officer McCleland had not been intimidated, and they had resolved things in the gymnasium's boxing ring, to Matthews' regret.

"Ah, gentlemen. We've been expecting you," Matthews said. He turned to lead them on. "Follow me."

"Do you mind telling us what this is all about?" McCleland demanded.

The Wing Commander spun on his heel and glared at him.

"In case you hadn't noticed, I believe you are a Squadron Leader and I am a Wing Commander.

So you can add 'sir" to every statement you make to me. Clear?"

McCleland was tempted to make a sarcastic comment. He strongly detested people who threw their weight around for the sake of it, but Matthews' time would come. For now he just counted to 20 in his head.

"Fair enough. Cut the cloak and dagger bullshit and tell us what's going on... sir."

Colin clapped a hand to his forehead and sighed. Matthews turned red in the face, fuming that his words had fallen on deaf ears, but he kept his temper in check.

"The senior officer here can explain it to you. Perhaps you'll show him more respect."

McCleland smirked to himself.

"Casey, I think you're constipated."

Matthews glowered at him. "Explain yourself."

Jim shrugged. "You're not spewing verbal diarrhea. Usually, you're the arsehole acting as a mouthpiece!"

Colin looked down at the floor, hoping it would swallow him at any second. Matthews seethed but after a few moments he forced a smile. It was not a genuine one.

"All I can tell you is that is of grave importance."

"When isn't it?" A pretty Wren overheard McCleland's glib remarks and smiled at him. Jim, having had his attention caught by the short brunette with brown eyes, returned her cheerful look with an impish grin.

"Pay attention, man!" Matthews said. 'This is an Intelligence section matter.'

Something you're lacking in, Jim thought. He nodded his head slightly. Now that was interesting.

Intelligence didn't usually play its cards close to its chest unless something big was happening.

This was most certainly not a bollocking session or a debriefing to suffer through. Generally there was a league time of several hours before any meeting, so this was very different.

McCleland gestured to his new cohort. "Let's see what he's got to say for himself."

He could swear he heard groans from Colin as the doors to the office opened.

FOUR

Jim McCleland and Colin Haltwhistle stood before the huge oak desk in the concrete walled office. The office was like all military installations: plain white walls that looked like they had been painted and repainted over the years. The lines from the brush strokes were still visible under the fresher layers of paint. Being deep underground in this cold war vintage bunker meant that there were no windows but an air conditioner pushed chilled air noisily into the room.

Paintings of various RAF aircraft lines the walls: Spitfires, Lancasters, Vulcan bombers, Tornados. On the wall behind the desk a huge map of the middle east was pinned up with guide markers pointing out places of interest.

And sat behind the desk was the formidable figure of Air Vice Marshal John Cartwright. What he lacked in height he made up for in sheer presence. Known as Black Jack to all, but not in his presence, Air Vice Marshal Cartwright was in his mid-50s. A stocky middle aged man of average height with wavy graying hair, Cartwright had the air of a roguish salesman rather than a senior Royal Air Force officer. He had a quick sense of humor and a witty quip ready for almost every occasion. But it was widely known however that he was a dedicated officer with a tough, no-nonsense style who had served in a V-Bomber squadron in his youth flying the Vulcan before taking over XV Squadron in Gutersloh, Germany, which was one of the first Panavia Tornado units. Cartwright wore the full uniform well, his left breast full of the braids of medals that he had been awarded. Haltwhistle could recognize the DSO and DFC ribbons among his campaign braids.

"Gentlemen, good of you to get here so fast," said Black Jack. He regarded them in turn. "Your reputations preceded you into my office."

McCleland guessed Cartwright was in some sort of Z - list department based on the set-up he had going in this dingy bunker. The older man flipped a manila folder open, and pulled out McCleland's and Haltwhistle's pictures and their personnel files.

Without waiting, Jim took a seat. Colin gaped at the pilot's insolence. He couldn't believe how brazen this guy was. The senior officer glowered at him over the brim of his spectacles.

"Oh yes, go ahead. Make yourself at home, McCleland," Cartwright said sarcastically.

"Thank you, sir."

The scowl continued, and Jim took the hint to rise to his feet. He and Colin then took their seats after being given permission to do so. The Air Vice Marshal thumbed through the file in front of him.

"Martin James McCleland. Squadron Leader and pilot leader of 101 Squadron, VC10s. Graduated RAF Linton on Ouse with excellent piloting aptitude and then trained at RAF Valley with a view for fast jet training. Served a tour in the Gulf and two in Afghanistan piloting Tornado GR4." He paused. "An unspecified incident caused you to request a recent conversion to heavies." He laid the folder down. "You went from supersonic jets to flying multi engine? That seems a retrograde step."

"I had my reasons, sir," Jim said simply.

"Really? Would you care to share that with us?" Cartwright was challenging him, testing him and McCleland knew it. What sort of man would take a seemingly backward step? He regarded the handsome pilot stood before him. His chestnut brown hair was parted from the left and swept back, with his fringe falling into a quiff. He stood tall and proud, his bulked up frame filling his uniform well.

"Not really, sir," was the simple, cool response, although he knew everything was available to the senior officer should he want to research matters. He probably already had.

"Yes. Lack of respect for authority has been noted on your file more than once." Cartwright's sharp comment was met with a vaguely amused expression from Jim. "Apparently, you like to do things your own way and don't care for superior officers' opinions of you. Your commanding officers have repeatedly noted your flippant attitude. I'm here to tell you, that that will not go here!" Cartwright continued reading. " 'Has the ability to devise unexpected and unorthodox solutions to problems.'"

His solution to the team gym exercise of getting from one side of the hall to the other was noted.

McCleland had offered the idea of throwing the rope through the rafters of the roof and swinging Tarzan like across the floor, a tactic that the invigilator didn't like at all.

"Apparently you said to the officer watching that there was nothing in the rules that said you couldn't do that."

"That's right sir."

Cartwright removed his spectacles. "Some might see that as flagrant belligerency."

Jim considered that for a moment. "Others might say it was thinking outside the box, sir."

Cartwright studied the irreverent pilot. "It also says here you don't care for having your name in front of the public."

"I don't see how doing my job warrants that sort of attention, sir. It just seems to single me out. That sort of thing isn't for me."

Cartwright nodded. He could understand the dislike of the limelight.

"Fortunately, McCleland we operate under the radar, as it were in this section, so you should have no trouble remaining incognito, you'll be pleased to know."

"Is there some point to this, sir?" McCleland quirked an eyebrow. He wanted to get on with matters.

Cartwright looked up from the file.

"Your cavalier attitude to authority and disregard for regulations is exactly why you have been chosen for this assignment. Both of your records state that you have 'criminal versatility.' "

Jim wasn't sure how to take that. "I'll have you know, sir, that I haven't been arrested once," he cut in, slightly offended. It was the first sign of annoyance or aggression he had shown.

"How would you explain your questioning by police when you were fifteen?" Black Jack was eyeing the pilot intently.

"I was never charged, sir." *Because they weren't smart enough to pin anything on me*, he thought.

The white cap was equally offended.

"I'm a Snowdrop sir. A proud one!" he protested.

"It doesn't stop your psychological profiles finding you both capable of operating on the other side of the law if needed," Cartwright said slyly. "As of now you are both removed from official Royal Air Force business and seconded to my section."

"But sir," Colin interrupted, something that he regretted, given how much his voice tailed off.

When he found his voice at Cartwright's questioning stare, he said "What about me? My record's clean."

Flicking over the second man's file, Cartwright read the particulars. "Christopher William Colin Haltwhistle." Colin disliked the use of his first given names intensely, settling on his preferred moniker before primary school.

"Flight Lieutenant," The AVM continued. "You were selected for pilot training, but withdrawn from the course by instructors. Graduated RAF Halton Police training. Seconded to SIB. Posted as flight commander. Long record of successful investigations." He paused. " 'Suspected of criminal methods to attain his goals. Never proven. Crack shot with handgun and rifle, winner of RAF pistol shooting competition three years running.' "

Black Jack laid the file down and looked up at him. Not as physically imposing as his new partner, Haltwhistle still cut a pretty formidable figure.

"If you are able to use less then legal methods to prove your suspects' guilt, that makes you as culpable as them. There's no room for maverick methods in the service."

Jim was looking at the other man, looking for any kind of reaction. There was nothing to give anything that Haltwhistle was thinking away.

"For the record sir, I always stay inside the letter of the law, but justice is what I'm most interested in."

"There's a big difference between the letter of the law and the spirit of it," Cartwright told him, looking for any telling indication. There wasn't one.

"You, Colin are the finest investigator that the RAF police service has. That is why you have been selected for this section," Harvey told him. "From now on you're partners, irrespective of rank, you're equal."

"What section might this be, sir?" McCleland asked, pausing before the word 'sir.'

Cartwright laid his spectacles down on the desk top, sat back in his chair and clasped his hands across his chest.

"I and my unit have been given broad discretionary powers to investigate and act on any unusual activity or threats to the security of the nation, specifically relating to aviation matters. Your tendency to do things by the spirit rather than the letter of the regulations, Colin, make you ideal." Black Jack regarded Jim. "I don't have to point out the flaws in your personality that single you out."

McCleland and Haltwhistle looked each other over. Cartwright rose from the desk and offered his hand to them in turn. "We're not officially active at this time, but welcome to the Airborne Intelligence Division, gentlemen. The cutbacks that the Ministry of Defence have implemented over the years have cut Britain's ability to defend itself off at the knees, especially post 9/11. Our armed forces are a quarter of the size they were forty years ago, and while we have equipment and people, we don't have anywhere near the capacity to push back against threats. Our job is to identify and neutralize those threats and to keep these shores a green and pleasant land. While we're attached to the RAF, we're not part of the service and we don't answer to the usual chain of command."

Jim laughed. "Sounds like a flying secret service!"

Cartwright smiled thinly. "In a fashion, McCleland."

For his part, Cartwright got down to business quickly. "Now that that's over with, gentlemen, again, thank you for coming at such short notice," he said in his thick Midlands accent.

He had Harvey pull the cord which switched the lights off and then turned on the overhead display. An image of Afghanistan's borders with Russia appeared. A red dot was highlighted, with a green line indicating an inbound course to the red dot.

Then Cartwright's whole demeanor changed. He paced around his desk to get a better view of the overhead screen. "I apologize for not being able to grant you any leave, but we have a very delicate situation to hand."

He pressed a control on the top surface of his oak desk. A model of a Russian supersonic bomber mounted on a stand rose out a compartment mounted in it. Its details and shapes accurately re-created in small scale.

"A dangerous development has taken place that we are in the unique position of being able to respond to."

Cartwright stepped behind the two seated officers.

"Thanks to the intelligence that we have gathered, we believe that the Russians are re-arming. An army, tanks, aircraft in a small town near the border with Afghanistan. We don't know what the town is called, but we've nicknamed it Happyville."

The red dot zoomed in on a circular settlement surrounded by desert to the north west and east and bordered by a mountain range to the south.

" 'Happyville?' A town full of scumbags and that's the best you could come up with?"

McCleland asked.

"Pay attention man," Cartwright snapped. "For further details, I'm turning this over to Group Captain Harvey."

Harvey stepped forward. Like Cartwright he was of medium stature, with thick salt and pepper hair but his most notable feature was his rotund, portly figure that did not seem to belong. He was still spoken of at RAF Halton of possessing an almost obsessive need to win. Renowned for his semi aggressive nature, his exploits during the first Gulf War were now required reading during basic training.

"Thanks." Harvey's clipped English accent cut the air like a knife. "Those tricky dicks are clever, and are not to be underestimated. We know that they have a network of intelligence officers throughout Afghanistan and beyond, and are all coordinated from here."

He indicted the red spot on the screen, which grew in size to reveal what looked like a barren, rocky arid desert, which on closer inspection covered in prefabricated buildings embedded into the rock. Huge hangars which could accommodate aircraft along with vast storage areas which could hold thousands of tons of weapons, equipment and vehicles were visible. Above them all, a vast control tower loomed over the northern part of the settlement looking not unlike some huge, impenetrable lighthouse overlooking a craggy cliff top.

"Happyville is located in Sector X-ray Lima 189. Bsased on information received, the Russians are gathering their top intelligence people in this one spot, for reasons that will become clear in a moment," Cartwright explained.

The view changed, and an image of Wing Commander William Clark appeared. Despite himself, Jim drew breath. He knew that Clarkie had requested and been granted leave. How did his immediate superior figure in this mess?

Beside Jim, Colin hunched forward in the seat. He didn't show a flicker of emotion, but McCleland knew better than that by his body language. Haltwhistle was quite close with Clarkie as well, having been recommended the position of the police section by him and was as concerned for his friend as Jim was, even if Colin would never admit as much in public. While he and McCleland had never worked together before, they had a professional respect for one another. This could prove interesting, but Clarkie's disappearance was worrying. They were both hoping for some good news, but he knew by Harvey and Cartwright's expressions that this was anything but good.

Harvey stepped forward. "We know that the Russians have abducted Wing Commander Clark, and our intelligence reports that he is being held at Happyville, awaiting interrogation. I don't have to remind you what Russian interrogations involve, Jim."

"No," replied McCleland grimly. "You don't." He remembered all too well Colonel Krasnov's leering face demanding information on the RAF's deepest secrets when they faced off a few months before. He guessed what was coming next and wasn't relishing the news. The reason why he'd been brought in to this matter was now clear to him.

"We suspect that someone of your acquaintance is behind this," Cartwright went on. The image changed yet again and Krasnov's unmistakable features appeared. McCleland could think of several words to say, none of them pleasant.

"No word on his right-hand man, Hantuchov. We believe that he is... not part of the equation."

"I was wondering what happened to the other half of the ugly club." McCleland tried to sound glib but even he knew he wasn't very convincing.

"Gentlemen, your orders are to get to Happyville, recover Wing Commander Clark before the Russians break him, and get yourselves home. It is up to you how to proceed with all of that but those are your mission objectives."

"Where was Wing Commander Clark last seen, sir?" Colin asked.

"We're not sure, Haltwhistle. The only thing that was recovered from his room was this."

Cartwright handed the Flight Lieutenant a card that was torn in half. Only half of the words could be made out: 'iana' and below it, 'rmez'.

"That part of the world is crawling with ISIS, the Taliban and Christ knows who else. All hiding in holes in the ground and none of them like us very much," Jim said grimly.

"You'll have to tread carefully then, won't you?" Harvey told them.

Haltwhistle started. "Have the Afghans or the Americans responded?"

Cartwright shook his head. "No. And no response to any of our messages. It looks like for whatever reason the Afghans are sitting this one out. As for the Americans, they think that this is an internal British matter."

The atmosphere in the room was getting colder by the minute. Jim knew when he was being tasked with a near impossible mission, but then he had been given near impossible assignments before.

Another thought gnawed at the back of Colin's mind. "Why would the Russians have such a large base that close to allied territory?"

"A good question, Haltwhistle," Harvey countered. "It would probably be in all of our interests to find out while you're there. This could represent a fundamental shift of power if they decide to go on the offensive."

Jim sighed a little more loudly than he would have liked. Cartwright smiled a little while Harvey glared at McCleland icily.

"May I ask how you expect us to infiltrate the Russian border without being detected or captured?" asked Colin.

On the screen the image changed to one of a helicopter. Haltwhistle guessed it was a security photograph taken just after the American infiltration mission in Libya some years before when they recovered such a helicopter and flew it out before the Libyans or Russians could respond and send a counter-insurgency team. The menacing lines and rounded glass canopy of the Mi-8 Hip were instantly recognizable It made for sobering thought as his understanding of what Cartwright and this new unit he had formed were proposing became clear. The MI-8 was a larger version of the infamous MI-24 Hind but was capable of carrying cargo and troops. Truly, a menacing proposition.

"The Hip is already prepped and on standby at Camp Bastion. Once there you will unload and take the chopper into the danger zone. It's a Russian type, and that should allow you to avoid suspicion and it should get you to Happyville. Once there, it's up to you how you want to proceed," the gruff Englishman explained. "I needn't tell you what sort of knowledge Clark has, you've both been around him for a long time. And his information would prove very useful to the Russians."

Jim thought for a moment. Even with the comfort of a Russian helicopter gunship, the risks of crossing into Russian territory and going to some heavily armed base with or without guns blazing were something he knew Colin was already calculating to some astronomical figure, and the expression on his partner's face gave away that he was not in love with this scheme at all. He had an awful lot more to lose than McCleland did, after all.

"What kind of backup are we due?" Jim asked quietly.

Cartwright and Harvey looked at each other. Slowly, Cartwright spoke, choosing his words very carefully.

"You'll have access to some equipment, but as far as weapons are concerned, you'll have to make your own arrangements when you're there. If you were caught with British equipment, it would blow the whole mission. We'll provide a pack radio and rations but to all intents and purposes, you are out on your own on this one, Jim."

McCleland was rarely a step behind, but this had come as a surprise.

"The Russians always use a special key to gain access to their bases. We don't have one to give you, so you'll have to... get your hands on one, if you follow my meaning," Harvey explained. A picture of what looked like a green jewel embedded in a piece of metal was displayed. Clearly, it was the key that they would need to obtain, somewhere, somehow.

"Plausible deniability, sir?" Colin asserted quietly.

"You get the idea, Flight Lieutenant," Harvey said.

Jim was genuinely expecting a tape recorder to combust spontaneously. The awkward silence was broken by Haltwhistle.

"Sir, have you considered that if we are discovered, especially with a piece of equipment that by rights we should not have access to, it could very well start a war?"

Cartwright half smiled. "Yes, it occurred to me." He paused with a mischievous glint in his eye.

"And your point is, Mr. Haltwhistle?"

Colin looked at the floor uncomfortably. Clearly no further questioning on this particular line of inquiry was invited. The grave silence and lack of eye contact said it all. Cartwright rose from behind his desk and turned the lights back on.

"In that case gentlemen, you had best make sure you are not discovered," he said bluntly.

"You will have the advantage of taking a special advisor," said Harvey. He pressed a control on his desktop. A side door opened, and an immaculately dressed, balding, middle aged man with a nicely groomed goatee beard entered wearing civilian clothes. He offered his hand to McCleland.

He had a grip like a vice, which belied his moderate build and quiet demeanor.

"This is Squadron Leader Melvyn Waters, Jim," Cartwright informed them.

"Retired," added the veteran. He had the air of someone who should be an accountant or a lawyer, not a retired RAF officer.

Jim nodded. Colin merely acknowledged him in his usual way. Then McCleland's eyes narrowed as he remembered.

"Yes! You were involved in Afghanistan. I remember reading about your maneuver with the Chinook. Nice move."

Waters grinned, a somewhat toothy but pleasant grin.

"Yes, that was a spur-of-the-moment thing but it somehow worked." He spoke with a slight nasally twang and sometimes fell over his choice of words. "Since then, I've been doing a lot of study on those... people."

It wasn't clear if he was referring to the Russians or the Afghans, but for now, McCleland said nothing.

"He has a lot of insight that should help you, Jim," assured Cartwright. "I think Mel will be useful on this trip."

Jim smiled thinly. "When do we leave?"

Harvey looked at his readout on the desk terminal.

"Your transportation should be at RAF Brize Norton about now. The Globemaster will need to be loaded and fueled, so you have four hours, tops."

McCleland and Haltwhistle looked over the images, the model, the maps and the assignment again. AID wanted this mission over and done with as quickly as possible. A lot was riding on its success and they were sending the best crew they had.

The fact that it was Clarkie in the firing line just upped the stakes that much more.

"Alright, we had better get down to Brize Norton."

"Take some time on the shooting range first," Black Jack. "You'll need to be proficient."

Cartwright offered his hand. Harvey merely half bowed, turned and headed through the doorway into his inner office. The door slid shut behind him. McCleland wondered what the issue was, but he was interrupted by Cartwright offering his wishes.

"Good luck gentlemen. Just get home in one piece."

Haltwhistle turned to leave but not before Cartwright surreptitiously handed him a thumb drive.

"Keep me informed of progress, Colin. Your code word for this mission is Rapier. Ours is Wrens Nest."

"Rapier? It makes it sound like you want me to disembowel someone." said McCleland wryly.

"Take that jeep out there," Cartwright thumbed the UAZ which the technicians had finished tinkering with. "And make sure you sign yourselves out a weapon each."

"What about my car?" McCleland was suddenly a little concerned about it.

"Don't worry, it will be taken care of," Cartwright assured him, but Jim wasn't mollified.

Cartwright winked as the door slid closed behind him then sat and considered what he had just put in motion.

"Why is it always the arseholes who are the best choice?" he mused.

FIVE

Colin turned the thumb drive over in his hand. Jim and Waters were waiting for him in the hallway.

"Is there a problem?" McCleland asked.

"Nothing that we haven't handled before, sir." Haltwhistle was still considering the drive in his hand, thumbing it thoughtfully. He'd inadvertently gone back to rank discipline.

"I told you, call me Jim. You heard the man, no rank privileges."

"What's that?" asked Waters, nodding at the small piece of plastic in Colin's hand.

"You'll find out soon enough." He didn't like keeping a superior in the dark, especially one with a reputation such as Mel Waters, but Cartwright had been unequivocal.

Haltwhistle nodded his head to Jim, meaning to move him along slightly, out of Waters' earshot.

He spoke in a low voice, too quiet for anyone to overhear. He showed his partner the thumb drive.

"Something for our eyes only."

The headed out of the armory and over to the UAZ. A handful of people were around, looking at them with curiosity, but clearly going about their own business. The White Cap showed the pilot leader the small piece of plastic.

"Sealed orders. You know what that means."

If he was surprised, Jim gave no indication.

"I half expected something like that.' He looked at Colin. "As a much smarter man before me said, this could be the beginning of a wonderful friendship."

The shooting range echoed to the sound of multiple gunshots. The paper targets set up on the runners were in various positions allowing each shooter to improve their aim.

McCleland didn't like the feel of the standard issue Glock at all. It was too light and flimsy in his hand for his liking, but it was accurate enough for him to hit the dangling piece of paper repeatedly.

Bringing the target back for him to inspect, he was pleased to find the neat bullet holes that had made their mark at thirty yards.

In the next gallery, Haltwhistle, with his own Glock in hand was pouring round after round into his paper hanger. Eventually the pistol locked back, empty. Placing the weapon down, he drew the target back. Jim showed his partner his handiwork.

"What do you reckon?"

Holding up his own thick piece of paper, Jim gaped at Colin's results.

There was almost nothing left of the head or torso of the drawn body's features. It was a case of almost relentless and perfect shot placement that had decimated the paper.

"Bloody hell," was all Jim could muster. He was simultaneously shocked and impressed by how accurate Haltwhistle was.

"Yeah, not bad for a swat, eh?" was Colin's reply.

"They weren't joking when it said you were a crack shot on that report!"

Waters inspected their handiwork and then shook his head at his own efforts. He was used to the Browning 9mm, which had a well-earned reputation for being about as accurate as a drunk trying to score a goal. He held his own target up for the two eager youngsters to have a laugh at.

"Not bad sir," Colin said diplomatically.

"Yeah, right," Mel said. He disappeared back in to the open atrium of the bunker.

"I hope he doesn't shag the way he shoots!" McCleland opined.

The three officers headed for the jeep. McCleland, however did it in a roundabout way and passed a slip of paper to the Wren he had spied a few minutes before. She quickly folded it up and put it in her pocket.

"Send me a text," he told her.

Seeing all this, Colin rolled his eyes and climbed in to the UAZ. Jim slid in behind the steering wheel. The 4x4 started easily enough and gave a throaty growl from its 2.7 liter engine. It was definitely a relic of the cold war, and it just oozed Iron Curtain charm. The seat was hard and uncomfortable, almost like something you would find on a bus. The whole interior was painted in a drab olive green which matched the exterior. The gear stick resembled a miniature RSJ and Jim could only guess at how clunky and lumpen the pedals and steering was going to be. From the outside it was hopelessly dated and did not look like it could offer the same sort of protection as a Snatch Land Rover or an Ocelot.

"I'm thinking that Cartwright chose this piece of crap because it would blend in where we're going," McCleland grumbled.

"I for one, would like to get in and out in one piece," Colin said.

"Best make the most of what we've got," Mel agreed from the rear seat.

Wing Commander Matthews scowled as Jim tried to make himself comfortable in the driver's seat. The senior officer keyed a switch that opened the double doors at the far end of the room which led to an underground passage.

"Well get out of my sight and stop filling my workspace with fumes!" he barked.

"Stop twisting for free, Shirley," McCleland answered him back with a smirk. He popped the clutch and left the aggrieved officer with a face full of burned rubber as Jim deliberately lit up the rear wheels.

"You arsehole, McCleland!" But it was too late, the UAZ was down the underground passage and gone. He trudged in to the office, and was not happy to see Cartwright and Harvey's faintly amused expressions.

"He needs to be severely disciplined!"

"Be my guest, Matthews, but I doubt it will change anything," Black Jack countered.

"He's irresponsible and insolent! He doesn't have a clue what the uniform means!"

"Some people might view such behavior a different way. I for one consider it an asset, especially at a time like this."

Realizing that he would not win this argument, the subject was changed. "What do you think the odds are of this working, sir? Especially with him on the team?" Matthews didn't so much ask as to speak rhetorically.

"I don't know." Cartwright steepled his fingers. He figured there was something more. "What's really on your mind?"

Casey folded his arms. "All of this has happened overnight, sir. Two weeks ago I was at a desk at Marham, and now we're all here." He paused. "And it came just after the Air Marshal's funeral. Coincidence, sir? No."

Black Jack studied him intently. "Aren't you thinking a little above your pay grade?"

"I'm sorry sir, but I was just interested in the timing."

"Any information that you need to know you will be informed of as and when I see fit, Matthews." The stern look on Cartwright's face told the Wing Commander that no further discussion of the topic was warranted.

For his part, Casey was chastened, in a manner that he wished McCleland would have been.

"I know you were close to Air Marshal Berry, Matthews. Did you see him before he died?" Black Jack asked.

"No sir. We had talked about me seeing his boat, but I never got to see it. He showed me pictures of it. It was a pretty thing."

Harvey was standing in the corner, taking all of this in. He wasn't sure what the AVM was doing, but he was intrigued.

As they drove down the dark passageway, the jeep's engine echoed from the tunnel walls. The narrow space had to be navigated carefully, but Jim, as was his wont, was not being particularly cautious.

"Do you like to piss off every person you come across?" Colin demanded shortly.

"Just the ones who deserve it. Anyway, this thing has got some poke!" was the gleeful reply from the driver's side of the car.

The UAZ emerged from an archway under Waterloo main station into the dawn breaking sunshine. McCleland turned right, then right again at the traffic lights, heading past Waterloo East. The Mustang was gone from its parking spot. Hopefully it would be in a car park, safe somewhere and not on the back of a traffic womble's tow truck. Unlikely considering the get out of jail free card was all-powerful. Turning north, the UAZ made good time getting through the northern suburbs and on to the M25. He could have taken the A40 to link up with the M40, but at this time of day, west London would have been a nightmare.

He was impressed with the gear change: clearly, the technicians had done some work to the transmission and it did not jolt or crash at each gear change.

Another bottle of soda was cracked and began to pass Haltwhistle's lips.

"Jesus, where do you put that? Don't you need a piss every hour?"

"I need it. It keeps me sharp," Colin argued. "I need the work otherwise I get really bored. And if I get bored, I drink this. On the flipside, I need it to concentrate."

Ninety minutes later, the strange Russian jeep turned into the main gates of RAF Brize Norton. A quick inspection of their passes and they were through the security checkpoint and heading onto the largest Royal Air Force station in existence. Lines of KC-135 tankers, iconic

Hercules C130 cargo aircraft and huge Globemaster transports lined the tarmac.

After the overnight rain, the air was fresh and the sun crisp. Jim brought the UAZ to a halt in front of the main office building and stopped by a low wall. An alert corporal opened the doors for them and they were escorted into the building.

The three made their way deep into the building, decorated in typical Ministry of Defence bright white.

Eventually they were shown into the station commander's office. He got up from his desk and saluted, which was returned. Group Captain Scott Williams greeted them warmly.

"Welcome to Brize Norton gentlemen. The arrangements have been made and your cargo will be loaded on time," he told them briskly. "I have to say these orders came through and took us all by surprise. A fully loaded and equipped Globemaster takes a while to turn around."

"It didn't exactly go down well with us either, sir," Jim replied. It was the first time Colin had heard him address a superior officer respectfully.

Williams smiled a little in agreement. Then he noticed Waters.

"Mel Waters! You old dog, how are you?"

"Oh, you know, surviving," Waters smiled.

"Mel here started as my co-pilot on Chinooks," Williams explained.

"How long will it take to prepare for departure?" asked Haltwhistle. He was not one for small talk unless he felt comfortable with the person he was talking to, and he really did not like hob- nobbing with senior officers.

"Oh a good few of hours. The cargo we've been told to load is not something that can be just thrown into the back of the plane."

"We also need the jeep we arrived in loaded, sir," McCleland said. Williams nodded and informed the corporal who had shown them in to take care of it.

Waters was genuinely pleased to see his old friend.

"Scotty! How the hell are you?" he asked Williams.

"Scotty? Don't you know you can't call a superior officer by his name?" Williams chided him good naturedly.

"Rank goes out of the window when you're retired," Mel said cheekily.

"I trust that 'er indoors is keeping you out of trouble." Scotty's smile was as wide as the Scottish highlands that he loved.

"Oh, she has her moments but I wouldn't trade her for anything."

"Does she fly?" Williams teased him.

Scotty and Waters each giggled.

"You could say so sir. A bit like the Chinook over Afghanistan!"

"Even in those days, you made do with what you had," Williams said.

Colin was enjoying them going at it. Familiarity would help a lot on a mission like this. If these people trusted each other, it was a major bonus.

"There's something strange about a group of RAF officers flying around in a Russian helicopter, though," Waters remarked.

At that, Williams looked surprised.

"Is there a problem, sir?" McCleland asked. He knew that secrecy had to be maintained but he had expected that the base commander would know what was being loaded into one of his aircraft, but decided to hear him out anyway.

"I didn't know that it was a Russian chopper. We all thought it was a prototype Apache or something. But the orders were.. well... cagey. You know how it is," Williams observed.

"It would appear that way, sir, yes."

"Have you been checked out on this helicopter? I'm surprised that they haven't put yourself through some sort of conversion course," Williams remarked. "I wouldn't feel comfortable sending three good men into an active war zone without the proper training."

"Well," Waters said slowly. "I've been told I'll be given some training on the go once we reach Camp Bastion by a specialist." He looked a little unhappy. "Quite honestly, I don't like it either, it feels like being thrown to the wolves."

Williams sighed in sympathy.

"Then you'll just have to find a solution and do the best you can. You may have to use it for a fair while on this trip."

"Yes sir," Waters said resignedly. He did not look happy at all. Everyone aboard knew the man did not like being under-equipped or lacking support. Anyone doing anything that could cause problems for the delicate job of piloting a chopper was a liability, especially a big heavy machine that he hadn't mastered flying yet.

"I think we should go and take a look at the loading and give everything a once over," said McCleland.

The others agreed unanimously. Williams had his staff car brought around and the four got in.

With Williams himself behind the wheel, they headed out onto the loading pan where their enormous Globemaster sat waiting. Its rear loading door was open like a huge gaping mouth ready to swallow anything that came near it. Right now it was about to swallow the carefully wrapped package that only the four officers knew it to be truly. They watched intently as the ground crew carefully lined the cargo up and inch by inch placed it into the cavernous innards of the cargo aircraft. Once it was secured, the UAZ was driven carefully into the back and braced ready for its journey.

McCleland, Haltwhistle and Waters made a beeline for the passenger door on the fuselage. Once on board, Jim and Mel headed for the cockpit to check in with the flight crew while Haltwhistle remained to check the cargo.

The two trained pilots headed in to the cockpit, which more closely resembled a computer center than the flight deck of an aircraft. Technology had pushed development onward of course, but Waters missed the cozy feel of old-fashioned dials and flight controls. Behind them in the cargo loading, technicians were working on fastening the rest of the cargo that the Globemaster would be transporting out to the lads in Afghanistan while others were checking manifests, making sure that everything that should be here was.

At the flight engineers' station, a sergeant was installing some sort of reader device. At McCleland's questioning looks, the young man spoke.

"It's to monitor the load and make sure it doesn't shift."

Jim nodded in understanding.

"Very good. Carry on, sergeant."

Across the flight deck, the pilot was showing Waters the captain's position and it's various controls.

"It's nice to be back aboard an aeroplane. They're quite a bit more sophisticated than in my day," observed Mel, looking over the cockpit.

"Chinooks, wasn't it?" asked the pilot.

"Yeah. Clunky by comparison to this but they get the job done."

Down in the bowels of the cargo section, the soft hum of the fuel bowsers pumping AVTUR into the massive wing tanks filled the air with their comforting throb. The huge power that the Globemaster possessed was at the moment not even active but even in that mode, the engines still looked hugely impressive. The electrical output the aircraft produced was enough to keep a small town in plentiful supply of energy for several days.

Flt. Lt. Haltwhistle was watching the final cargo load being slid into place when three technicians working on a shipping order caught his watchful eye. He had been trained to observe, to pick up on anything unusual, any behavior that seemed out of place. His natural nose for trouble had earned him a good reputation as a police officer and in the trade training had earned him the almost inevitable nickname of Sherlock. It was a moniker he had managed to shake off.

The three young men were checking over the cargo, which was fair enough, but it was the conspiratorial whispering and the odd body language that had got Colin's attention. They seemed like they were trying to hide something as they worked.

Haltwhistle slowly crossed to the men huddled by the cargo pallet, making sure not to draw attention to himself.

"Whoever set this machine up really just had to throw it on and hope for the best," said the first technician.

"Rather inappropriate to question the work of an experienced officer isn't it?" said Colin.

The young man jumped and turned around. He clearly recognized Haltwhistle for who he was, and knew his reputation.

"Oh sir, I didn't mean to sound like I was..." He was stumbling over his words.

Colin interrupted him off with a smile.

"A good engineer knows that sometimes you have to improvise with the tools that you have."

The younger men, three corporals by their rank emblems started to go back to their business but with Haltwhistle's presence, they seemed even more eager to please and just get their work over and done with and get out of the officer's way. The three corporals went on to check another load of spares, clearly hoping and praying that this Flight Lieutenant would just disappear. Colin watched them work and how different their body language and indeed their conversation was now that they knew that someone was watching them. But still, the thought niggled at Colin's mind. Why were they so keen to hide what it was they were doing with the pallet?

The white cap observed them checking the crate of tools for a while longer, amused by their efforts to get their work done.

"What was so interesting about the load earlier?" he finally asked them.

The second corporal stood to attention. He was in his early 20s and keen to please.

"I'm sorry sir?"

"Well, the three of you seemed very interested in something to do with that last pallet of spares. Let's take a look at it, shall we? I want this unloaded and opened, now."

Haltwhistle was curious enough to do a complete unpack and repack inspection. The crate was full of vehicle components which he guessed was for Land Rovers. There was nothing untoward in the crate, but Colin checked the pallet itself.

"Are you quite satisfied, sir?" asked the first corporal, the one who had been furtive in his behavior.

"I'll let you know when I am," was the measured reply. 'So I'm intrigued, what was so special about this?"

"We were debating if the contents matched the manifest, sir," explained the first non- commissioned man, an eager, sandy haired young man.

"Yes, well we wouldn't want a mistake, would we?" Colin agreed. He looked around at the other cargo.

Everything seemed to be normal, but he intended to double check everything once they arrived at Camp Bastion. The third corporal was speaking in hushed tones to the other two. He had been very quiet since Colin had accosted them but something he said caught his weary ear. Something about Russians.

A thought caught him.

"Young man, who said anything about Russians?"

The color drained from his face. He looked at Haltwhistle for a second then spoke.

"Well just in case you're heading that way, or back to Helmand Province," he said quickly.

Colin frowned. Usually when he suspected something, his instincts were right, and he suspected something now.

"What's your name, corporal?"

The technician shuffled and looked at the floor.

"I asked you a question. I expect an answer," Haltwhistle insisted.

"Sutton, sir."

Colin was about to comment further, but he was interrupted by McCleland who had come to find him.

"We're needed."

"On my way."

As they headed away from the three corporals, Haltwhistle intended to talk to that technician further about his offhand comment before they took off. Something did not sit right with him. He mulled over it as they made their way back to the cockpit of the Globemaster. The doors opened and he stepped into the spacious flight deck.

"All cargo is on board and secure," the pilot told them. The view from the cockpit windows showed the ground crews taking their equipment and backing away to the edge of the apron.

"I need a few minutes to talk to one of the men out there," Haltwhistle said urgently.

The pilot shook his head. "Sorry but we're on a tight schedule. Takeoff is in 15 minutes. I need to ask you all to take your places."

Jim noticed how frustrated Colin looked.

"We'll talk about it in a bit," he assured him.

Haltwhistle did not look the least bit mollified.

The tractor that was to tow the Globemaster to the taxiway was being hooked up to the nose wheels. The flight crew began preflight checks and started up the huge engines, two on each wing.

"It's time, gentlemen, take your seats," the co-pilot told them.

They retreated to the crew area and took a seat each, next to Waters, who was already belted in and had his nose buried in a book.

McCleland did not mind flying at all, hell he was a fast jet pilot but he didn't like being not in control. It was a common problem for most pilots. He settled back and pulled up a playlist on his iPod. The eight hour flight needed some classic rock, he thought. At last that little part of the plan was done. Next to him, Haltwhistle looked decidedly unhappy.

Seated on the other side of him, Waters noticed Colin's displeasure "Is something wrong?"

"It can wait, sir. Apparently everyone else isn't interested," Haltwhistle answered.

Mel shrugged and went back to reading his book.

"Just Mel is fine, Colin."

Unless he was close with someone, the junior officer was reluctant to be too familiar with a senior, but he went along with Waters' wishes.

"Fair enough Mel. You're familiar with the area?"

"Yes, I was on the front lines," Mel replied. He seemed to drift off into reverie. "But it was a long time ago."

"That would explain why Cartwright considers you an asset on this mission."

Changing the subject, Colin produced several maps of the area surrounding Happyville, and folded them so that it was manageable.

"I think it would be a good idea for you two to work together," suggested McCleland, noticing the maps. He was happy to defer to Colin with something like this, knowing how sharp his mind was.

"Fine with me," Waters said.

The two began a deep conversation about the lay of the land and what hiding places there were surrounding this makeshift town. The maps had details of ridges and tracks that would be ideal for hiding a helicopter in and driving a jeep along, so that seemed to solve that problem, but of course seeing something on a map and then actually seeing it for real were two different things.

The chances that there would be scouts and lookouts around was high.

"You can tell that you are definitely familiar with all this," Haltwhistle said.

The older man shuffled uncomfortably.

"Those missions were just a job I did, Colin. They were no more of a job than what you're doing now. I just accepted it as part of my duty of wearing the uniform."

Colin seemed deflated. He may be an officer and a gentleman but he had no flying experience and had never seen active duty. All of this was very new to him. Despite being almost the same age as Jim, he had a lot of boyish enthusiasm about him.

"But sir, not to put too fine a point on it, but you're a legend."

Waters gave him a wan smile.

"If you say so. All I wanted to do was get home to my family. The legend thing... Well, let's just say I did what I had to do. I wasn't always happy about doing it either."

Jim smiled from the other seat.

"His enthusiasm is infectious, Mel. He's a fast learner."

Waters nodded but still seemed uncomfortable. Colin decided now was a good time to broach the subject of what had been playing on his mind.

"I need to put this out there."

This time Jim knew that something was wrong. Haltwhistle did not usually act in this way when technical issues took precedence.

"What's the matter?"

Colin filled them in on the encounter with the technician. He looked grave and spoke in hushed tones.

"I'm not trying to be a doomsayer, but it seemed off. I think Corporal Sutton should be watched."

Jim could see where his partner was coming from, but at the same time he had to give the benefit of the doubt. But then considering the orders he had been given, any kind of leak could be catastrophic.

The intercom buzzed. In the cavernous cargo area, the voice buzzed and bounced off the huge metallic tube that made up the inside of the fuselage.

"Ready for takeoff, please fasten your seat belts," came the captain's instructions.

Haltwhistle quietly wished that he was the one at the controls, but his dreams of being a pilot had been dashed when he performed poorly during basic flight training. Try as he might, he just could not get the hang of the workload and the inevitable chop followed. It had been a major kick in the teeth, but his talents in other areas had been noticed and he was soon happy in his SIB position.

Through the porthole windows, they could see the airfield had been cleared and the huge aircraft had finished its taxiing. They were lined up at the end of the runway. Then the roar of the engines as full throttle was applied filled the cargo area and the change in motion caused the airframe to shake some as the collective power of the four engines boosted them down the runway.

At the right moment the sensation of movement changed as the Globemaster lifted off the tarmac and into the Oxfordshire sky. The airfield receded rapidly behind them as they climbed above the clouds. Far below the land was various shades of green and individual town could be made out.

Jim always liked seeing the world from this perspective. It gave a feeling of being able to see over everything and everyone.

Once the engines settled back from the takeoff and altitude climb, the vibration and noise in the aircraft diminished to where they could talk in normal voices. Reflecting on what Colin had told him, Jim made a decision.

"I want you to double check everything on board that we are taking with us. Report anything that you find, no matter how small. We can't take too many risks."

"I was intending to anyway," Haltwhistle was glad for some decisive action but wished it had been done before takeoff.

The familiar hum of the engines filled the aircraft as it headed out across the English Channel.

As much as he enjoyed seeing his homeland, out there where the action really was, was where Jim truly felt he belonged. As for Colin, he had turned a distinct shade of green.

SIX

Clark searched his person for anything helpful that would help him out with his current predicament. He remembered he had a small pad stylus in his pocket and reached for it. He looked down at the manacles on his ankles. Hmm, a simple lock that could be picked. Clark looked over and saw the guard eyeing him.

He gave the guard a smile and thought about a way to do this without being noticed. He lay back on the bunk and smiled. He would have to bide his time. It was something he knew Black Jack would do. In fact if it was Cartwright in his place and not him, Bill was sure his maverick superior would have escaped by now. He kept an eye on the guard who glanced at him from time to time but mostly stared ahead. He's probably wondering why he got stuck with such a boring job, Bill thought.

"Doing anything good out there?" Clark called. The guard grunted something and turned away.

Now was his chance. He took the stylus and started manipulating the lock, twisting the pointed piece of metal one way then the other as he had seen in a demonstration one one of those training courses that the higher ups liked to throw at their people, just in case you were captured and locked up.

As he worked, he remembered a time when he was a kid back in Bristol. His father has locked him in his room as punishment for back talking his parents at the supper table. He was just 13 years old. Sent to his room in disgrace, the resourceful if mischievous young Bill had successfully picked the lock to get out and had headed over to a friend's house when the going was good. Upon sneaking back into the house unnoticed or so he thought later that night, he was confronted with his father, livid at Bill's deceit. A month's grounding and no ball game privileges were the punishment. The memory of his father's withering look and disgusted tone of voice brought a smile to Clark's face, and he recalled how he had turned the lock on his door using a tin nail and tried to do the same now.

Footsteps outside alerted him to the approach of someone. He quickly hid the stylus and lay back. Krasnov's stony face matched the walls of the cell. The door was unlocked and the Russian general stepped in to the room.

"Quite comfortable, William?"

Bill simply lay there, unmoving, not looking at his captor.

"Come now, William. You will have to co-operate sooner or later. Save yourself some pain and let's be reasonable," Krasnov's tone was genial but menacing all at the same time. He grinned his sinister grin.

Bill finally, lazily sat up.

"Oh, it's you again," he sighed.

"Yes William, it's me." Krasnov sat across from Bill's bunk again. "It's time we had our little talk. I am very interested in the British strength and movements around Camp Bastion and northern Afghanistan."

Krasnov was nothing if not persistent. He looked expectantly at his prisoner.

Bill let out a low groan. "I told you, I have no knowledge of any of that sort of thing."

Krasnov's eyes flittered for a moment. "William, I have no desire to harm you. In spite of what you may have heard, we Russians have a code of honor which we stick to, but my patience is limited. Do not force me to use... different methods."

"Bollocks to your methods Krasnov. Bollocks to your honor, and bollocks to you too," Bill spat.

Krasnov looked resigned. "Is that your final word, William?"

Bill simply laid back again, immobile, silent, looking at the ceiling of his dank cell.

"Very well, Wing Commander. I had hoped to spare you of this, but I see you leave me no choice."

He signaled for the guard at the door to come over. He had to duck to get in the low doorway.

To Bill, he resembled an American Footballer that he remembered seeing in when flicking around TV channels.

"Take this person to the interrogation room. Prepare him for interrogation."

The guard unlocked the manacles and started to lift Bill from the bed. Clark chose that as his moment to strike. He jammed the stylus into the man's forearm, deep and neat. A spurt of blood gushed from the wound and the guard howled. Clark was on his feet and kicked the bigger man in the ribs, then bolted.

The big man ripped the small, jagged, gnarled piece of metal from his skin and threw it across the room after the human, who was now through the doorway. For his part, Krasnov had his automatic pistol drawn and ready. He dashed after his prey, who proved to be astonishingly light on his feet.

Bill threw himself headlong along the stone clad corridor. In parts it was patched with metals and was bathed in brown and dark green light. There were soldiers running towards him from the other end of the hallway, leaving Bill with few options to escape.

He launched himself at a doorway to his right, which thankfully opened at his shoulder dive into it. A stone staircase lay beyond. The Englishman was jumping down the flights of six steps at a canter. He heard the feet pounding from above as his pursuers kept up their hunt of him. He came to the first landing, slipped and fell on the slick floor, bashing his knee as he fell. He let out a gasp of pain and struggled to his feet, then headed through the door and down another corridor, almost identical to the one on the floor above.

Dammit! He cursed to himself.

From somewhere behind him he heard Krasnov shout out. "Stop him at all costs!"

The pain in his left knee was almost unbearable and Bill was limping. He knew instinctively that he had torn a tendon. More importantly he knew that his chances of getting out of... wherever it was that he was now had just taken a blow as big as the fall he had taken.

He rounded a corner and ran straight into a burly Russian who looked like he wanted to rip him limb from limb. Clark spun and fled, only to see Krasnov walking towards him, holding his gun.

It was trained on his heart and Bill threw up his hands in surrender, knowing it was hopeless. He lapsed into unconsciousness as the blow from behind overwhelmed his senses.

Pain. A blinding light. A wince inducing headache.

Bill felt like he was outside his body, floating and not really there at all. But the pain in his head and his knee was enough to make it feel like he was stuck between sleep and waking up. He was aware of voices but couldn't make out what they were saying.

Thoughts of laughing with his friends, worrying about filling out another report on time, his life on the base, his military training and his past adventures races across his mind. But it felt like he wasn't in control of his thoughts. Memories of Joanna and the pain of his divorce, his father growing ill and infirm, his way of dealing with it and the bitter aftermath came flooding back.

Then thoughts of seeing action in the Gulf. The guilt of hearing that one of his men had been shot down and probably killed, his pain at the loss of his brother. The joy at buying his first car, the glee he felt at having his first girlfriend. Him gaining his wings. His first meeting with his sergeant on the first day of basic training and thinking what a bastard he was, and the initial animosity he felt towards his father-in-law. It was like someone was looking at the worst memories he had in the dark corners of his mind.

Bill shut the thoughts away, then became aware of what the voices he had heard were saying.

"It's not working. He seems to have a resistance to the treatment," said a voice.

"Have you tried the different settings?" another voice responded. It sounded familiar but Clark couldn't put his finger on who it was.

"Yes. it's almost a brick wall level of resistance."

"Can you give a reason for this?" the familiar voice asked.

"I'd say he has incredible control over his mental state and his emotions. It must have given him a mental barrier that I can't get around. We're going to have to find another way."

"That is most unfortunate," said the familiar voice. Krasnov. It was Krasnov, Bill now realized.

"Increase the power level."

"If I do that it could induce a cardiac arrest, there will not be much memory to recover if he's dead."

"I don't care," was the cold reply. "Do it."

"His brain functions will start to break down."

"It's worth a risk. Do it."

Images flashed in Bill's mind. His childhood and his playing in the fields outside of his home.

His initial realization of wanting to be a pilot. His first instance of drinking alcohol and the tangy taste it had left. His parents' dismay when he came home drunk for the first time. The pain in his head increased to the level of a migraine. Then that feeling of floating returned, as if he was there but not quite in himself. It felt like his mind was being emptied, all his thoughts were being sucked from his being. Clark shut his mind out and he felt his soul returning to within him.

"It's not working."

There was a crash of a fist hitting equipment and smashing noises.

Krasnov left the room, leaving the doctor and his prisoner. He was frustrated by the lack of results. A prime catch like William Clark was in the palm of his hand and so far he had not been able to do much with it. Clark had been wired up to a set of electrodes which would apply electric shocks to his person, depending on where the electrode was connected to. So far the results were limited to inactivity on Clark's parts, violent shaking or yells of pain depending on the severity of the electric shocks applied. So far, Krasnov had the results of his knowing what Clark's name rank and number were, that he was stubborn, refused to co-operate and so far had resisted all electric shock treatment. Not exactly much to go on.

Krasnov trudged along the dark hallway to his office. Once he was behind his closed door he poured himself a strong vodka. He didn't usually drink alcohol but now he felt like something strong to energize his senses.

His desk was large and full of mementos of victories in battle. A Bowie knife, an old style Browning 9mm pistol. A painting of his battalion, which he had commissioned after a victorious Encounter hung on the wall behind him. The window to his left gave a vista out over the town. If His wife was here, she would undoubtedly tell him to do something else, to take his mind off Things, as an answer would come. She had an insight that was startling at times. He thought for a few minutes as he sipped his vodka. It had a sting and a burn that went straight to the brain that he liked. Then his eyes widened in realization. His wife did indeed have a sense for solving problems.

"Of course!"

He turned to his desktop terminal and sent a summons to the man who could solve the Maddening problem of the unhelpful RAF officer now languishing in the laboratory.

Across the Russian Federation, deep in a bunker lined with grisly trophies of victories hard won, A stocky man sat sharpening a large ceremonial knife. Carefully and with great attention to detail, the man admired his handiwork as the edges of the blade became sharper and sharper.

Intermittently testing the blade's cutting ability on his withered, scarred fingers, the man was finally satisfied with the knife and placed it carefully in its long leather sheath. Next, he turned to his revolver, custom made. It wasn't the standard Russian Nagant design. Featuring the finest white bone as its inlaid grips and fitted with an attachment to allow the knife he had been working on to connect, the revolver was an upgraded version of a typical GRU assassin's.

His name was Vladimir Ulyenkov. He enjoyed preparing his weapons. It gave him great satisfaction to make sure his arsenal was at its best. Anything less would not be worthy of him.

In fact he enjoyed preparing everything that he became involved with or used to assist him.

Known as one of the best "fixers' in the Empire, Ulyenkov's job to the casual observer was anything but repair. Any threats to the state, incidents that required high level, in-depth investigation, any job that required a resolution that was messy and inevitable for the perpetrator always seemed to land in Ulyenkov's lap. A famous incident that had led him to murder the treasurer to the Polit Buro, who as it turned out had embezzled significant funds from the military budget had made him a formidable reputation who could be called on to fix situations that other people would have either washed their hands of, or done it in a ham fisted way.

His focused lifestyle precluded him becoming involved with anyone. He had tried it as a young man and found the whole experience of having to indulge a female's emotional needs an annoyance that he could not be bothered to put up with. Females could be so unpredictable and that did not sit well in his measured existence. As for younglings, the idea of raising and teaching a child was just as distasteful as putting up with a woman's emotional outbursts. No, his profession was all that he needed and all that mattered.

And now he had a job to do. An intriguing offer from Krasnov. Not that he cared much for him; he was too given to talking to people than just telling people the way a situation should be handled. He was soft. Not the sort of person who should be in control at all.

But the call for help and the offer of an interesting assignment had come. A job he would take pride and great pleasure in doing. He arose and left his bunker. This William Clark would prove to be an interesting challenge.

SEVEN

McCleland watched as the European coast drew itself under the aircraft which was cruising along at 40,000 feet. From this height, the Earth looked pitifully small. While towns and cities were visible, individual people were most certainly not.

Colin felt the thumb drive in his pocket which Cartwright had given to him and now that they were clear of the British shores, they could view whatever orders were on the drive and find out what all this was really about.

"Wait one minute and then head for the bog," Colin murmured to his friend, just loud enough for the pilot to hear him. Unclipping from the seat, Haltwhistle made his way to the Hind and disappeared behind it, making it appear as if he was checking on the payload. Waiting for the right moment, Jim headed for the lavatory in the far corner. Once out of eye line, he made his way around the packaged crates to his partner, who was waiting with a laptop. Sliding Cartwright's thumb drive into the USB port, Jim watched as Haltwhistle opened the sealed orders.

'Password required,' the legend on the laptop screen read.

Jim keyed in his details and the screen changed.

The video carried the usual Top Secret for Ministry of Defence Officers Only warning. Over the next few minutes, Jim and Colin watched what information the video contained. Once the display screen had gone dark, the two were in silence for a moment.

"Now it all makes sense," said Colin finally. "It would explain our recent run ins with the Russians." McCleland pursed his lips.

"You can say that again. We're going to have to tread very carefully with this one. Any kind of slip up will have far worse consequences than an all expenses paid stay at Lubyanka," he agreed.

Colin clasped his fingers together, which he did when he was deep in thought.

"Fortunately, we do have an element of surprise on our side," he thumbed at the UAZ. "But we have to come up with a way of getting in to this place without being collared."

Jim simply smiled. "I'm way ahead of you mate. We already have something on board that can help."

Haltwhistle's eyebrows lifted in surprise.

"Cartwright supplied some Russian uniforms. They're in my holdall."

"I think you'll find that's a breach of the Geneva Convention-" Colin started.

"That's not a popular club with psycho Russian generals, mate." Jim's expression was a perfect poker face. After a moment, Colin backed off.

"Yeah, good point," he conceded. He grasped that they had transport and a way to get in.

"I can see a bit of a problem though," Haltwhistle went on. "It's a good job we didn't bring any of our gear. It'd stick out like a sore thumb. We need Russian equipment."

Now there he did have a point, Jim thought. Dammit, he had forgotten about that. "We can probably get some from the locals. The Taliban use all that stuff."

If Colin's chin had been any lower it would have clanged on the floor.

"Have you got any idea how to do that? We can't just go up to a bunch of Taliban and ask them for their guns," Colin pointed out. In a whole country full of hostile people who wanted to kill them anyway, three RAF officers even dressed as Russians would be conspicuous in the extreme.

In fact, appearing as Russians would make them feel about as welcome as a fart in a spacesuit.

But Colin looked thoughtful.

"What's whirring away in that mind of yours?" Jim demanded.

"I do have an idea. But it'll have to wait until we get to Camp Bastion."

Exasperatedly, Jim pressed for more.

"Don't keep me in suspense mate, tell me what you have in mind."

Once Haltwhistle explained his idea, McCleland seriously considering calling the men in white coats for his friend. He could not believe what he had just heard. Not only was it crazy, but it was a surefire way of getting killed if they got found out.

"Why not?" Colin reasoned. "You're the one who said dress up as Russians, why not this too?"

McCleland didn't have an answer for that one.

The rest of the flight was pretty uneventful. They had to climb to 60,000ft to avoid a thunderstorm over Eastern Europe and it got quite bumpy for about half an hour but once the Globemaster had cleared that, the run to the Middle East was pretty uneventful.

The enormous beast began the long descent into the huge base from about 60 miles out, and touched down at 4:00pm local time. Brought to a stop, the three officers got up and stretched, then headed for the door once it was safe to do so.

They stepped down into the unrelenting sun of the desert. It was unspeakably hot. Hotter even than Iraq, Jim thought. The air felt heavy and the desert dust was immediately a nuisance. A camp commander was waiting for them, standing beside an Ocelot.

Cartwright had taken care of everything, Jim thought.

"If you'll come with me," he offered. Haltwhistle shook his head.

"I'd like to oversee the unloading of the cargo," he replied. Jim nodded to him as he and Waters were grateful to find some protection from the oppressive heat in the armored interior of the Ocelot. The Hip looked both impressive and oppressive. It stood purposefully on the pan and had been placed under guard to prevent any interference. McCleland, Haltwhistle and Waters slowly stepped around the strange looking helicopter. its odd shape grew on you over time and it's graceful, if threatening lines became appealing. From its flanks, wings on either side held several weapons pods from which evil looking gun and rocket ports were mounted on each side.

"Did you check out all those crates for whatever it was you were looking for?" Jim asked of Colin.

His partner shook his head.

"Yeah, I couldn't find anything."

"I've never been up close and personal with one of these before," said Waters. He was still Taking in the chopper and wondering to himself if he could fly this thing.

"I thought you saw action against them?" Haltwhistle looked puzzled "That was with the Hind's, but it wasn't face to face."

Jim was circling the front of the helicopter, looking up at its beak like nose.

"I can't say much about the Russians, but they did nice work here."

They continued the walk around of the chopper as several ground crew looked on curiously.

Although they were in a security protected area, they were still close enough to be seen.

Haltwhistle did not like that. Too many prying eyes for his liking.

"I'm not sure why it's so big on the outside, because the cockpit is tiny by comparison. It has a compartment which could be used to transport troops or weapons or limited cargo. I would say this thing is one of an older batch built, about 30 years old," said Mel.

McCleland was staring up at the gun ship, taking it's lines in appreciatively.

"Didn't you manage to outturn and outrun one of these with the Chinook?" Colin asked Waters.

"Yeah. I didn't know if it would work. I pretty much set the thing to fall out of the sky and turned and ran before he knew what was happening. He nearly turned himself inside out trying to keep up."

The white cap was genuinely impressed. He had seen such a move being demonstrated at an airshow and had not believed what he was seeing. "Brilliant move."

"Those days were interesting. It was touch and go but we looked out for each other," Mel agreed.

Waters and McCleland climbed up into the narrow stepped cockpit and into the chopper. It was cramped and claustrophobic inside. The crew compartment was painted a pale blue but it was the cramped feel that made it feel oppressive. McCleland slid into the cockpit in the very front of the Hip and slipped into the co-pilot's seat, which was equally limited for space and decorated in the same way but had an airier feel, being enclosed in a huge Perspex bubble. It had reasonably up to date avionics screens but there were a surprising number of antique dials that gave away the age of the machine.

Waters made himself comfortable in the pilot's seat. The bulkhead in front of him was a mess of switches and knobs and buttons which as a technician demonstrated controlled flight functions. It looked like someone had thrown the buttons at the console and an engineer had simply screwed them down where they landed. There was no rhyme or reason with the way they were arranged, and to an untrained person it looked impossible to decipher. The visibility was good though, Mel thought. A large bubble canopy gave good visibility. The seats were similar to the ones in the jeep: bare metal with fabric covering and looked extremely uncomfortable to sit in beyond a few minutes. His backside was going to feel like a toaster after a while.

The actual controls consisted of a cyclic similar to the Chinook's that fit snugly under his right hand, and a collective which was fixed to a mechanism behind the seat that he knew controlled the upward and downward movement which held sway by his left hand.

Talk about old-fashioned! Despite how old and out of place it felt, Jim found himself liking it, and was making himself at home in the gunners' compartment. Out in front, the canopy curved underneath. If they had been aboard a Hind, the long barrels of the 7.62mm machine guns would have pointed threateningly outwards.

Waters had made himself as comfortable as it was possible to in the pilots' chair and was getting used to the controls. It only took him a few moments to be at home at the controls of a working aircraft again.

"Hello, chopper," Mel said softly.

"I bet it feels good to be back at the controls, doesn't it?" Jim called up from the front seat.

"Yeah. Yeah it does." Waters had to admit it was a nice feeling to be back in the cockpit.

Colin came up the ladder beside Waters and poked his head over the top of the cockpit side. The older man was relaxing back into the pilot seat, and looking over the control readouts with a faraway look in his eyes.

"I think I see why Cartwright wanted you on this mission. You being familiar with these things is a great asset."

"Let's not stand on ceremony," McCleland said. "Let's get going. We've got to get where we're going and fast."

"I need time to prepare," Haltwhistle countered, annoyed that Jim was disregarding his idea.

Reaching for the starter button, Waters pressed the control that would start the engines and get the huge rotors above them spinning.

An earsplitting grunt was emitted from the engine cowling accompanied by a plume of black gray smoke. The power plant clattered, gurgling and finally was silent.

Colin was aghast. If the engine failed to fire, then they wouldn't get anywhere fast and without proper cover, the whole endeavor would have to be abandoned.

"Try it again," he insisted.

Another press of the engine starter gave the same result. The exhaust belched more dark clouds, but the engine stubbornly refused to fire up.

"Bollocks!" Jim cursed.

Waters climbed down from the cockpit and signed the form declaring the aircraft unserviceable.

He handed the clipboard back to the crew chief while the ground crew immediately began climbing all over the stricken helicopter.

Haltwhistle came up with the only solution open to them at this point.

"Pub?"

With little else that they could do until the Hip was in working order, the three retired to the mess, where the drinks began to flow. From Colin's point of view, it allowed him extra time to perfect his plan.

Mel looked wistful. "It was a long time ago when I was a pilot. But it was at a time when things were dangerous and we had to improvise to survive. Those legendary missions as you guys called them... we had to accomplish them regardless of the risk. And I had to get us out of some tight spots."

Jim understood completely. "Probably another reason he wanted you along with us."

Waters leaned forward in his seat.

"I've kept in touch with your missions as well. It looks like you've been in some tight spots as well."

"Oh, there were a few, but we always found a way out," McCleland said.

Mel smiled. "Just as we did."

By the expression on his face, Jim had remembered something.

"Your falling-out-of -the-sky trick was required study in basic," he said.

Waters smiled a little. "Yes, that was certainly an interesting one."

"How did you come up with it?"

The older man took the controls as if to emphasize what he was explaining.

"We were on patrol and delivering supplies to the guys at the front when this Hind popped up out of nowhere. Its pilot tried to outflank us as we running parallel to him. To throw him off I brought the chopper up into a steep climb and rolled over the top of him. It scared the hell out of them and when we came out of the fall, we turned and ran before they could get a lock on us," he explained. He was using his hands and moving them to underline his meaning. "It was pure instinct and it wasn't authorized to do it."

"An unauthorized flight move? I bet your CO loved that." Colin looked puzzled. Anything like that would earn a severe reprimand now without official approval.

"It was a different time. When you're in the firing line, authorization tends to go out of the window. No time for clearance, just do what you can to save the ship and crew. The CO was alright with it... but he did give me a bollocking and told me not to do it again!"

His stomach began to tell him that he needed something to eat. "Let's get some grub down us. I'm starving," Mel told them.

While Jim picked over the almost inedible mush that passed for chicken curry, Mel and Colin tucked in to some spaghetti, which looked about as unappealing. Retiring to their room they discovered that they had been allocated a communal bedroom with simple camp beds and a chest of drawers each.

It was all that was available, but it would do. Setting up a makeshift bar in the corner, Jim produced a bottle of Glenfiddich whiskey, two six packs of bitter and a bottle of Smirnoff vodka complete with cocktail shaker and glasses.

"Where have you been hiding that?" Colin demanded. "How did you get that past security?"

Jim winked. "I have my ways."

Mel eagerly took a can of ale for himself while Colin, who himself liked a glass of the dark stuff and was not much of a spirit drinker.

The frothy beer had a nice crisp taste.

"I can tell you're from the home counties, mate!" Jim teased him.

"I'm from Derby," Colin corrected him as Jim proceeded to crush ice into the shaker, pour some vodka and sweet white wine into it and shake the metal flask vigorously for a few moments.

"Vodka Martini. How do you take it?" he grinned.

Mel nodded. "Straight."

"I wish I had some lemon though. I never have it with olives. Too salty for me."

"You do realize that a Martini served like that is just a watered down drink that is being ordered in a wanky way, don't you?" Colin took his turn to tease Jim. Mel laughed in agreement. "Only amateur cocktail drinkers take it shaken."

"Yeah, so what?"

"It makes you look like a snobby cockwomble. And shaking it bruises the alcohol."

Jim took a sip of the concoction, the sharp bitter taste was good. "Has that shandy gone to your head already, Col?"

The three of them laughed. The tension that had been building up over the last 24 hours lifted off them and they relaxed.

"Can I ask how old you were when you graduated and were posted?" Colin asked Mel.

Waters was enjoying the back and forth between the two younger men. He had been made to feel welcome by them and it was nice to be back, involved in a mission. But the thought niggled at him: it would have been nice to be at home with the wife and kids, though. He just hoped that this wasn't a one way trip, and the way things were shaping up he was not putting good odds on it. If he had known what was in store, he would have said a big fat no when the offer from his old commanding officer had come.

For now, he humored the two of them.

"Twenty one. It was just a huge exciting adventure to me. And at the time, I had what I thought was a great posting. My first time on active duty was really exciting."

Waters remembered the first time he had been on a live RAF station and how impressive it had been. It was no less so now. Camp Bastion, despite its location was a truly impressive place.

"I was lucky to have a good CO. The chinook was always well maintained and the guys I was with were great people to work with, but the bloody thing always felt like it was about to fly apart, but I wouldn't have traded it for anything."

The veteran had a faraway look in his eyes. The memories came flooding back whenever he spoke of his time on the squadron.

"I would have loved to have been aboard." Haltwhistle was genuinely interested in the older man's stories.

"Can you tell me about some of your other adventures? I read about you, but I wanted to hear your view on things."

Waters sighed. He had retold his stories too many times. He had once overheard someone else telling them and embellishing for a group of incredulous students. He had been quick to correct the errant officer for that. If there was one thing that he didn't like, it was embellishment. Still, Colin wanted to hear it from the man himself, so Mel obliged him. Jim too seemed interested in hearing from the horse's mouth.

"We were on patrol and our way back to camp when we were chased by the Taliban. It was pretty nasty. They were faster than us and better armed somehow. We suspected they had got them from somewhere. We wouldn't have lasted long in a fight, but we checked out the area and found a cave close by. The CO ordered us in. The Taliban thought they had us pinned down, so we had to come up with something. We played dead and set up some stuff to protect the cave mouth."

Jim and Colin were agog. This was not something that they had expected to hear. They were expecting to hear more about his encounters with Russians.

"All I can say is we made it out in one piece," Mel finished.

"That's amazing," Colin breathed, impressed.

Waters smiled thinly.

"It was where I learned everything there is to know about the locals, Colin."

EIGHT

Aboard the cramped confines of the Chinook, registered BW, Pilot Officer Mel Waters was seated at the co-pilot's station. Unlike an aircraft in which the captain sat on the left, in a helicopter, the commander of the aircraft took the right-hand seat. To his right, Squadron Leader Peter Nichol waited for further instructions. The small cockpit was abuzz with activity. Ahead of them, six other RAF Chinooks hung, awaiting whatever fate should befall them as they headed over the rugged reddish brown terrain of northern Afghanistan.

The Chinook had proved itself in the Falklands, where the only surviving example after the others had been sunk during an Exocet attack had performed brilliantly to ferry troops to the front. Now it was on duty again: a covert mission behind the lines in support of the Mujaheddin.

In fact the Falklands stalwart, Bravo November was at the head of this squadron.

Waters had passed his pilot training aboard a Westland Wessex, and had initially found the Chinook a very different beast, but with some perseverance he had got through conversion training and was now established on the squadron.

Since becoming captain in his own right a few years previously, Nichol had led the Wokka- Wokka on several missions overseeing the nation's security in various parts of the world. The number of officers of Celtic descent in the squadron had led the unit to be dubbed the Starship Scottish.

The other choppers in the squadron were a mixture of newer and older variants of the type, cobbled together from whatever the RAF had available in the area. This sector, despite being under dispute by the Russians and the Afghans was far out from the RAF's usual patrol and defence duties. However the Mujaheddin had begged for help and the government had agreed to support them.

Loaded with supplies, the six Chinooks were headed to a rendezvous to drop them off. Flt Lt MacDougall, the chief officer in the back was ostensibly second in command of the chopper by rank, but Waters, being the co-pilot was in reality.

Now the Chinooks that had been sent in faced a deadly situation.

"I'm picking up a group of contacts approaching from the north," reported Hoy, checking his radar screen.

Through the windscreen the blips grew rapidly to become the formidable shapes of a squadron of MI24 Hinds. Each looking evil and each packing a hall of a punch.

"How many do you think?" wondered Nichol.

The scanners whirred and beeped. The crew watched intently, waiting for the machine to finish it's processing.

"Fifteen, sir."

There was a murmur of apprehension.

"They outnumber us over two to one," gasped MacDougall.

Nichol sat back in his seat. If there was going to be a fight, which looked increasingly likely then they were not going to last long, the firepower that the Hinds had at their disposal would see to that. The intercom crackled.

"All gunships, this is Squadron Leader Rouse. Assume standard defensive pattern and await further instructions."

The six Chinooks arranged themselves in a rough diamond formation. The intention was to dissuade any threats from approaching them while giving each helicopter a clear field of fire, not that the Chinooks had much of that by comparison. The Chinook at the head of the squadron did not waver in the face of the leading Hind.

"Ready all the weapons," ordered MacDougall from behind them, his rough Scottish accent seeming to bounce off the bulkheads.

The cockpit light provided a moody atmosphere as the status readouts dotted around glowed red and green.

"Here they come," said Nichol.

Ahead of them the fifteen Russian helicopters closed in. These newer attack choppers looked ominous compared to their clunky predecessors. A bit like the Humphrey compared to the Chinook, mused Waters.

A rough voice growled across the bone dome headpiece.

"You are intruding in the territory of the USSR. Land and surrender, or we will open fire."

Rouse's voice cut in. An experienced man, Jonathan Rouse had a no nonsense approach to command, and pretty much everything else. He was very work orientated, professional and alert with a tendency towards aggressive tactics. He generally spoke with a slightly slow lispy tone and tended to drop parts of words, but he was still perfectly understandable.

"This is Squadron Leader Rouse. We are on a humanitarian mission in this region. Please do not impede us. Withdraw, or we will be forced to defend ourselves."

"Rouse. I am Commander Ulyenkov," the Russian voice growled. "The USSR claims this region as our own. You will stand down, or I will personally take pleasure in blowing those American built pieces of junk out of the air."

The Russian ships seemed ever closer, just itching to open fire. There were tense faces in the cockpit.

"I say again," Rouse said insistently. "We are on a humanitarian mission and mean no harm to anyone. Withdraw immediately."

Hoy checked the records, but there was no mention of a Ulyenkov in any of them. He must have risen through the ranks quickly or been posted somewhere beyond the reach of Ministry of Defence intelligence records. The Russian was as immovable as any of them had encountered before.

"I am not in the habit of quibbling. Especially with RAF jackals, Rouse. Now leave or be destroyed."

"Come now, Commander. I'm sure we can resolve this in a more peaceful way. Would you be agreeable to meeting in person where we can discuss this properly?"

Ulyenkov snorted loudly.

"British words mean very little to me. I am giving you and your hangers-on there one minute to turn tail or the next thing you'll see is the desert floor as your armada is immolated."

Rouse's response was succinct.

"Then prepare to take your best shot Ulyenkov, because we are going on whether you like it or not."

The line went dead.

"The bloody fool!" MacDougall spluttered from behind Nichol's chair. "He's just started a war!"

"Stand down, Niall," the captain told him.

The Chinook rocked as the first burst of tracer fire lanced across their bow, blinding the two pilots for an instant.

"Return fire!"

MacDougall opened up with the starboard beam machine gun, peppering the Hind as it passed.

The Russians turned and came back in with MacDougall taking pot shots at them. It seemed to hold them off.

Waters had never been in a battle before. Just months before he had been sitting in his academy graduation class and now he was on the frontier, staring death in the face. The nearest Hind blasted at them with it's devastating machine gun and rockets. The Chinook shuddered under the barrage of fire.

"Evasive!" shouted Nichol.

They managed to avoid the round of rockets, but the hail of incendiary bullets impacted. The starboard cockpit windows splintered into shards of Perspex and the console promptly exploded in Nichol's face, launching him backwards to the floor. He screamed in pain, and it was obvious his vision had been impaired. Hoy went to work with the first aid kit while Waters fought to keep the floundering Chinook airborne. He held the cyclic tightly, feeling the helicopter still under his control. He remembered a tactic that he had read about in an old book on World War Two fighter pilots. He aimed the big, bulky double rotored machine at the Hind head on and rolled the ship over at the last moment, allowing MacDougall to shower the underside of the Hind with machine gun fire. The Russian machine spun wildly out of control, flames spitting and smoke pouring from it's port side engine cowling. The rocky desert below them was itself a mass of smoke and flame from the battle.

Hoy did not have the time to congratulate the young man on his tactics or piloting skill. He was tending to the wounded pilot whose face was singed and bloody from the tiny shards in his cheeks left there from the explosion of the windscreen.

Waters brought the Chinook around on a second target. In front of them, the lead aircraft had engaged three of the Hinds and was exchanging heavy fire, while one of the Chinooks bloomed as it was hit by a volley of rockets and the relentless assault by the Russians resulted in it's total destruction. The aft section of the nearest Hind came up directly in front of the battered RAF machine.

"Fire!" Waters was almost on his feet, red faced and determined in his course of action.

MacDougall let loose with another burst from his .50 caliber machine gun, which found it's target. The Russian gunship disappeared in a yellow-green cloud of flame and spinning wreckage.

"We have another one of those bastards on our aft port quarter. Closing," Hoy called, calling from his machine gun post.

"On my mark.. I have a plan. Be ready," Waters said quietly.

Behind them, the Hind closed in for the kill. The Chinook was smoking from the punishment it had taken, but it was still flyable.

The Russians probed closer, with its air to air missiles ready to strike them. Still the Hind ventured closer.

"Now!"

The transport chopper groaned as Waters applied emergency reverse thrust. The sudden deceleration nearly hurled everyone forward and the cargo they were carrying slid worryingly toward the cockpit, despite being tethered to the deck. But somehow, the gunship held together.

The missile flashed past, as did the Hind which passed to their port side dangerously closely.

"Open fire!" Waters bellowed.

The aft section of the helicopter gunship glowed and pieces of debris spun from its hull, but it somehow remained in one piece. Its robust build quality managed to absorb some of the furious blasts of the Chinook's weapons, but enough damage had been done.

"They are withdrawing," said Hoy incredulously. For the Russians to back away from a fight was almost unheard of, but the proof was right there in front of them. The remaining Russian helicopters moved away from the remaining RAF machines, decreasing in size until they were mere pinpricks against the stark background of rugged peaks and dusty desert plain.

"I want to see what they're up to," Rouse snapped tinnily over the damaged microphone at no- one in particular.

The dust in the distance gave away that the Russians had formed a line but they hovered just below the horizon. Three of the Chinooks had been destroyed but the sheer ferocity that the RAF squadron had displayed had forced the enemy back. For now.

MacDougall checked the damage control readouts.

"We have some hull damage, our port engine took a nasty hit that we'll need to check out and the captain has been seriously injured."

Waters thumbed the control to the intercom.

"This is Golf Echo Romeo, come in."

Rouse replied in a tinny sounding voice. If things had been different, Mel would have been tempted to laugh at how silly he sounded.

"I want a full damage control party on all damage immediately. I don't want to be caught out if they decide to come back for a second round."

A Scottish voice answered him. "Golf Lima Bravo here, we're in one piece but our co-pilot is down."

Mel frowned. That was good news. He knew the co-pilot, Pilot Officer Montgomery had graduated at the same time as him and he was a good guy.

"All remaining ships reform on me and carry on. Let's get this mission over with," Rouse said in determined tone.

"Yeah," came a cynical reply. "And get shot to shit on the way back."

Rouse was absolute in his intentions and was clearly not in the mood to be back talked.

"That is quite enough. We will discuss this when we land."

A short time later, Mel Waters found himself sitting in a circle under a starry sky. The remaining Chinooks were being patched up by the engineers that had been assigned to each aircraft, and whatever tools and spares they had were now being put frantically to work. The supplies had been handed over to the Mujaheddin and the tribesmen had mysteriously vanished as quickly as they had appeared from the rocks surrounding the landing site. Quite impressive considering they were mostly on horseback. Their leader, a man who answered to the name of Navjit had laughed at the gifts and led his people away as soon as they had what they wanted.

Rouse had insisted on no camp fires as that would give away their position in an instant if the Russians were still out there, which none of them were in any doubt that they were. Now here they were, sat in the middle of Afghanistan contemplating their fates.

Nichol was being ended to. His burns should heal but they needed to get him back to camp quickly. Hoy had patched him up as best as he could and he was resting for the time being. As the senior officer available of his particular chopper, he had been ordered to attend after Rouse had called a cabinet of war as he called it of the commanding officers of the remaining Chinooks.

Now he found himself alongside some illustrious company. Flt. Lts. Sytner and Reeve, two men as uncompromising as they come, of the BK sat next to Sqn. Ldr. Gravett and his first officer Plt.

Officer Harvey of the BY. Gravett had gained notoriety by taking part in the Falklands, flying a Humphrey under heavy and sustained fire at Goose Green. Of the two, Harvey was the more jovial personality, but there was a long standing animosity between himself and Wing Commander Cartwright, the squadron commander.

For now, they were keeping their mutual dislike in check, while Gravett remained characteristically businesslike.

"The question, gentlemen, is why the Russians sent to many choppers into this area," Rouse was saying.

"This area has been under dispute for years but they have not made an aggressive attempt to take territory until now. I want to know why."

"I would have thought the answer fairly obvious," said Sqn. Ldr. Soper, his number one. "They want to destroy the Mujaheddin and anyone who tries to assist them."

"Noted, but I'm sure there's more to it than that."

"I say hit them now, and keep hitting them," said Sytner. Reeve nodded in agreement. "Hit them now and then they might get the message."

"In case you hadn't noticed, sir, we have just had a very costly engagement. I'm sure that you can tell that three of our crews will not be coming home again," MacDougall countered.

"Yes I saw that. All the more reason to hit them now," Sytner shot back hotly.

"Mason," Rouse told Sytner. We are down to three ships while they still have eleven. Those are long odds."

"We got them on the run though, didn't we? We shouldn't let up the advantage." Sytner was resolute.

Rouse and Gravett simply looked at each other across the table. The sandy haired Gravett shook his head.

"Your opinion is noted, Frank," was the only riposte.

Sytner looked genuinely disappointed to not be putting up more of a fight. Waters had been keeping quiet, letting the senior officers have their say. Perhaps they would see it as him speaking out of turn, but it was worth taking the chance.

"May I speak sir?" he asked Rouse. The senior officer nodded curtly.

"Sirs. There is obviously something in this area that they want badly. This whole part of the country is close to the borders with Russia. From the air it looks worthless, just hills and mountains, but what do the mountains hide? Whatever it is, it could be very valuable." Waters was nothing if not impassioned, and he could tell that his words were having an impact. The older heads were paying attention to him. It was a nice feeling. Emboldened, he went on.

"If the Mujaheddin need our help, it would be in our interests to check out whatever is around here, and report it."

"And how do you propose to do that, kid? As your crewman pointed out, we're all out of men,"

Sytner said sourly.

"We could send a search party out to see what is around here."

"We tried that a few years ago. It failed dismally," Harvey responded. "Who let this guy in to this meeting?"

"I did, Tom. And you should be thanking him because it was this man who came up with those acrobatics that you were so impressed with," Rouse told him bluntly. "So show some respect.

You know, that thing that you struggle with?"

Harvey stared daggers at Rouse and snorted but said no more.

"This young man is right," said Gravett. "If the Russkies have something big going down, then we could be in serious trouble."

"Hell, they may already be here and that's why they were so keen for us not to be," agreed Sytner, finally showing some interest.

The officers rose and looked around at each other.

"Let's put together a search party. One person from each crew. That way the risk is shared. It's too late to head out now, so we move at first light," Rouse said.

There were nods of agreement before they broke out their sleeping bags and tried to get settled for a night's sleep in the desert. The temperature dropped rapidly once the sun went down, and tonight was no different. Waters and MacDougall huddled in their all-weather overcoats and sipped on coffee from a heavy duty thermos flask.

At last, Mel began to feel sleepy and he dozed off into sleep. The feeling that anyone could be Around who could jump out at them at any time meant that someone kept watch on two hour shifts. Sinter took the first watch, his Browning 9mm set in his hand and a grim expression on His face. Somewhere in his sleep, Mel wondered how these people got the thought of their Friends going down in flames out there.

"You don't you just get used to it," said Sinter.

Mel opened his eyes and rolled over.

"Sorry, what?"

The older man was still sat in the same position that he had when Mel had fallen asleep. He Looked down at the young charge.

"You were talking in your sleep. You said how we live with seeing the death and destruction Of our friends," Sytner said solemnly.

"This will be experience for you. Probably not good, but experience anyway." He weighed up Waters carefully. "You did well out there, Waters. I'm impressed with you."

Waters beamed with pride. The young man was clearly touched and emboldened.

"Thank you sir."

"Don't let it go to your head. You still have a lot to learn."

Harvey took over from Sytner and Waters dropped off into a dreamless unconsciousness. When Mel awoke, the first shafts of sunlight were starting to peak over the craggy ridge of hills to the East. He pulled himself up from his drowsy slumber and smoothed his uniform down. The senior Members of the squad were already deep in discussion.

"Alright," announced Rouse finally. "Myself, Waters and Gravett are going on Recce. The rest of you, keep working on the choppers. We'll probably be getting out of here in a hurry."

Mel hadn't expected to be chosen considering he was the only serviceable pilot on his crew. Still it was the chance to show what else he was made of.

"Then we headed out into the hills and that's when things got very interesting," Waters finished.

Haltwhistle was agog with interest. He and McCleland had sat for the previous ten minutes in silence listening to the veteran's story. "What happened then?" Jim was eager to hear more.

"It can wait. Now. Tell me, about one of your adventures," said Mel. He had had enough for the time being of going over old and sometimes painful memories.

"Oh I don't know. I've not faced anything so dangerous as you two. I'm just a desk hugger,"

Colin said modestly.

"That's a load of crap mate," Jim told him. "You solved that thing about the aircraft that supposedly disappeared."

"What was all that about?" asked Mel, intrigued.

"Well," Colin began. "I worked out that someone was ferrying something he shouldn't have been out of the country. What he was doing was taking off, flying at low level with another plane so that on a radar screen it looked like one aircraft and at the last moment, the one guy would turn away for landing while he went on below the radar horizon. It was simple, really."

"That's impressive!" Mel told Colin.

"No, not really. It was just reading through the air traffic reports and matching them with the aircraft signed out from the airfield that I suspected. I was just doing my job."

Jim shook his head. He couldn't get his head around why Colin was so self - effacing. He didn't seem to take pleasure in his own achievements or smarts, or if he did, he didn't show it.

Although he wore his heart on his sleeve, McCleland was tempered by experience so had avoided the accusations of being arrogant or big mouthed. Well, to those close to him he wasn't!

"What would you like to hear about?" Jim asked Mel.

"You served in Afghanistan. Any good stories?"

McCleland shook his head. He did not particularly want to open up, as much as he respected the older man. "Not really I was in my Tonka flying at 10,000 feet above those on the ground, so I was in the rarefied atmosphere. No face to face stuff."

It was a bare faced lie. He had indeed faced off in person, but he had no desire to talk about it.

Waters smiled. He knew McCleland was hiding something but was far too gentlemanly to say anything.

They went back and forth for a while, sharing notes on their respective adventures and how much of a different challenge a helicopter was to a jet bomber. Colin sat back and let them go at it, enjoying the pilots comparing notes.

"I would say, Jim that you've enjoyed the same kind of adventures that you Mel had the pleasure of taking part in."

McCleland smiled a little. "It was certainly a good challenge."

NINE

Just as he had said he would, Colin Haltwhistle arrived in Camp Bastion's vast medical center.

He sought a top plastic reconstructive surgeon who he knew from basic, Dr. Dave Thompson. If anyone could be trusted to not ask too many questions, he could. Thompson had become acting chief medical officer in light of recent events and was deep in working on a report when Haltwhistle knocked at the door of his office. Thompson was highly organized to the point of OCD, and he had had the office rearranged and tidied to suit his working preferences. The medical unit was mostly quiet, except for a nurse treating an unfortunate squaddie's elbow, the result of an accident in the gym.

"Not interrupting anything am I?" Colin asked from the door frame.

Thompson looked up and smiled. "Sherlock! Where the hell have you been hiding?"

"Oh, God, don't start that again," Colin groaned.

He ushered his old friend in and they shook hands enthusiastically. It had been six years since they had last seen each other.

"What's a dazzling personality like you doing in this shit hole? What can I do for you?"

Colin plopped himself down in the seat opposite Thompson. He looked around to make sure the nurse was not in earshot before he spoke.

"Oh, I'm fine. Getting by."

"Seriously, what the hell are you doing here? The last I heard you were doing Sherlock Holmes type stuff?" Thompson was genuinely surprised and pleased to see Colin.

"Yeah a bit of that, but at the moment I'm in a hurry and I need help." Colin cut to the chase quickly. He hadn't much time and while catching up sounded great, he had a job to do.

"What I'm about to tell you, you can't tell anyone OK? This is completely confidential and can't be spoken of with anyone else on the camp," he informed the good doctor.

"Yeah sure. Now what's on your mind?" Thompson thought there was some sort of medical issue that was to be kept private. He did not expect what Haltwhistle now requested of him. He felt like laughing but given Colin's serious expression once he had explained the situation, he knew this was serious.

"Yeah, I think I can do that. I would need to have some time to prepare that for the three of you, and I would need to take molds of McCleland's and Waters' faces but I think I can do it." Then he smiled. "I wouldn't go to a fancy dress party though if I were you!"

Colin made a face. "I don't see why I'd want to go to a party dressed like that, I'd be disemboweled."

Thompson knew Haltwhistle better than to know he wasn't serious and let it slide.

"Never mind. I can get it ready, but I will need to see the three of you to get everything set up."

"Let me know when you're ready, mate. I have to get back to see what else is in store for us."

Then the Flight Lieutenant turned on his heel and was gone.

The nurse popped her head around the doorway, curiosity getting the better of her. She had released the squaddie in short order, being more interested in knowing what Haltwhistle's visit was about.

"Anything I should know about?"

Thompson simply smiled broadly and went about his work. The nurse cocked her head, knowing when she wasn't going to be told anything and went back to work.

TEN

Colin rose from the table and went to the mess room door. The room had cleared out in the time that they had been talking and Haltwhistle was now taking advantage of the quiet. He locked the door and came back. Jim suspected he knew what his partner had to say.

"You're not about to produce paddles and a gimp mask are you mate?" he said lightly. He knew that this was serious and he was trying to be as cheerful as possible.

"I've been checking Russian intelligence channels on and off while we've been traveling so far."

"Russian intelligence? What for?" asked Waters.

Haltwhistle retook his seat and produced what looked like an iPad and stylus. He opened yet another bottle of Mountain Dew and took a deep drink from it.

"Bloody caffeine addict!" Jim joked.

"I think we're in for a lot more trouble than what we've been told," Haltwhistle explained.

McCleland stood up and leaned against the table, perching on the edge of it.

"I'd go along with that. Behind the lines is always a risk, but the mission still has to go ahead."

Waters needed answers. "Could you two please tell me what the hell is going on?" he asked in exasperation.

"I think the reason you were brought aboard with this and why we've been given a Russian chopper will become clear in a moment. For this mission to work, we to get hold of that key. It's the only way we have of not raising any eyebrows when we get to wherever it is we're going," Colin explained.

"Go on," McCleland knew not to interrupt Colin when he had an idea.

"I have been checking the database for any member of the Russian intelligence services. I think that to really be able to pull this off, we need to head to a city in Uzbekistan and go from there."

"What city? What are you talking about?" Waters was genuinely confused.

"Mel, erm... I think that the reason you were arm twisted into this was not so much because you know this area, but that's important, it's because you're the best chopper pilot that Cartwright knows of. But as I was saying. Gentlemen, it's in our interest to get hold of Russian guns, explosives and the like and IDs to allow us to blend in. I've already got the camp surgeon to put together for us certain things which will allow us to go unnoticed as Russians, but we need to get hold of guns and kit."

"Mate, we can't just waltz into a shop and buy AK-47s," Jim protested. "And what about this key?"

"Actually, you can if you know the right places to go," Mel told them. "The nomad traders do business with just about everyone. If you need to get hold of anything, they'd be the ones to track down."

"Exactly," Colin said. "So I'm thinking we should head for Temez, it's a city near the Turkmenistan border to get our hands on this stuff."

"Turkmenistan? That's a fair way from where we're going to end up," McCleland pointed out.

"True, but with the way the supplies to this Happyville place are coming and going, it won't raise any questions about odd routes flown."

"Oh, fair enough," Mel understood now. "But what about this Russian intelligence business?"

Haltwhistle changed from images of maps on the iPad to pictures of Russians in uniform. Severe looking types, all of them. "That brings me to my checking on Russian Intelligence. I've found out that a guy called Ulyenkov is due to be in Temez in two days, and is heading to Happyville afterwards. I think we need to erm... you know... get his co-operation."

Colin brought up an image of Ulyenkov on the iPad screen. The image was fuzzy, obviously taken surreptitiously. But even a blurry photo showed he had a vague similarity to Jim's features.

Waters started.

"You said Ulyenkov?"

"Yeah. You know of him?"

Waters felt a cold finger running down his back. "Yes I do. But it was a long time ago." Mel shook his head.

A run in with that man was the last thing he wanted. McCleland, noticing his advisor's discomfort pressed on.

"I'm sorry, but how do you plan on getting him to see things our way? I don't think a Russian interrogator is going to be that inclined to help us. Unless you fancied a one way trip to Chernobyl's reactor core."

Then Jim realized what Colin was about to suggest. He could already feel his heart sinking. For his part, Haltwhistle had a devilish gleam in his eye.

"Oh no. No way, no and never in that order mate." Jim was wagging his finger to emphasize the point.

"If he were removed and replaced by someone impersonating him, then we might, might just make this work. Ulyenkov travels with a couple of lackeys, which explains why there are three people actively taking part on this mission. And you looking like this bloke helps too. The fact that in your file it says you can speak Russian makes you perfect."

Jim went white. "You read my file?"

"Course I did. I wanted to see what kind of guy I was being given to work with."

McCleland knew where this was going, and he didn't like it at all. "You mean I should impersonate this dude?"

Colin's response was succinct. "Yep."

"Mate, I'm not an actor! I can't put on a silly voice!" He effected a Russian brogue. " 'We have ways of making you talk, comrade!' See what I mean?"

Jim simply glared at Colin in the usual way he did when he wasn't thrilled about something. For his part, Haltwhistle simply returned McCleland's grim expression.

Waters looked deeply uncomfortable and tapped his glass of shandy.

"What you're proposing is at best crazy and at worst could start some seriously bad shit. And for what? This whole scheme is mad!" he exclaimed. "This is not what I signed on for! I was told I was simply to be an advisor!"

"I think you can thank Black Jack for all this," Jim responded lightly.

"If you have a better idea, I'm all ears." said Colin, folding his arms.

"Look at it this way," Jim said. "All you have to do is fly the chopper. All I have to do is pretend to be some psycho for a few days!"

"That shouldn't be too hard for you," Colin grinned.

Jim grimaced. "Fuck off, man."

The helicopter was undergoing final ground checks and Waters had chosen to grab a cup of coffee while the final checks were made. Mulling over his drink in Camp Bastion's vast mess hall the following morning, Mel Waters wondered if his vast experience would be enough to get him through this, a mission he had never asked for. Being dragged away from his family for a week was reasonable. He had had to spend extended time away when he was on active duty, but this had been a bolt from the blue.

He was 49, a time when his contemporaries were resting comfortably, spending their down time with their loved ones and writing their memoirs. Waters had enjoyed a fulfilling career. Never being a flamboyant man, he instead had earned a reputation for being methodical. He had been forced to come up with inventive maneuvers to save his helicopter and crew, yes but they were always carefully considered. He rose through the ranks before taking a transfer from front line duty, instead becoming an instructor at RAF Halton.

Shunning the responsibility of outright command of a squadron, he nonetheless got the thrill of being back out in the field. Certainly appealing for a pilot, especially when he had been told it was to work with a special operations section that had just been set up. He had red about the RAF's previous special service division, as had most people in the service. It was all the more pleasing that his old commander, John Cartwright had been the one to approach him. A fine if unshowy man rather like himself. But Jim McCleland and Colin Haltwhistle represented a new breed of officer, one that was prepared to take risks, and despite what Colin said he was young and therefore prone to throwing caution to the wind. Mel had heard of the two by reputation only but now that he had got the chance to actually met the men, he was able to form a real opinion. It was a good one but it also raised a lot of questions, so he decided to ask the man who had put him up to this. He really needed a drink stiffer than coffee after learning how they wanted to proceed with this scheme.

"What's going on, Mel?"

"Sorry to trouble you, I just had a few things to ask," Mel explained to Cartwright.

Cartwright had not expected a call, but he had a lot of time for his men, even if they were retired or no longer in the service. He also knew that Mel wouldn't contact him unless something was on his mind.

"You look like you need to talk," Cartwright said over the video link.

"You bet I do. These two guys. They have just come up with the daftest scheme I've ever heard."

He filled Cartwright in on the details of what they had proposed.

"Well, that's pretty extreme but I gave them a wide latitude with this, so the ball is in their court."

"Do you know what could happen if anything goes wrong?" Waters exclaimed.

"Mel, I'd keep your voice down if I were you. You don't know who is listening." Cartwright was clearly happy to go along with whatever his two young charged had in mind, no matter how crazy. Mel knew he had lost before the argument had even started. He felt dejected.

"I was just thinking. What am I doing here? I'm a bit long in the tooth for this sort of thing."

The older man sat back in his chair.

"We've come a long way since we were both young. You were almost scared to get things wrong in case your commanding officer laid into you as I recall."

"Yeah, I was quite sensitive to start with," Waters agreed. "What do you think this is all about, sir? A Russian helicopter and a Russian jeep all this stuff about rogue generals..." His voice tailed off so as not to alert other people in the mess hall, who may or may not be listening.

"Things will come out in the wash, I'm sure. We got involved in some cloak and dagger stuff in our day," Cartwright replied matter-of-factly. He knew a lot more than he was letting on, Mel was sure of it.

"We did, but nothing this extreme."

They sat and shared a look. It had been several years since they had seen each other, but it was like picking up where they had left off, even if it was through the limited means of a webcam.

"How have you been, John? Air Vice Marshal of the RAF, third in command. You've done well for yourself."

"I can't complain. I get kept busy. A bit too much red tape from people who don't have a clue but like to think that they do, but you know how it is. The big man here I could live without, but he lets me do my work without looking over my shoulder."

Mel leaned forward. "I've read about that. It's not good."

"Yeah, well it's office politics and it's everywhere, so get used to it. Anyway, I suspect this is not about pushing paperwork, so what's on your mind?" Cartwright brought things back to matters at hand.

"Yeah. it's about my new colleagues."

Cartwright grinned. "Are they pulling on the leash?"

Mel liked how Cartwright could defuse a difficult moment with a joke. "No, they're behaving for now. What are these two actually like? Do I need to know anything?"

John thought about the question. He could mouth the usual platitudes but they wouldn't answer what Waters was really asking: Would Haltwhistle and McCleland's actions put him at risk or worse?

"Jim thinks he's right in his own mind. He's a straight shooter. He takes risks but they're always calculated. He's capable but he's a rough diamond. If he listens to Haltwhistle, which is one of the reasons I put them together then he will be fine," he answered.

"I've spoken to him a little when we were checking everything out, but I need to know what he's like as a person."

"He's good. Quite brash at times, but I doubt you'll be placed in great danger. Colin is calmer and doesn't rush in, so he's a good influence."

There was an audible sigh of relief.

"What you're saying is, I won't be taken by surprise again then?" Mel ventured hopefully.

"Mel, relax. You'll be fine."

His good ardor was quickly undone as soon as he walked in to the medical center. Waters could not believe what he was seeing.

He had been told to close his eyes while Doctor Thompson took a mold of his face so that he could manufacture the pieces he needed to transform the retired Royal Air Force officer into a fearsome Russian officer. Now he was seeing the fruits of the good doctor's labors.

In the mirror a severe tanned looking man with a drooping mustache and cropped hair had replaced the balding, amiable looking, middle aged gentleman he was used to seeing. Waters was horrified. This was not what he had come out of retirement for.

This whole thing was getting completely out of hand. He remembered something his father had told him at a sports event he had had to enter as a kid. *Son, never volunteer for anything, because as sure as you stand here, you will be the poor sap who gets volunteered anyway.*

Well, now he was seeing the point his old man had made all those years ago!

Across the office, McCleland and Haltwhistle were similarly outfitted with features which made them look as if they had a permanent scowl and distinctly unpleasant natures. All that was missing was the usual Russian uniforms.

Jim was checking himself over in the mirror, while Colin looked on. He was surprised how close his appearance matched Ulyenkov's.

The Russian's picture was stuck to the mirror and all Thompson had to do was follow the image.

"I don't think I'm going to win any beauty contests in this get-up," he sighed.

"Yeah, you definitely wouldn't win Miss Universe. But you might pick up one of those tennis players with the funny long names!" Colin replied.

Jim looked at him thoughtfully. "I've never had a Russian girl. I'm not sure I could put up with all that comrade stuff."

Mel could hear the sarcasm dripping from Colin. "In any case you should make for a very convincing Russian."

McCleland gave him a look that could freeze water, not too difficult with the face he was now wearing.

"You could pass yourself off as a decent representative of the Iron Curtain yourself, mate. The good doctor did a nice job hiding your ugly mug! I feel like Martin Landau."

Happy that the disguises were good enough, the group removed the hair and face appliances, but the facial makeup that Thompson had created was difficult to wash off. Only repeated scrubbing would begin to have an effect. Waters again thought of how he had got himself into this as he recognized his own face again. He promised himself he would not speak to John Cartwright again for a very long time if he somehow got out of this in one piece.

Colin checked his watch.

"It's nearly time," he said. "They should have the chopper by now."

Jim nodded and looked at his partners in crime. "Let's go."

ELEVEN

Jim stood on the pan, waiting for Waters to return from his test flight. He checked his watch. He had been gone for about 20 minutes. He knew from experience that a check flight could last up to an hour. The ground crew had worked tirelessly over the last two hours to get the Hip in to serviceable condition and the call had been welcome.

The sun was sinking low in the sky, so he reckoned it may be that the veteran was going to get in some night flying as well. It would probably be needed.

Colin rejoined him with a sly smile.

"We're all sorted," he said cryptically.

"That sounds dodgy!" McCleland replied.

The light was failing quickly. Around them, spotlights lit up the base and the faint shouts of orders being barked as the guard changed could be heard. Jim knew it was nearly time to put the first part of the plan into operation. He also knew that their next actions would raise a few eyebrows if word got out. He just hoped he didn't get any more cloak and dagger assignments for a while after this.

He glanced around him. Fortunately, there were no nosey parkers hanging around, but when the Hip came back in to land it would undoubtedly pique some interest. The base commander had been very helpful in getting together a handful of people to guard the chopper, and McCleland hoped that military discipline would keep everyone else at bay. But this new mission was something that had never been contemplated, let alone attempted. A thousand things could go wrong, and there were so many doubts.

Having Waters along was a blessing. He had seen and done more in this area than all of them put together, so it gave some measure of comfort. He could guide and advise around potential obstacles.

The familiar beat of rotor blades on air giving a comforting whump-whump sound grew faintly from the west. The noise grew steadily as the helicopter approached. Its nose searchlight was switched on and grew brighter the closer it got until as the chopper crossed the threshold of the airfield, the noise and light became overwhelming. With Waters at the controls, the big Russian machine touched down gently, throwing up clouds of dust and sand. The rotors slowed as the noise died away and the small, stocky man climbed out of the pilot's seat. Waters had a satisfied smile on his face. He took his bone dome off and headed back to where his colleagues were waiting. His trainer just nodded and walked off, heading back to his billet.

"How was it?" Jim asked.

"It just took a bit of getting used to," the older man grinned. He had clearly enjoyed the experience.

"Do you think we're ready?" Colin asked them both. The three looked around at each other.

"We don't have the time to not be. Yeah. I think we're up for this," Jim said. If they didn't do this now, then the chances of recovering Clark in one piece were slim to none.

The base commander had been as good as his word, posting several guards. Haltwhistle had voiced his concerns about leaving the helicopter unattended, but Jim assured him that would not be the case and Colin's mind was put at ease. Taking the helicopter in, Jim was still impressed by how imposing the thing was. Menacing, full of power and looking mean just at a standstill, resplendent in its desert camouflage scheme.

McCleland wiping his face, still grimy from the hastily removed makeup. He stopped by the ladder up to the forward cockpit where he would be sitting.

There was a sense of expectant trepidation in the air. The UAZ had been loaded somewhat awkwardly into the Hip's aft compartment. How it had been loaded was a miracle as the jeep was too large in reality, but a few modifications, such as removing the canvas roof and the unhooking the helicopter's loading doors had helped. Waters took the helicopter's log and signed it, officially turning responsibility for the aircraft to him.

"Report."

"Everything is ready, sir. All cargo loaded," said the crew chief.

"Very good. Any sign of anything in the area?"

The chief was confident. "None at this time."

"How about the weather, not going to be caught by surprise are we?"

"No, sir."

It's going well so far Colin mused. Then he thought ahead. All three of the helicopter's occupants would be needed to go in to the city itself which would leave the helicopter unprotected. They needed someone to come along.

"Are you fully rated with weapons, chief?" he asked.

"Of course, sir, but -"

"You're coming with us. I'll square it with the base commander."

The techie looked more than a little put out. "I have my orders and duties sir! If I fail to report, I'll be in the shit!"

"Well now you've got some new orders, chief. Get on board." Colin turned to McCleland. "Once we're airborne, code a message to Cartwright. Inform him of our current status and tell him we are proceeding with the mission. Make sure you use the call signs to open and close the message."

He nodded. "Will do."

McCleland ducked into the cockpit and stepped down into his seat. "Alright." He punched the button on his seat that he knew would start up his weapons systems. "My watch says it's time."

Mel sat in the pilot's seat and began running through his preflight checklist while a team of ground crew went over the engines and rotor blades. Once they were satisfied, Mel gave his instruments a one over and flicked the switch that he knew would turn the engines over. They whirred and turned slowly at first, gaining speed with each rotation until they caught and the familiar beat of rapidly turning rotor blades filled the cabin. Dust plumed into the air as the blades caught the air. Waters pulled up on the collective and the Hip lifted off the ground, pitched forward and gained height. The chief, not used to being airborne looked a little pale.

"Bring us about and head northeast," Colin said through his headset. He was designated the navigator and had plotted a course for them that would take them away from patrol routes and therefore prying eyes.

From the other end, Waters' voice sounded strangely resigned. "Wilco."

The Hip turned smartly on its axis and headed away from the base towards the mountains in the distance. Keeping low to stay under any radars that anyone watching may have set up, the helicopter skimmed the ground as it went on its way. Behind them, the camp gradually faded from view until it was gone.

From the flight engineer's station, Haltwhistle watched as readouts whirred and flashed as it checked the helicopter's workings. The readouts were labeled in Russian, which was a course he hadn't taken, so he kept himself to himself and studied his maps again.

"Can I ask what the plan is?" asked Waters. "Are we sticking to what we discussed earlier, or do you have any other good ideas?"

"Well, I've been thinking. I think that if we are going to disguise ourselves we need to have the right equipment. What we were talking about, and what Cartwright talked about, you know?

Weapons, radios and that sort of thing. We need to get hold of that stuff pronto."

Jim shot back. "Hold on. Let me just bend over and pull this out of my arse!"

In the pilot's seat Mel rolled his eyes. He could do without the schoolyard banter.

Colin ignored the jibe. "I checked the latest intel reports. There are no bazaars out this way where we could get stuff like that, but if we headed for the Turkmenistan border, there's a city called Termez."

There was reason to Colin's line of thought. The piece of card that Cartwright had handed to him back in London had led Haltwhistle to scour the maps of the local area. The only place that he could find that matched what appeared to be printed on the card was the city of Termez.

The chief didn't like that notion at all. "You need to be careful going that way. The Taliban are thick around there. We'd be heading straight in to a trouble spot."

Jim frowned. "That far north? I thought they were towards the center of the country."

The NCO just looked him sideways. It was enough to know he was sure about what he was saying.

"That part of the world has vast poppy fields. I'm sure you know what poppy seeds form the basis of."

Colin understood immediately. The manufacture and effects of opium and in turn heroin was something he had read up on in great detail. Its effects were grim and devastating. But the sale of poppy seeds and their subsequent conversion into the highly addictive and deadly drug was a hugely valuable - if despicable – commodity.

"That would explain why there are Mujaheddin around there. It's funny, the biggest export the country has and the Taliban want nothing to do with that stuff."

"There's good and bad everywhere, mate," Jim replied.

Mel considered all the information shared for a moment.

"No margin for error, eh guys?"

The dark, stony look that his two friends were giving him said it all. But what Colin had said about them needing suitable equipment made sense.

"We still need those supplies. I think it's a risk worth taking, but we'll have to be really careful.

Let's go there, find what we need and get the fuck out of Dodge nice and quietly. The last thing we want is to get involved with drug smuggling," said Haltwhistle.

Waters and McCleland agreed wholeheartedly with that statement.

Mel adjusted his controls and the view ahead of the helicopter shifted again as he changed course and headed for the city. The chopper turned to the left. The mountains were looming ahead of them and they had to get across the range in order to reach the city.

"Estimating arrival in two hours, eight minutes," Colin informed them, checking his maps and looking at the air speed dial. "That gives us enough time to fill in Cartwright on what's going on."

"I'll take care of it." Jim rose and went back into the hold.

In his office based in the converted air raid bunker deep below the Waterloo stations, Cartwright paced around the assembly area, deep in thought. He had been used to sending crews out on difficult assignments and his best officers into situations where danger was just around the corner, but this was different. There was a lot more at stake than recovering Bill Clark, but at the moment he had to focus on other work to pass the time.

Then a voice disturbed his thoughts. Despite himself he jumped slightly. Trying to quell his anxiousness, he turned to see Casey Matthews with a radio headset in his hand. Harvey came over from the bank of computers to join them.

"The message you were waiting for has just come through sir," Matthews offered, somewhat reluctantly Cartwright thought.

"Put it through."

He retreated to his office with Harvey in tow. Switching on the video link on his computer terminal, he got a shaky picture of James

McCleland, who was sitting in the confines of the helicopter, still wearing standard desert kit.

"Rapier calling Wrens Nest. Come in."

Cartwright nodded. "Wren's Nest. Go ahead."

"Mission proceeding as planned. Plotted course for first touchdown point. Please stand by Wrens Nest. Rapier out." Simple, straight forward. The image of Jim was cut and the camera image went dark. Cartwright smiled to himself.

"Come home in one piece, lads." he muttered.

He then asked Harvey to have Wing Commander Matthews join them. In a moment, he was in the office with his hands clasped behind his back.

"Our men are on their way. So far, so good," Cartwright told him.

"That's good to hear. Did they say what their plan was?" Matthews asked.

The Air Vice Marshal shook his head and came around the desk.

"No. And I doubt they will let us know specifics. We did give those guys a broad remit to get things done with this one and perhaps it's best not to know."

"Perhaps too wide, if I may say so sir," Matthews replied.

Harvey and Cartwright exchanged a look.

"Really? Why do you say that?" Harvey demanded.

Matthews swallowed a little and chose his words carefully.

"McCleland's a maverick sir. He has a history of disobeying orders and how should I say it... 'interpreting' regulations to suit his own wishes? That sir, in my opinion makes him unsuitable to command, let alone lead a mission like this."

Cartwright considered this for a moment. Then he waved the Wing Commander to take a seat.

"If you had reservations about McCleland, why did you mention him to me before? I brought him in based on what you said."

Harvey was not impressed with Matthews' attitude either.

"Exactly because of his maverick nature. Despite his reputation for ignoring the rules, he gets results," said Casey stiffly.

"I see," Cartwright leaned against the desk to one side of Matthews. "You've commanded a flight before. You've been out there. You've had to order men to their death, haven't you?"

"Of course I have, sir. What's your point?" he said slowly.

Cartwright eyed his subordinate with curiosity.

"It's not exactly a secret around these parts that you and McCleland don't get on. It's a fact that you chopped Haltwhistle from his flight training as well, despite him having good aptitude is it so?"

Matthews did not like being put on the spot like this. He had a nice clean record. Why was he copping flak?

"Haltwhistle was a command decision. He couldn't co-ordinate the instrument checks or his directional flying. He wasn't good enough."

Cartwright pressed on. "In fact as I recall, you ordered two of your crew on a dangerous mission that had unfortunate consequences."

Matthews shifted uncomfortably in the seat. "That's right. As I recall it was one of your crew who came up with the idea for that risky mission."

Black Jack held up a hand to show that Matthews should stop talking.

"That's beside the point. You know what it's like out there. These men have to face death in some way every day. The rule book takes a back seat when people's lives are at stake and situations never seen or heard before events crop up on a regular basis. I see the manual as just that. A guidebook. Actual experience and a gut instinct is generally what brings our people home safely. If those boys are flying by the seat of their pants, then that counts for something. You may have given me the options on people, but it was me who made the final choice on this. And it was my choice to being you in to this section. So, you'd better remember which side your bread is buttered on. Clear?"

Matthews look chastened, then he stood up. "I'll try to remember that, sir."

"Dismissed," Cartwright said softly.

Matthews saluted then turned and stalked out.

"What do you think, sir?" Harvey asked.

"It's too early to tell.' The head of AID looked at his chief of staff. "Dressing down a little, aren't you? What happened to your lapel pin?"

Harvey reached up and touched the empty button hole. "Sorry sir, I must have forgot to put it in this morning."

"Don't forget it tomorrow."

Harvey did as Matthews before him had done and left the office. Cartwright watched them as they left, then flicked a button on his desk intercom.

"Bring me all of the records on Air Marshal Berry's death and the inquest in to it. Every word written about it."

***

In the cargo compartment, Haltwhistle had finished packing away the internet dongle and shutting down the laptop. Space was at a premium, so even the computer case had to be stowed carefully. A field radio and its accompanying power pack sat in a backpack.

Water flasks and rations were stored in another. The jeep barely squeezed into the back of the space. Fortunately, the aft fuselage opened outwards so that when the helicopter landed it could be reversed out. He had finished packing the computer into its space aboard when something out of the port side windows caught his eye. It was small and faint but the movement it was making was unmistakable. He ventured into the cockpit and peered out of the port side hand windows for a better look.

Yes. There it was.

"There's a helicopter off to our port side. I'd say about four or five miles way," he told Mel.

That was not news McCleland or Waters wanted to hear, especially as they were so close to reaching the border with Uzbekistan and the city of Termez. Jim craned his neck to look out to the left.

The unfortunate crew chief, still not happy to be have been essentially press ganged in to this mission was now facing the possibility of enemy action.

"We need to turn back," he insisted.

"Too late for that," Waters replied.

The helicopter was only a small speck against the skyline, but it looked as menacing as any that would usually be in this region. It appeared to be heading away from them, taking a lazy path in a straight line from left to right against the ridge of hills that it was flying over. If they could see whoever it was, they likewise could see them. Waters did not want to take any chances.

"I'm taking her down to the deck," he said.

Almost imperceptibly, the other helicopter also seemed to change course. The movement was hardly noticeable to the untrained eye, but an experienced airman could see there was a definite shift. Could they have seen them? Or was it a coincidence? Were the people on board after them?

All of those questions flashed in Mel's mind.

"Bring us in to land," Jim said. "We'll wait for them to move off."

"They could attack us while we're parked, sir," the chief pointed out. "We'd be a sitting duck!"

"A chance we'll have to take."

The whine of the rotor blades faded as Waters slowed and dropped the chopper to the deck. He nudged the Hip gently onto the ground and shut down the engines. The helicopter was now about four miles distant and still on its course which if they were still airborne would have brought them to intercept eventually. The crew were apparently completely unaware of the Russian machine now sat on the ground behind, watching them. For several agonizing seconds which felt more like minutes the three RAF men watched the helicopter as it faded from view.

The chatter from its engines and rhythmic beat of the rotors faded in to the distance along with the sight of the aircraft.

"Do you want me to take off?" Mel asked.

"No. Let them go for a bit. Put plenty of distance between them and us," Jim replied, still studying the horizon.

McCleland sat in his seat, waiting and watching. He knew that if they were detected, then a failed mission would be a mild consequence of what would follow. They would undoubtedly be arrested and charged as spies. The equipment on board would be enough evidence of that. A long stay in a jail or worse would be the result. It was not an appealing prospect. He looked at the worried face of the chief.

"Sorry for dragging you in to this, sarge," McCleland said.

"It's too late to worry, sir. I'm here, so I'll grin and bear it."

Jim was about to give the word to take off and continue, but Colin was still looking skyward. It was a good move to do so.

"Sounds like there's another chopper out there. Looks like it's following the same course as before."

The gray bulk of the second helicopter rolled across their path, but it was much closer and looked far more menacing. Mel could make out the battered paintwork on the side of the fuselage, a legacy of hard work and little solid maintenance, typical of Mother Russia.

There were no markings of any kind. All they could do was hope and pray that they hadn't been seen, but at this close range, maybe a mile there was no chance of not being so. The gray shape ghosted as it passed, but barreled on apparently oblivious to their presence, following the same course that the first chopper had headed, until it too was gone.

"That was close," breathed Colin.

"Too close," Jim agreed. "Can you track their course and work out where they were going?"

"Looks like the same place we are. it's the only thing around here," Haltwhistle said finally, looking up from his map and slide rule.

Perhaps they were not in trouble after all. If they were headed to the city too then it may have been completely innocent. But doubt niggled at the back of Jim's mind.

"Alright. Let's get this show back on the road. How close are we to Termez?"

"Not far at all. Fifteen miles maybe," Colin replied.

Mel rubbed his stubbly chin thoughtfully. "How about we drive into town from here? There doesn't seem to be anyone around and it's far enough away that we wouldn't be seen landing or anything like that."

"I like that," Jim smiled.

As the nominated driver, McCleland backed the jeep out of the helicopter. It took a few minutes to put the canvas roof back in place and load the equipment, but it was done. It was roasting hot and the desert gear they wore barely beat the heat back. His brow soaked with sweat, Colin climbed in to the back seat of the UAZ. As the rear door opened, a soft metallic thump sound came from somewhere at the back of the vehicle.

"Did you hear that?" Colin asked them. He rocked the jeep as best as he could, and the soft thumping noise was heard again. He got down on his knees and looked at the underside. It looked normal, but there was something, he was sure. Maybe a suspension arm was loose?

"Rock it again," he called out to Jim. He did as Colin had asked and the thudding sound came again. Haltwhistle fumbled around, he thought he knew where the sound was coming from. He reached up above the left rear leaf spring and felt something small and square in his hand. He pushed and pulled it until it came loose. Wriggling out from underneath, once he was on his feet he showed Mel and Jim what he had found. It was a small metallic box with an aerial wire and a flashing green light on top of it.

"It's a tracking device," Waters said. He turned it over in his fingers. He pushed the aerial in to the metal body and the light ceased.

"Where the fuck did that come from?" Jim demanded rhetorically.

"How the hell should I know?" Mel shot back.

The mission was now in serious jeopardy. If they were being watched, then those helicopters...

"I knew I should have checked everything again!" Haltwhistle was cursing himself.

"What's done is done. Don't beat yourself up," Mel told him.

"Should we turn back for Helmand?" the chief asked, half hoping that they would. It seemed as if that was inevitable and it would have suited him down to the ground.

"We need to let Cartwright know," Colin started urgently. "We might be being watched right now!"

Jim took the small device from Waters' hand and crushed it beneath his boot heel.

"Problem solved." He looked at the sky and worked out the sun's position. "It'll be dark soon, so we need to move everything quick, just in case there are any prying eyes. If I take the jeep and meet you..." he looked at the map that Colin had been looking at earlier. He pointed out a spot a couple of miles to the east that appeared to be surrounded by hills. "...here. That'll be a bit of security."

They agreed to the plan, and Jim set off in a cloud of dust. As the sun set, the Mi-8 took off and made the short jump at just above ground level to where McCleland was waiting for them, as good as his word.

Once Waters and Haltwhistle had disembarked, they set up camp quickly. Colin was still furious with himself at the oversight. He prided himself on being thorough. Hell, it was his job to be thorough.

"I've been thinking," he said. "Remember when I told you I saw those three guys acting strangely in the back of the Globemaster?"

"Yeah," said Jim, understanding.

"I think one of them was trying to find a place to plant that thing and once my back was turned, the little prick did it."

Mel nodded. "That makes sense. Do you remember his name?"

Colin frowned trying to remember. Southern? Sowter?

"It'll come back to you," Jim assured him.

"We need to give base a heads up."

He took out the laptop case and loaded the computer up. Once it was set up, he opened a line to Black Jack.

"Rapier calling Wren's Nest. Come in."

At last, Cartwright responded.

"Tracking device found on jeep. It must have been planted during the loading at Brize Norton."

He went on to explain about the technicians, and requested that they be held in custody for the duration of the mission.

"That can be taken care of, Haltwhistle. I wish to speak to all three members of the team."

Cartwright leaned forward and stared straight at the camera.

"You have permission to abort mission. Repeat: abort mission."

The chief looked more than a little relieved hearing those words. He was expecting the group to pack up and fly back immediately, but he was reckoning without McCleland and Haltwhistle's adventurousness.

Jim responded immediately. "We've come this far, we're going through with it."

They expected Black Jack to order them to abort, but his expression softened. "Very well. We will remain here for the duration. Wren's Nest out."

The screen flashed off and went dark.

"I wish you had consulted us before making that decision," Mel said irritably, looking at the NCO, who looked as if he had been slapped.

Jim simply gave him a look that said any argument was doomed to failure. "I'll let you know when this becomes a democracy."

"We need to change into those Russian uniforms," Colin said, changing the subject and hoping to head off a row. At the same time, he agreed wholeheartedly with his partner's instincts.

Climbing out of the jeep, they went around to the back and began unpacking their kit.

"Do you think one of us should stay with the chopper?" Mel asked, looking around at the group.

"We'll have to," Jim told him. "But it'll be fine."

Colin looked a little guilty. "Myself, Jim and Mel will be going in to the city, Chief... I want you to stay here and guard everything."

Despite everything, his sense of duty and honor was foremost in the Sergeant's mind. "Yes sir. You can count on me."

Colin nodded. "I'll make sure you get some sort of award for this. Thank you."

"Wait a minute," Mel commented. "If we go into town dressed like the Russian army, we're going to be about as welcome as AC/DC at an opera performance. We need to come up with something else."

He had a point there. Being formerly part of the USSR, Russians would probably not be welcomed with open arms, and knowing the area as he did, they had to defer to his superior knowledge. Jim looked in the backpacks and then at his two friends thoughtfully.

"Do we have any tea towels?"

Colin sighed. "Oh God. What have you got in mind now?"

A few minutes later and resplendent in their Russian disguises, McCleland's suggestion had resulted in the three of them dressing themselves in sleeping bag liners that were tied to resemble Bedouin robes.

Some parachute silk in a storage locker of the helicopter came in handy to make headdresses.

They looked passable. Colin was surprised how well this idea had turned out.

Now it really was time for this plan to be put into place. So far they had been lucky, but things could get extremely messy if their disguises didn't work, or if the people watching out for the tracker got clever. And being among a city full of potentially unfriendly people did not fill Jim with much joy.

"Alright, let's try this again," he said.

The next few days would be very difficult he mused as he started the engine. It turned over and growled in to life. The rustic vehicle contrasted well with the equally antiquated helicopter that it had been paired with.

"Good luck," Jim told the chief. "If there are any problems, radio us."

"Yes sir."

Pulling away from the helicopter, the UAZ bumped over the dusty, rocky road as the last strains of sunlight disappeared behind the hills to their left. The jeep shook and rocked over the stony track as they made their way towards the main road that was highlights on Colin's map.

Through the windscreen, Haltwhistle saw that the road was in a steep sided valley whose sides veered up steeply, allowing only one way traffic. It reminded him a bit of Dovedale in Derbyshire, and he wondered what it would look like in daylight. At last, the ground became smoother as they neared the road. A weathered road sign stood forlornly; it's writing in Arabic with English beneath it.

Following the directions, Jim turned left and began the journey into Termez. The headlamps had been refitted, like everything else and they lit up the dark highway very well. The occasional goat crossed their path, but nothing that was too dangerous. Jim revved the jeep up and put her in to top gear.

TWELVE

As they neared the city, the glow in the sky told them that this was a bustling metropolis that was busy. Being the biggest settlement in this area, they were bound to find something, surely?

"Do you guys have any idea how we go about finding, let alone getting hold of these supplies?"

Colin asked.

"You were the one who came up with the idea, mate. Didn't you check in to it?" Jim shot back.

"Well since Mel knows this part of the world, I thought I'd let him work that part out."

Waters merely smiled. "There are a lot of traders who come and go," he explained. "What they usually do is hang around in the bars in the evenings and do their business there where there are too many people around for anyone to cause a fuss."

"What we need then, is to do is find a dive and hang around there until someone dodgy-looking shows up and then talk to him?" Jim was being sarcastic. But Waters just nodded.

"That's the general idea, yes."

"I didn't think they had bars in Muslim countries? Aren't they against booze?" Colin looked puzzled.

"These old USSR nation states still have a lot of Russian influence. They still have bars that serve vodka and that sort of thing, so it's not a worry," Waters told him.

Jim smiled. "Well, there's a relief!"

McCleland was enjoying himself. He loved a challenge, and especially since the discovery of the tracker, he was even more determined to complete this mission. Someone was out to stop them so he took that as a challenge to be beaten. He also knew it was time to give away a little more information on the mission, but he had to be careful what he said, so as to not put too much out there. He was about to inform them, but Colin beat him to it.

"I did some more checking. Our man, Ulyenkov should be here this evening. We find somewhere to park and grab him once he shows up," he said matter-of-factly.

"This Termez place is a big city dude. He could be in one of a hundred places!" Jim protested.

"He always stays at the biggest hotel in the city," Mel said quietly. "We should be able to track him down there."

They had reached the outskirts of the Termez. The outlying buildings looked ramshackle and it was obvious that poverty was rampant here. People huddled outside, their belongings gathered around them. It reminded Jim of the homeless of London. As the jeep headed further into the city center, the buildings became more impressive. Relics of the USSR were everywhere: some of the buildings reflected the totalitarian bad taste of the Iron Curtain. They were stark and imposing, built of gray stone. The city's main square had various statues and monuments to a regime now thankfully in the past. Termez was an odd place, an amalgamation of Russian and Arabic influences, two more conflicting ideologies that would be hard to find a match. It had been founded 2500 years before and had been conquered by Alexander the Great at one point.

Colin produced three passes from his inside pocket.

"Here. I had these made. They should pass muster if we get stopped."

Jim looked down at the security pass he had been given. It had his photo, Ulyenkov's name and information written on it. Colin and Mel's passes were similarly labeled and marked.

"How did you come up with this stuff?" Mel asked.

"As I said, I had them made. I copied the details from a pass I found on the information I had."

Jim was taken aback. A police officer was able to do something like that? That didn't seem kosher somehow. "You falsified these?'

Colin's sly grin gave the game away.

"Do you know how illegal that is? No wonder Black Jack said you had criminal versatility."

Colin simply smiled. "It's not illegal if you don't get caught. And anyway, I'd like to come back in one piece, so I'll take anything for an edge."

That gave Jim food for thought. It wasn't as if he himself hadn't resorted to tactics which were not 100% legitimate before.

"Fair enough. We need to get to this Happyville pretty quickly after that. I don't think Old Bill is going to tolerate Russian hospitality for much longer, if I know him," he replied.

Mel looked at McCleland from the passenger seat with a mixture of curiosity and understanding.

"You mean he knows we're coming?"

Colin leaned forward. "Hold on. You mean to tell me that my checking of the whats and whys has made me guilty by association with this scheme, and that you knew who to target."

Jim smiled. "Yeah. Old Bill knows we're coming, but it's up to us to make sure it's a surprise. We can't risk him giving us away." He looked at the incredulous expressions on Mel and Colin's faces. "Don't feel bad Col. You're not guilty by association. You're just guilty."

"It was a bit of a coincidence that this Ulyenkov fella was the individual who was called in," Colin insisted.

Jim said nothing in response.

From the passenger seat, Waters was not impressed at all. "I'm risking my neck for something that was all pre planned?"

McCleland thought for a moment about how to phrase his next statement.

"From what I understand from the old man. We had to have an excuse to get behind the lines and a rescue mission seemed a good idea."

"You mean to tell me that this whole thing is a put on?" Waters sounded bitter. "I thought I'd left all this see no evil, hear no evil bullshit behind when I retired!"

He returned to his thoughts and cursed the fates at being roped in to this crazy plot. His mood was getting darker with every minute. He felt used. He just wanted to get home as quickly as possible.

"I've got a question, Jim." Colin asked.

"Shoot."

"How did you convince him to be the one to get himself captured? You know him as well as I do, he would not be so open to risking himself."

Jim grinned broadly.

"That one I can give you an answer to. You know how out there Old Bill is when he's not thinking straight. Black Jack gave the orders. Throw in a couple of bottles of whiskey and my old commanding officer is... well... a bit off the wall."

***

Cartwright always enjoyed visiting Old Bill's quarters. Unlike himself, who spirited his personal achievements away in his safe, Clark wore his success on his sleeve. His certificates and qualifications to fly an aircraft, his commendations and photos of his service were clearly displayed in his mess quarters.

Added to that, Clark shared a passion for antiquities and old knickknacks with Black Jack, and his work area and living quarters were decorated with old books and ornaments that he had collected over the years. A walnut mantelpiece clock adorned a corner cabinet that must have some value to the base commander. It gave the space a feeling of being lived in. By comparison, Haltwhistle's house was as clinical as his personality, and his preference for order to made the atmosphere even more oppressive. It made Cartwright wonder how Haltwhistle's wife put up with it. Of his friends, John enjoyed visiting with his immediate subordinate officer more.

Unfortunately, this visit was not a social call.

"Sir, are you crazy?" Clark demanded. "There is no way this going to work!"

"Bill, trust me. We will not be far away. Think of it as serving Queen and Country," Cartwright countered mildly.

Even to him that argument sounded weak. The two were in Clark's mess, and Old Bill, having just finished a 10 hour shift had retired. When John came knocking with a bottle of Glenfiddich 15 years, the older man had willingly let him in. It was only after a couple of glasses had gone down, Cartwright had hit him with what he had in mind. Even in a not quite sober state, Clark could see how difficult what John was proposing was.

"You want me to willingly let myself be rounded up by the Russians just so you can ride to the rescue?"

"There's a bit more to it than that, I assure you but that's the long and short of it, yes."

Cartwright held firm. "Based on the fact that you are who you are, the person they'll more than likely send to talk to you is someone MI6 has been after for years. We could eliminate a grave threat to these waters in one fell swoop."

Old Bill slumped into his favorite chair. He set his glass on his desk and considered Black Jack's proposal again.

He was as grouchy as the Air Vice Marshal had ever seen him.

"Why me? Why not you? You're younger and I could come and get you."

John gave him one of those looks that told Clark that no matter how much he protested, Cartwright had made up his mind, and was probably acting under orders that he wasn't aware of yet.

"Because last time it was myself in the firing line. there's enough action to go around."

"That's pretty thin, sir," Clark scowled. "Who put you up to this?"

"With the diet requirements I'm forced to live with, thin is what I'm used to," Black Jack shot back.

Clark harrumphed loudly. "That's not funny. I asked you a question, who put you up to this?"

"I can't tell you any more at the moment. it's for your own safety. We don't want you talking too much if they hook you up to one of their machines, do we?"

Clark could read between the lines. Damn the Official Secrets Act!

"You said there was a bit more to it than saving my life. What more is there?" Old Bill was not in the mood to be messed about, especially if he suspected, as he did right now, that he was simply a decoy.

Cartwright simply folded his arms and stared at his subordinate.

"Oh. I see. You can't say any more." Clark understood all too well. Orders and all that. "I still don't see why I need to risk my neck."

Cartwright poured him another glass of whiskey and sat down across the desk from Clark.

"Because you're excellent bait for this assignment. You're a high ranking officer. that's enough for the Russians to be interested. And there's a bottle of this fine stuff in it for you as well when we get back."

"Usually it's me trying to get you out of a funk with a shot of the good stuff. Now it's you doing the reverse."

Clark was a highly skilled leader of men and was good under pressure, but then was also a very capable air force officer and was more than able to operate outside of his area of expertise as he had proved during the time Cartwright had known him. He just had to be convinced. For his part, Old Bill was desperately thinking of ways to talk his unruly subordinate who he had had to reign in more than a few times out of this, as futile as that may be once Jim had made up his mind about something.

"Jack, I am not one of those secret agents that you enjoy reading about in those books of yours. I really don't know if I can pull this off. And what happens if our friends break out some of their infamous torture methods? I don't want my training or my life going out of the nearest window."

Cartwright had to admit that Clarkie had a point there. He had had experience of something similar some years before and it had not been a pleasant encounter for him. For now, he knew he had to nail his contrary friend down.

"I assure you that will not happen."

Old Bill harrumphed again and drained the rest of his whiskey. He knew this was a lost cause.

John would no doubt come up with some excuse to twist his arm if he refused, and probably incite whatever orders that he had been given of course, but Clark knew John would only do that as a last resort.

"Alright," was the resigned comment. "I can tell you're not going to leave me alone until I say yes. But you'll owe me big time for this, sir."

Cartwright poured another glass of whiskey for them both.

"Cheers."

But Old Bill did not feel charitable. He did however feel the need to get drunk after agreeing to such a nonsensical scheme.

"One thing Bill. don't breathe a word of this to anyone. Not family, not any other officers, no- one."

Clark opened his mouth to protest, but Cartwright cut him off.

"No one. This is top secret and must not be discussed with anyone, not even the other officers on base. I can't stress this enough."

Old Bill sighed and drained his whiskey in a single gulp.

"Alright, I hear you. You don't have to beat me over the head," the Group Captain was swayed by John's expression. For Cartwright to leave even his closest confidantes out of the loop was unusual, unless his orders were explicit. Damn the orders, damn the fates, damn Jack for being such a close friend.

Waters kept his annoyance in check. He still wasn't sure how he had wound up here. He felt like Daniel in the Lion's Den having traveled aboard a contraband Russian helicopter with two foolhardy younger guys. In his day, this sort of assignment was left to the government's network of spies and mission specialists but apparently times had changed. Either that or McCleland had been especially chosen for this for some reason, which no doubt would come out in the wash. A run down looking bar appeared to their left as they drove off the main square. Music blared from outdoor speakers and a couple of men smoking cigarettes lounged by the entrance. "Juliana's" flashed in neon lights above the door.

"I'd say this looks promising," Colin commented absently, taking a peek at the torn card again. If Clark had been here, then here was the place to go from.

"Alright." McCleland pulled the jeep to a stop just up the street from the bar and switched off the engine.

"Do they speak Arabic or Russian here?"

"A mixture. People from all over come to these parts so take your pick. Whatever you do, don't speak English. We don't know who may be hanging around and not one of them like us around these parts." Waters climbed out and stretched a little. The seat was crippling. He started walking down the street. He could definitely do with a stiff drink.

"I think he's pissed off," Colin noted.

Jim nodded in agreement. He understood completely.

"Yeah. And he has every right to be upset, but with things the way they are, the less he or anyone else knew, the better. Let's try to keep it that way."

The night air was cool. The streets were fairly busy with people bustling about but they were giving the bar that Mel had chosen a wide berth. A greenish purple haze filled the air as it's garish neon lights illuminated the night. This was clearly pretty well off the beaten track or else it was a harbor for the lowest of the low, Haltwhistle thought. The wooden front of the building was comprised of timbers which were old and some splintered. The rest of the facade was fashioned from cobbled together metal sheets assembled to give an impression of a respectable store front.

"What the hell kind of bar is this?" Colin wondered as he opened the door.

"You ready for this?" Jim asked from behind his shoulder.

Haltwhistle wasn't sure what he was getting himself in to by going in here, but needs must. It had been his idea to pursue this.

"Not really, but let's do this."

The door opened and they stepped down into the bar. The air smelled damp, but it was perfectly dry. The place was dimly lit and clad in unfinished metal. It had clearly been built by someone with limited money and resources but was determined to own such a place. The ceiling was as patched together as the rest of the place. Parts of corrugated metal, metal road signs and sheets of metal plating had been bolted or welded together and the whole thing looked like it could fall in on itself at any moment.

Only two or three patrons sat in the place, so it was really early or really late for any action.

Jim knew he had to take a chance or else he would stick out like a sore thumb. He strode up to the counter and took a seat. The bar was decorated with a mixture of ornaments and objects: a set of knives were set against the opposite wall from the counter, along with various trophies indicating victory in combat or competition.

An impressive looking curved weapon hung above the bar itself. It must have been some sort of sword, but McCleland had not come anything even close to it in his travels. He admired it for a while. It may be a dangerous device, but there was no questioning it's beauty.

"It's a shashka," whispered Waters. "Ceremonial sword."

The proprietor, an older woman with long black hair came over and smiled at them.

"Yes? What will you have?" She spoke in broken English. If they responded in kind, this could rumble them.

Jim looked at the menu on the wall.

"Straight vodka." He said in his best Russian dialect. "Make it a double."

"Make that two," Waters put in from beside him. His pronunciation was a bit off but it conveyed what he wanted well enough.

The bartender turned and went to get their drinks. Colin appeared on Jim's other side. The bartender came over with their drinks.

"Thank you. The same for my friend here."

He took a swig of the vodka. It seemed to be a local brand that he had not come across. It had a spicy flavor similar to ginger or cinnamon but it was much stronger. It was pretty good actually.

Mel seemed to be enjoying his beverage as well.

"I'm going for a piss," said Colin. He got up and headed for the lavatories, off to one side of the room.

What he really wanted, of course, was to check the place out. He made his way past the piled-up boxes of alcohol through the rickety door that led to the rear of the building. Empty crates and sacks lay strewn all around. He searched through them, looking for any clues.

If Clark had indeed been here, then he may have left some details behind that could be crucial.

There was nothing of note amid the debris, so Haltwhistle retreated in to the building and took a look at the gentleman's room. A good look around the rank, putrid smelling lavatory revealed a cuff link, silver cut in to the shape of a red, white and blue roundel. An RAF cuff link if ever Colin saw one. Clark had certainly been here, but frustratingly, there was nothing else to be found. He rejoined Jim and Mel, who were still sipping on their drinks.

"Anything?"

"I'll tell you later."

Then a large hand clamped down on Jim's shoulder from behind. He turned to find a large, burly man wearing a turban glowering at him.

"Ulyenkov! Bastard!" he spat.

Oh shit, Colin thought.

THIRTEEN

McCleland slowly turned in his chair and gave the offending party as good a menacing glower as he could. He rose from his seat.

Beside him, Mel felt the color drain from his face. *No, no, you're inviting a bloody and messy confrontation by challenging him like that!*

"I would advise you to take your hand off me, if you know what's good for you," McCleland snarled. "I trust you know who I am. If I were you, you'd be advised to go about your business."

The big man let out a roar of fury and backhanded McCleland, a move which nearly landed Jim on the floor. Colin attempted to step in front to block a further attack, but the man pushed him aside, sending Haltwhistle sprawling.

Fortunately, Jim saw him coming, and kicked out, catching the bigger man in the side of his knee. He went down to the floor, giving McCleland enough time to get up.

"You murdered my brother!" the aggrieved man howled. He drew a large, vicious looking knife with a serrated blade and slashed viciously at Jim. For his part, the captain jumped back out of the way but still felt the tip of the blade cut into his shirt. As the big guy swung again, Kirk took advantage of his momentary openness and drop kicked him in the chest, then smashed down with his fists on the bigger man's face. The man fell back but still had the knife in his hand.

Haltwhistle again attempted to intervene, but Waters pulled him back.

"That would be seen as a severe dishonor to Jim if you interfered," he whispered as softly as he could. Colin realized his mistake and watched as his partner continued to go toe to toe with his assailant. He lunged at Jim again and the blade slashed the air dangerously close to his face.

McCleland was tempted to pull his gun from his waistband and blow this wanker away, but remembered that for the moment he didn't have a sidearm. In any case, it would have drawn attention, not that he wanted this attention right now! Instead, he grabbed a rickety wooden chair and parried with it, knocking the knife out of the big fellow's hand. Jim smashed the chair over the man's head, stunning him, and then shoulder tossed him, hurling him through the air to the ground, landing on his back.

The man, who Mel now knew was an Arab thrashed and managed to get up, but he had been disarmed by Jim who grabbed him by the wrist. A good side kick to the mouth sent the Arabian sprawling backwards and he crashed through a table which cracked and splintered under his weight. The impact with the floor put the big man out cold. Jim stood over him, then handed the knife to the bartender.

"Sorry about that," he said apologetically.

"Think nothing of it," the bartender grinned. "Best entertainment we've had all month!"

McCleland and Waters drained their glasses. He drew some cash to pay but the bartender turned him down.

"It's on the house."

Jim smiled appreciatively. Then a thought struck him.

"Excuse me. Me and my friends are trying to buy certain items, could you help us?"

"It depends on what you want to buy," the bartender replied.

McCleland looked around. "It's not the sort of thing that you could buy here." He leaned in closer. "Would you know where we could buy weapons. We lost ours and need to obtain some."

The bartender looked dubious. Then she laughed.

"I'm sorry gentlemen, but you're in the wrong place to buy anything like that. I run a bar, not a gun store."

Waters drew closer and spoke in a conspiratorial whisper.

"Can you tell us where we can get some?"

The bartender laughed again. Her guffaws seemed to make the walls shake.

"You're not from around here are you? You can't buy any weapons in this area."

Jim looked down at the floor. He sighed.

"Alright. Well thank you anyway. Again, sorry about the mess." He nodded towards the still unconscious Arab who lay sprawled on the floor amid the broken furniture.

They retreated to a booth with another round of drinks. Colin was more than a little dejected.

Based on what Mel had told them, a place like this was a good crossroads to meet people engaged in business of the type that they were trying to get involved with.

"Apparently our friend Ulyenkov is well known in these parts," said Colin dryly.

"No shit!" Jim responded, favoring his jaw where the enraged Arab had clobbered him.

"You could say that. He's not just a GRU agent, he was responsible for all sorts of... bad things in these parts." Colin went quiet.

Jim gave his friend the most horrified look that he could remember. "Now he tells me!"

"Are you alright? That was a hell of a knock you took," Waters remarked. McCleland winced but put a brave face on things.

"I'd say that this was a good way of testing the disguises that we're wearing. So far they're working."

Haltwhistle's observation was right on, Jim had to admit. His jaw ached where the big dude had knocked him sideways when he mistook him for this Ulyenkov character was testament to that fact.

Their conversation was interrupted by a pretty dark haired young lady in her late 20s who approached the table. She resembled the bartender in some ways and Colin guessed that they were related.

"I heard you are interested in buying some things that you cannot usually buy in a bar," she said.

Again, she spoke in broken Russian. "There is no need to speak in our native language. I know that you are not from here."

Jim looked her up and down. She was trim so kept herself in shape. She had bright eyes and a pallid complexion. She was of medium height and wore heels to make up for the difference.

"Would you care to join us?" Mel asked.

She sat down in the booth with them. "My name is Juliana."

Colin smiled to himself. The eponymous bar must be named after her. Her name must be the one on the business card.

"What you are asking for is difficult to come by but perhaps I know of someone," the girl continued.

Jim looked over at Colin and took a quick sip of his drink.

"Could you introduce us?" Jim asked.

The girl thought for a second. "It could be possible, if I can contact him. But it would cost you."

"And how much would that be?" Mel demanded, fed up with the cloak and dagger stuff. The young lady looked offended.

"There is no need to be rude."

Jim quickly jumped in, sensing an opportunity here. "I'm sorry for my friend. He's just had a bad day. What is your price?"

She looked at the table and then at McCleland. "Fifty thousand."

There were murmurs of consternation. That was more than they had been allotted for this trip.

Mel was sure they could find some elsewhere for a lot cheaper, and that was without a finders' fee. He was about to say so but Jim beat him to the punch.

"Is that price open to negotiation?"

Her expression softened a little at him. "Perhaps."

Jim returned her smile. There was an impish gleam in his eye which Haltwhistle picked up on instantly. "Then… perhaps we could go somewhere else and talk it over? It is kind of confidential, after all."

"I'd be happy to." She looked at Colin and Mel, then back at Jim. "But just you."

She rose from the table and McCleland went with her, following her lead.

"If you'll excuse us." He grinned at his colleagues as he and the girl disappeared behind the bar and deeper into the building.

Colin gave an incredulous shake of his head. "Oh, for fuck's sake," he grumbled.

"Literally!" Mel said dryly. "No prizes for guessing what he's up to, is there?" He downed the remains of his glass in appalled derision.

Waters took another glass of the local alcohol. Haltwhistle, having no taste for the peppery flavor of the local booze, abstained.

***

The thick pile of papers that had been compiled about Berry's demise took quite a while for Cartwright to digest. He was not the fastest readers, preferring to savor the details on offer in a book, but that kind of relaxed perusal was not in order here. The boat's explosion had been sudden. Moored at a lock, the narrow boat had gone from being completely normal to floating debris in seconds with no warning. The crime scene reports pointed to the flotsam and jetsam but no specific details. Interestingly, an interview with the lock keeper was conspicuously absent.

It was enough to pique Black Jack's interest.

"I am going out," he said as he left his office. "I'll be a while."

"Do you think that's wise, sir? With our current situation?" Harvey asked, straightening from reading a report.

"We all have to go from a walk from time to time," was the brusque reply.

The lock was peaceful. Weeping willow trees lined the towpath which led to the lock keepers' cottage and the pub beyond. The scorch marks where the boat had exploded were still in evidence, cordoned off, but the remainder of the canal basin was open for use to everyone else.

Cartwright knelt and looked at the moorings. The forensic people had removed anything of interest or use, and their reports had been absorbed, but the lack of an interview with the one person who had probably seen something in the area.

He strolled along the canal, seemingly taking in the peace and tranquility of the place to anyone watching. Making a beeline for the pretty cottage beyond, Cartwright did not expect anyone to answer.

The house looked like it had not been occupied for some time, despite it retaining its crisp appearance. A sharp tap on the door however brought a frail man to it.

"Hello?" he asked.

"Afternoon." Cartwright presented his ID card. "Can I ask you a few questions?"

"I don't know anything," was the man's plaintive reply.

That definitely caught the AVM's notice. "I never said you did, sir. I'd just like to ask a few questions, that's all. It won't take five minutes."

Reluctantly, the man let Cartwright in. The low ceilings and narrow rooms gave away the cottage's age.

"What can I help you with?"

"Were you here when that boat exploded a few days ago sir?"

The hesitation was obvious. "N-no sir. I was away."

Black Jack fixed his steel blue eyes on the slight figure before him. "I do not wish to doubt your honesty, but I need you to be as open with me as possible. You were here weren't you?"

The lock keeper sat down. "Yes I was."

"That's better. Can I ask who or what you saw?"

"Just before the boat blew up… it smashed the windows in my greenhouse! It ruined my tomatoes!"

Cartwright smiled a little. "I'm sure you can grow some more, sir. Go on."

The older man looked at the floor. "I saw someone near the boat. It wasn't the owner. Someone else."

Leaning forward in his own seat, the RAF officer pressed on. "Did you see his face?"

The older man shook his head. "No."

There was a sigh. "Was there anything distinctive about who you saw?"

The lock keeper thought a little, his face showing that he was thinking. Patience was a virtue in times like this, but Cartwright, never the best at biding his time was becoming agitated and trying to keep it in check.

"I think he leaned over to his left when he walked. Like he had a limp or something."

That stirred something in the back of the AVM's mind.

"Thank you, sir. You've been a great help."

"I don't know if I have, but have a good day," the older man replied, showing his visitor out.

Cartwright took his leave and walked back along the towpath. The dark scorch marks on the grass and gravel made a good point from which to look for anything that had been missed.

A thorn bush on the other side of the path seemed a good place to start. It had not been pruned, therefore not checked. Wrapping his hand up, Black Jack pushed in to the lower recesses of the thorny plant and felt around. A close look was what was really needed but he did not have a pair of clippers to hand, so this would have to do. He slipped on his leather driving gloves and resumed his search.

Soon, something small and circular in shape was felt. Reaching to grab whatever it was, Cartwright found a small round circle of metal and turned it over in his hand.

"Well, I'll be damned."

***

It was about an hour later before McCleland returned to the table alone. He looked a little the worse for wear and his clothes were rumpled, but he had a wide grin on his face. He sat down heavily in the booth where Haltwhistle and Waters regarded him with irritation.

"I don't suppose we need to ask how it went then?" Colin said.

"No need at all," was the simple reply. Jim sat in silence still wearing the smile which made him look very self-satisfied. He seemed to be lost in thought.

"Well don't keep us in suspense. We've been sat here for the last hour while you got your end away," Mel grimaced.

McCleland looked at them both pacifically. "We have ourselves a deal. And it didn't cost us a penny."

"How did you manage that?' Haltwhistle demanded. "What did she do? Knock a grand off for every time you banged her?"

Jim looked at his friend with a quirked eyebrow. "Col, I do believe you're jealous!" He took a swig of his now stale vodka. "No, she's a lovely girl. Very classy."

"So classy that she shagged you just moments after meeting you." Haltwhistle wasn't jealous, he was just disgusted that his friend had stooped to such low-rent methods to get them what they needed.

"All girls are classy. As long as they're fit and up for it!" Jim was beaming as he filled them in on the deal. "The girl knows this guy called Aziz who could possibly help us out with our request. It'll take a few hours to get in touch with him, and then she'll take us to meet this guy."

"Hold on, you talked all this over while you were…?" Haltwhistle snorted.

"No, that'd be too much of a mouthful." McCleland's smug grin was beyond aggravating.

Colin harrumphed loudly. Apparently Jim had no time for ethics as opposed to factual, analytical solutions. Two wildly divergent approaches to get the same results.

"I'm not even going to imagine how you sorted all of that," Mel commented, still unimpressed.

"We can't leave the chopper forever, we have to get back to it!"

"It'll be alright for a couple of hours. It's not as if we left it unattended, is it?" Jim countered.

"I'm surprised you could set all this up, all things considered," Colin added, his arms folded across his chest.

A nonchalant shrug from McCleland was his response. "What can I say? I can multitask."

If looks could kill, Haltwhistle's expression would have left his friend in a six foot hole in the ground.

Juliana had left instructions with McCleland to pull around to the back entrance of the bar when they returned. It gave them until 3AM. Heading out of the bar, Jim went back to the UAZ and they dutifully climbed back in to their venerable steed.

"Let's just go and find this Ulyenkov guy," Jim said shortly.

He started the engine and pulled away from the kerb, heading back into the city center.

"Where did you say this bloke was going to be?" Colin asked Mel.

"He always stays in the biggest hotels. He's flashy like that. He's not showy with what he has or what he's about, just in his tastes."

"I hate to ask this, but how do you know so much about this bloke?" Colin's detective instinct was piqued.

Mel sighed. He had left this part out of his retelling the helicopter battle incident. He had not revealed who the pilot of the Hind had been. "He wasn't always a KGB and GRU man. He used to be a pilot. I... came up against him."

It was Jim's turn to be taken aback by his friend's behavior. "And when were you planning to share this?"

Waters was defensive. "Well, I didn't think I'd go head to head with him again. I had hoped I'd never see him again. He's not someone I want anything to do with." Mel was already regretting telling them anything.

"Well neither do we, but we don't have much choice," Jim said acidly.

It was all falling in to place. If Waters had fought this guy before, no wonder he was so unhappy.

He didn't want to face him again and if he knew what Ulyenkov was capable of, then he probably didn't want to be within a hundred miles of him. It was all getting a bit intense. Still, if Mel knew where he was, then perhaps they could remove him from the equation and solve the problem before it even started?

"OK, from now on, no holding back information. Between any of us. Agreed?"

Colin snickered despite himself. "If that's the way it is, was the girl good?"

McCleland stared daggers at him. "Go and get your dick wet."

"Apparently, you just did!" his friend retorted.

Jim changed the subject. "Alright. which hotel do you think he's in then, Batman?"

"As I said, he'll go for a classy, showy place. With that in mind, let's look for the biggest one in the city."

"It shouldn't be too difficult to find this man. He does look like me after all!" Jim was trying to be flippant, but it fell flat.

FOURTEEN

In downtown Termez, the team scoured the district searching for a location that fit Mel's hunch.

While quite stark, some of the buildings were genuinely impressive. The roughly hexagonal Archaeological Museum was particularly eye catching with its huge doorways framed by pillars.

Finally, a large structure of concrete and glass that reached into the sky and labeled 'Gostinitsa Surkhan' loomed ahead. It was a vast pale gray building that looked as oppressive as the regime that had originally built it.

"That'll be it," said Waters.

"Are you sure? There might be other places..."

"Colin, I'm sure. When you realize the kind of man he is you'll understand."

"Well, that's all fine and dandy, but I prefer a bit of hard evidence," Haltwhistle insisted. Jim pulled the jeep to a stop in an alley across from the front and they crossed the street as unobtrusively as possible.

Approaching the main door, Waters tugged on Jim's arm. "We should take the back way. Less chance of being seen."

"We need to know what room he's in, don't we?"

"It's gonna look funny if two guys who look alike have been seen in the same place, innit?" Colin hissed.

"That doesn't mean that he couldn't have left the place for a drink or something, does it?" Jim headed for the reception. His colleagues' lack of imagination and clear apprehension was sure to get them caught out. At this point it was vital to put on a commanding front.

For his part, Haltwhistle was certain that they were about to be executed.

Stepping up to the wooden counter, its scratched surface gave away the hotel's age. Jim drummed his fingers in an impatient manner. An older gentleman looked at him a little sheepishly.

"I'd like my room key please," McCleland said.

The number on the pigeon hole gave away that Ulyenkov was indeed staying on the top floor but of course, the key was not present.

"I'm sorry, but the key is not here. I can have a porter -"

A curt wave of the hand cut him off. "That is not necessary." Jim stalked away towards the lobby where the stairwell and lifts were.

"This way. Best to take the stairs." Mel led the way to the top floor where the penthouse suites were. At the far end of the dimly lit corridor, a man stood in a doorway, trying not to look like he was standing guard and failing miserably.

"Okay, so what do you have in mind? We can't exactly go up and knock, and Oddjob there isn't going to open the door for us either," Jim said. "We don't even have shooters!"

"Neither do they," Waters replied. "This lot don't carry firearms." At McCleland's questioning look, Mel said "They use knives instead."

"Sort of like unpleasant Gurkhas then?"

"That's one way of putting it, yeah!"

Haltwhistle was looking along the corridor. "We could make like we're going to our room?"

"Nah, they'll have scoped the place out. They'll know if he's in there or not," Mel told him.

They slunk into a doorway. Hiding didn't pose too much a problem. The corridor being as dimly lit as it was meant that the three could duck into an alcove and blend in easily. But time was not on their side.

Jim looked at Colin and nodded towards the bin that he could see. Its metal structure would certainly get attention. Realizing what McCleland had in mind, Haltwhistle slowly put his foot against the litter bin and tipped it over with his foot, making sure it clanged on the polished stone floor.

The guard looked towards the noise and approached to investigate, only to be met by a fist in the jaw from McCleland. While Colin dragged the unconscious form of the guard away, Jim and Mel had reached the doorway.

"You wait here, me and Col will check it out," Jim said as softly as he dared. If this guy was GRU he could have all sorts of gizmos on them right now. Another reason to hurry this up. He grabbed a tray with a vase of fruit from a table lining the corridor and took a deep breath. He knocked and waited to be greeted.

He and Colin pulled their headscarves down to disguise their faces as best as they could.

Finally, the door was answered.

"Da?" boomed a voice in Russian from the darkness. "We don't want to be disturbed!"

Two figures appeared at the doorway, one was tall and muscular built but the other was of average height. The tall man wore a long cloak while the shorter individual was dressed in what appeared to be a Russian officer's uniform. Instead of a sandy brown tunic it was black, and he wore a large metal sash over his right shoulder.

In his best Russian which was admittedly ropey, Jim claimed to be room service. Astonishingly the ruse worked.

The smaller man was not armed, his knife laid carefully in its scabbard on the bed and he motioned them to come in.

Jim slowly came into the room from the shadows, trying to be as casual as possible. As he got further in to the room he saw who he was looking for. A little shorter than himself, this guy was eyeing him carefully.

He had an incredible presence matched by intense burning eyes, and looks that virtually matched his own behind the disguise.

Ulyenkov. The man he had to impersonate. Jim knew that he would have to take him hand to hand options extremely limited. If this man was indeed a killer by profession, taking him on without a weapon could prove to be a lost cause.

"Deliver your food and get out!" grumbled the big fellow.

McCleland remembered the challenge that the guy in the bar had made to him.

"You killed my brother!" he barked in his best guttural voice. The snake eyed Russian simply smiled thinly and stood up, then noticed Jim's appearance.

Colin was horrified. Ulyenkov grinned a very unpleasant looking grin. From his right boot he drew a ceremonial dagger that looked positively evil. He turned it over in his hands like it was a toy and he was waiting for the right time to plunge it in to Jim. Then Ulyenkov and the smaller man suddenly sagged and fell to the ground. Mel appeared out of the shadows from behind them, his hand wrapped around a heavy glass vase. He had hammered them into submission with the glass, which incredibly had not shattered.

But maddeningly the big man had been out of reach and was now tearing into Colin Haltwhistle.

Jim attempted a flying kick to the head, which sent him across the room, only for him to come back at them swinging a collapsible table as if it was a sword.

"Oh shit," groaned Jim. Maybe this hadn't been such a good idea.

He went at Mel next, twirling and jabbing the metal legs of the table at his face. For his part, Marvin blocked as best as he could, but he still got caught on the cheek. Throwing the table aside, the brute lunged viciously at Waters, swinging his fists. A loud clang as the Russian's hand smashed into a wardrobe door and the yelp he gave caused Mel to swing quickly with his two fists clamped together. He caught the bigger man in the side of the head and knocked him down.

Despite the blood now dripping from his cut cheek he took advantage and Waters kicked out as hard as he could into the other man's face. The Russian groaned, pulled a dagger of his own and tried to get up to attack the smaller man, but Colin, now back on his feet was on him in an instant but a swift blow from a porcelain vase to the back of the head put him on the floor, out cold before he could do the job himself. Jim sighed with relief while Waters smiled, then flinched when the pain on the side of his face got too great.

"Where did you come from?" McCleland demanded.

"It'd help if you looked for more than the main door." Mel wiped his hands.

That would have been nice to know that a few moments ago, Jim thought. "Still not enjoying the adventure?" he asked instead.

"I'm warming to it," the retired officer responded. Despite the physical altercation, the fight had energized him.

"Thank you for sparing me what could have been a very messy encounter," Waters said somewhat cynically, wiping the blood from his countenance. The room was a shambles: smashed furniture and damaged crockery was everywhere.

"What are we going to do with this lot? We can't kill them. Too much noise," Jim noted.

Haltwhistle looked around and noticed the bathroom. The three of them dragged the unfortunate squad into the toilet cubicle and gave them a shot of morphine each from the first aid kit in Colin's knapsack.

"That should keep them down for a bit."

Thinking quickly, Jim searched each of the unconscious men, looking for this infernal key that they so urgently needed. But none of them carried anything barely resembling the gadget. If it was here, he couldn't find it.

Locking them in the cubicle and then doing the same to the bathroom door just sweetened it. It would be a few hours before they could get free. A few hours that they could use to get ahead.

"Let's get the hell out of here," Mel hissed. He had had his share of Termez' hospitality. For his part, Waters snatched up the knives that the goons had left lying around and handed Ulyenkov's to Jim. Then he stuffed the other in to his waistband.

"It's a shame they weren't packing guns," Colin said. "We could have saved ourselves a trip."

Pulling around the back of the bar as Juliana had told them to, the three sat in silence. Colin checked his watch: 2:50am. Ten minutes before time. Haltwhistle severely doubted that the girl would show at all and they had been had, especially based on how his friend had manipulated the situation earlier. He was still unimpressed with Jim's methods despite his actions in the hotel room when the big lug had tried to get his hands on his neck and Jim had literally stepped in.

"I'm telling you, she ain't gonna show up," he said quietly. "We should just go back to the chopper and move on."

"She'll show. Too much money to be made for her not to put in an appearance. And we still need the stuff that this Aziz guy has got," Jim countered.

"I thought you persuaded her to cut us a free deal?"

Jim looked at Colin. "I did. But she'll still get a lot of dough from this Aziz guy for getting him customers."

Haltwhistle grimaced. "Sounds like she's a drug mule for him."

"I don't like this at all," said Mel. "We need to get back to the chopper before Ulyenkov wakes up. We've already been far too long."

"We will. I don't think this will take long at all," McCleland assured him.

"I hope not. I could do with some grub," Colin cut in. He was still nursing his jaw where he had been hit rather hard.

"If my guess is right they will be close by. They don't want to get too far out in to the country because of all the other tribes around," Waters explained. "This part of the world is full of different tribes who all hate each other. They keep themselves to themselves and only come out when there's money to be made or a battle to be fought."

Juliana appeared from the back doorway and waved to Jim when she saw him at the wheel. He beckoned her over and she climbed in to the rear seat behind Mel.

"Hello again," Colin greeted her, trying to be as casual as possible.

"Hullo." she said warmly, her eyes shining. She had a glow about her, the legacy of a few drinks and Jim's influence. The smell of alcohol hung around her.

Haltwhistle was aghast at what he felt were immoral methods. "You might want to make an appointment with the local clap clinic when we get back. You got this girl pissed as well? Where are your ethics man?" he hissed, leaning forward.

"Ethics have small bearing on tactics," was the glib remark from the driver's seat. "I got her on side and then convinced her to cut us a deal."

Haltwhistle shared a glance with Mel, who looked similarly disgusted.

The jeep pulled off and Juliana gave Jim directions, who headed out of the city center. He made a mental note to get more fuel in this thing when they got back to the chopper. They were heading south east out of the city, roughly in the direction of where the helicopter was parked.

They were back among the run down shacks and back alleys of the more seedy parts of town.

Eventually reaching the city limits, they seemed to be indeed heading into the countryside with its wild ridges and untamed wilderness, but after a mile or so, the girl told Jim to turn left onto a rocky track that appeared on the left. In the front passenger seat, Mel honestly believed they were being driven to their executions. The track became rougher and more uneven as they climbed up into the hills. It was definitely a path that was less taken and the ground became even more rocky, it's sharp edges dulled by years of erosion and rainfall. Above them the hillside sheared dramatically upwards into craggy peaks strewn with boulders while to their right, the hillside dropped away into a wide valley with a river winding its way along it, lit up by the half moonlight.

It hadn't escaped Colin's notice that they were driving in the direction to where the helicopter was parked. For him, this was becoming too dangerous. The need to get back to their transportation and go on their way was becoming the major priority.

At last the track stopped climbing and they came to a wide plateau. Juliana instructed McCleland to stop the UAZ. He did and sat back, waiting. Mel did not like the look of this place. Not the scenery, which even in the milky moonlight was stunning, but it was a prime spot for an ambush.

Fortunately, they were only a couple of miles or so from where he knew the Hip sat waiting for them.

The clip-clop of hooves on stony ground alerted them that someone was coming. Jim was ready to start up and head off, his hands on the controls.

"It is fine, Bodie. We are expecting them," Juliana assured him, her words slightly slurred and her cheeks rosy from the booze.

Colin mouthed 'Bodie?' to Mel, who simply rolled his eyes. But the white cap realized that Jim had given her a false name to protect them.

He relaxed back into the seat and watched through the bug stained glass as a pack of maybe 12 horses held together with harnesses came around the corner from their left. Three men dressed in headdresses, robes with thick scarves around their necks and faces were leading the equine convoy. Each horse had large saddlebags draped across their backs, but didn't look large enough to hold the weapons they were after.

Juliana clambered out and went over to see the three men.

"Who are that lot?" Colin murmured.

"The local Mujaheddin," Waters replied. "This could get very messy. We'd be best leaving now!"

Juliana turned and beckoned for the others to join her. Clearly, their noncompliance would scupper this arrangement. With that in mind, Jim and Colin cautiously got out.

"Are you sure about this?" Haltwhistle said conspiratorially.

"Do we have much choice?"

Juliana spoke to the three tribesmen in Arabic and then turned to them.

"We are waiting for your order. We apologize for the wait."

"No worries," McCleland shrugged. He noticed something glinting in the moonlight that was half perched out of the man's pocket. It looked like metal.

Haltwhistle had also seen the implement. The bulge in the man's jacket gave away its shape. It seemed that this man did regular business with the Russians.

"Is business good?" he managed to effect roughly.

"It suits me," the man replied. "We were not expecting you in person, Mr. Ulyenkov. When Juliana told me that someone wanted to buy weapons we were not expecting you. Your shipment is on the way."

Not wanting to give anything away, McCleland thought quickly. "I want to... make sure of my investment."

Haltwhistle had been observing all of this and his concern was beginning to grow. If Ulyenkov was doing a deal, what could he possibly be dealing in?

"Do you work with anyone or is there some places you wouldn't go?" He was aiming to get the gentleman to start talking, but the man was suspicious.

"That's my concern."

Jim and Colin stood kicking pebbles and stones down in to the valley to pass the time.

Headlights from down there meant that someone was now driving up a steep road towards them.

The unmistakable rattle and chug of an engine filled the air as the truck strained to pull up the rocky incline.

FIFTEEN

The radio cracked at that moment. Jim and Colin shared a concerned look. It could blow their cover.

"Come in, Mr. McCleland or Mr. Haltwhistle." It was the voice of the crew chief.

"We read you, go ahead," Colin answered, his voice hushed.

"I think I've got company. You need to hurry, I don't know how many there are!"

"Shit!" Mel cursed.

"We're on our way. Try to hold on. Out." He quickly switched the radio off. It was perhaps a little callous but at the risk of being discovered, it was necessary.

The rumble of the approaching engine morphed in to an ancient truck trundled to a halt, facing the pack of horses. A swarthy looking gentleman climbed down from the cab on the driver's side while his passenger got out and went around to the back.

Looking on, Waters was horrified. This guy was one of the Taliban. This entire deal hinged on Jim and Colin not being discovered. If they were, they would be swiftly executed.

The driver went to the back of the truck and opened the cargo compartment.

"Come," said the first man, who must have been Aziz. Beckoning to his potential buyer, he shone a torch in to the back, illuminating the cargo. McCleland did not have to see much to realize that they had a whole arsenal in the back of the truck. Guns of all types and descriptions sat neatly on racks attached to the sides. Body armor, mines and different types of explosives sat on the floor.

Other equipment such as goggles and night vision gear which Colin recognized as British MoD was also available. Among the horde was a cache of AK-47s and several buckets of ammunition for them which Jim scooped up. Colin let out a low whistle of disbelief as he took in the collection that Aziz had available. He helped himself to a couple of Tokarev automatics and several clips and several magnetic limpet grenades.

"I wish to be paid," the driver demanded impatiently.

Colin set down his knapsack and withdrew several notes, handing them over. The man took them, examining them hungrily while Jim loaded their haul into the back of the jeep. For her part, Juliana made her way to the truck and made herself comfortable in the cab.

Satisfied, the truck's driver gave a nod of thanks to them then turned over some of the cash to Aziz and began to unload the saddle bags from the horses. Aziz and his two friends worked with the two gentlemen to load packages of what appeared to be sackcloth covered bundles.

Colin watched and felt the hairs on the back of his neck standing on end, realizing what was going on.

They had just funded a drug deal, he was sure of it. Seemingly helping them to load the truck, he deliberately dropped the package he was holding and heard something inside rip. The unmistakable smell and sticky, smooth feel let him know that this was indeed a parcel of opium.

"Holy shit," he murmured. So Ulyenkov was involved with smuggling heroin! There was no way the package could be taken for anything else. He placed the bundle into the truck and backed away to the jeep.

"There must be at least a year's supply of dope here!" he hissed through gritted teeth to Jim, who looked at least as uncomfortable with that revelation as Colin felt. He clearly had no desire to be a drug pusher either.

"Let's beat a hasty retreat, shall we?"

"Our Mujaheddin friend has a key. I'm sure of it. We need it."

"Well, let's leave and then follow him."

They both got in the jeep smartly and Jim started the engine, aiming to make for the gap behind the truck to get back on to the track down to the main road.

Unfortunately, a heated argument between Aziz and the driver of the truck broke out.

Shouting in Arabic and finger pointing quickly escalated to where things looked very ugly. The representatives of the Taliban and the Mujaheddin, two groups never on the best of terms were now about to make the mutual dislike public. The sound of gunfire filled the air, giving a persuasive hint that a bloodletting was now in the offing.

Aziz fell to the ground as the truck driver stood over him with a pistol drawn, then he opened fire on Aziz's two companions in quick succession and finally turned towards the jeep.

"Let's get the fuck out of here!" Mel insisted. Not just for their own safety, but the chief's.

But their way out was blocked by the truck driver's friend who was now holding a formidable looking machine gun on them.

Instinctively, Jim's acquired automatic was in his hand and the jeep was rolling as the automatic weapon opened fire, peppering the side of the UAZ with a hail of lead. Fortunately, the armor plating that had been fitted protected the occupants well. Colin's Tokarev was in his grasp and he fired on the driver as a sharp crack from the pistol, its muzzle spitting flame dropped the gunman, the machine gun firing wildly as he fell. The hail of multiple stray bullets hit the truck's fuel tank.

The resulting huge explosion was as inevitable as it was spectacular. Forty gallons of fuel ignited instantly which was almost immediately joined by multiple rounds of ammunition and poorly stored explosives immolating. The combined explosive force lit up the valley almost as if it was daylight, as a deafening wall of noise echoed around the hills. The sheer violence of the blast caused rocks and boulders to fall from above, causing the horses to bray and scatter, making down the hillside in a virtual stampede in their attempt to flee the rock fall.

Colin dived out of the jeep, ran to the slain Mujaheddin and searched their persons.

"Col! What the fuck are you doing? Get back here!" Jim shouted.

The heat from the explosion was almost overwhelming but he managed to retrieve what he had seen in the man's pocket. A piece of brass with an emerald green jewel that matched the picture that they had been shown back in London.

He jumped back in to the safety of the vehicle as Jim gunned the charred UAZ down the rough track as fast as possible without busting the suspension to pieces.

"I got it." Colin held the small object up for the others to look over.

"You nearly got yourself killed!" Jim chided him. "Don't pull that shit again!"

At the same time as they were making their escape, the chief, a .50 caliber in his hands sat on top of the dune, the helicopter to his back. He was sure he could see or hear movement from nearby, but in the pitch darkness it was impossible to be sure. After his radio call, he had been forced to wait, hoping that his colleagues would reappear shortly.

He kept his eyes fixed ahead, but scanned as best as he could. He thought he heard a rustling from the left as if someone was trying to scale the sand dune. He made sure the fearsome weapon was cocked and ready. A lone figure appeared over the top of the drifting sands. The sergeant waited. Two more people appeared, following the first, who pointed at the helicopter. Clearly they wanted to either steal or destroy the machine.

The .50 caliber rounds roared from the barrel, cutting down the three people in terrible and foreshortened fashion. There was a tribal cry from below and two more people appeared, heading up the sand bank towards the chief. Waiting to the last moment, they too met their doom, falling backwards down the fine grain.

How many more could there be? And where were they?

"Come on McCleland, where are you?" he said to himself in a low growl.

The road finally, mercifully appeared ahead of them. McCleland skidded in a controlled drift, kicking up the dust and stones as the jeep fish tailed from the sharp turn he had just done. They were back to the helicopter faster than they could have imagined.

Finally able to speak, Jim asked "Is everyone OK?"

"Yeah," breathed Colin. Mel nodded gravely. Then they realized.

"Juliana…"

She probably had not suffered. It more than likely had been quick and painless.

The UAZ bounced back along the track that it had traversed earlier. Just a minute more and they would be at the helicopter. The stark shape came in to view around the next rocky outcrop and Jim skidded to a stop. He leaped out of the battered, bullet ridden vehicle with Colin and Mel close behind.

"Mel, check the chopper." Haltwhistle sprinted up the sand dune behind the chopper, while McCleland went up the dune to the front of the cockpit. Moving around the top of the ridge, he crouched low. He counted six dead bodies, but no sign of the chief.

Something soft underfoot got Colin's attention. He stopped, looking down. The robes and blood stained form of a shawl wrapped man were at hand. He grimaced. Kneeling down, he turned the corpse over. He couldn't tell which clan the man was from.

"Over here," Mel's voice came from in the direction of the chopper.

They both scrambled down the dusty bank and made for the side door of their steed. They could hear a low moan.

Waters was knelt down next to the chief. His chest was soaked in blood. The two younger men looked grimly at their seriously injured colleague. A few feet away, another dead body lay, a large knife clutched in his dead fingers.

"Sirs," the sergeant said weakly. "There was a dozen of them." His spent machine gun lay by his side. "I won't be joining you for the rest of the mission. I'm sorry." His head lolled to one side and he slumped down.

Haltwhistle's jaw was tight. He was to blame for this happening. "If I hadn't forced him to come along, he wouldn't be dead."

"That's the price we all pay for keeping the peace, mate," Jim reminded him gently. The thought of Steve after they had ejected from the Tornado was in his mind. Life was deeply unfair at times.

Mel checked over the helicopter's structure and systems and made his report. "No damage. He must have fought them all off and one of them managed to get him at the last. I told you we should have got back here sooner, but oh no, you two had to get in the middle of a tribe war!"

McCleland looked around. "What's done is done. We can't take him with us. We'll have to bury him here."

"It doesn't seem very fair to do that," Colin said quietly. He had never ordered a man to his death before. It was not a pleasant feeling. He removed his dog tags, rank and any other identifying markers and slipped them in to his inside pocket.

He looked at the jewel embedded in the burnished metal that he had retrieved. "All of this death and destruction for this." He looked at the hard green crystal. "Chrome Diopside. A Russian gemstone."

"Is there anything you don't know?" Jim asked, trying to keep things light, but it fell on deaf ears.

Colin was turning the dog tags over in his hands.

"These'll be returned to his family."

"Yeah, well let's get out of here before ours end up as part of the collection belonging to this clan as well. I don't fancy being turned into a kebab," McCleland insisted, ignoring Colin's horrified expression.

Haltwhistle was wondering more and more how his partner was so offhand at such horrors. He was certain that he was going to ask to return to normal duties if they managed to get home.

A short time later, the stubby helicopter, refueled and loaded took off, turned away from the lights of the city in the distance and headed for the border with Uzbekistan. In the cockpit, the tension was near breaking point. The last few hours had productive but at an awful cost. Two dead and both innocent parties to all of this.

"I hope that they won't get found for a while," Waters mused from the pilot's seat. He was enjoying this trip less and less and just wanted to get back to his quiet life and his cottage in the country. He was getting too old to be running around the world getting involved in derring-do escapades, and especially didn't want any more death and destruction on his conscience.

"I doubt they'll be a problem," Haltwhistle replied. "Even if they do manage to get out, the shot I gave them should keep them at bay for a good few hours."

He thought for a moment. "Jim, I've got a question."

McCleland shrugged. "Go ahead."

"It seems very convenient that Ulyenkov was the one to be headed in the general direction we needed to take. Did you know about it beforehand?"

Jim simply shrugged and a non-committal look crossed his features. "It'd make sense for one of the Russian's top people to be headed to this Happytown place to interrogate Clarkie. The fact that it was this Ulyenkov guy was just a bonus."

"Happyville," Colin corrected.

"Well, whatever the fuck it's called, it was a given they'd send one of their fixers."

Fortunately, Colin didn't press the issue. Jim sat back in his chair and treated the bruise that was growing on his face. Even under the dark makeup, the swelling was becoming noticeable. It would not make for a good impression if Ulyenkov the assassin was seen to be a weakling, especially as they were going to a very public place. Of course, the real guy would be in disgrace and dishonor and would want revenge if he got out of the city that they were now leaving behind.

And who knows what he would be capable of?

Jim shook away the thought. He had enough to deal with in the coming hours without a crazed killer on his tail as well but if he was to pull this off, he had to know about his new nemesis. He should have read up on him before this, but it was never too late.

"How much do we know about this dude anyway, beyond what you told us?" Jim asked around his companions.

"I think Mel should be the one to answer that, Jim."

SIXTEEN

Waters and MacDougall sat in a glade, surrounded by withered trees which looked like they were severely lacking of water. The hillside stretched upwards behind them, covered in yellowed grass and scrubby looking bushes. It was almost unbearably hot.

Drought was clearly blighting the country. Overhead the sun beat down relentlessly on the arid landscape. With little in the way of shade, Waters found himself beginning to sweat profusely.

Close by, Sytner was crouched down watching a cluster of buildings at the bottom of the hill below them, at about half a mile distance. He waved them over and raised a finger to his lips. He waved his hand, gesturing for them to keep low and out of sight. Once they were with him, they saw Gravett beyond, hiding behind a large piece of plant life that resembled a cactus, but with far sharper and nastier looking spikes.

"You appear to have been right, Lieutenant," he said in a low voice. He handed over a pair of binoculars.

They were equipped with a shield attached to the upper rim to kill sunlight glare. MacDougall took them first.

"Look down there. That village."

The binoculars zoomed the view in until it fixed on the settlement. MacDougall let out a low groan.

Russians. Lots of Russians were among the sun baked buildings. Some went about their business, others were keeping a watching brief.

MacDougall handed over the binoculars to Waters.

"You were right. They beat us to it."

Waters took in the view. He hated being right.

"What are your orders, sir?"

"Higher up needs to know about this and fast," MacDougall said firmly. He took out a field radio to call it in.

"What can they do? They're hours away. Even a message would be bounced back by these hills, or picked up by them. We need to do something ourselves," was Sytner's emphatic reply.

Waters scanned the surrounding area area. The village was in a low valley surrounded by hills which reached shallow ridges on both sides. Baked by the sun, they were like the hills behind them, various shades of yellow and gray. Because of that, anything unusual would stand out easily. Something like a mining operation or military activity. Like the one he had spotted at the far end of the valley.

A trail of smoke stretched into the sky pumping out noxious black clouds of chemicals into the atmosphere. The smoke appeared to be coming from the foot of a craggy hill, which meant that someone was working on something deep underground.

A huge spoil heap lay on the other side of the encampment, giving a persuasive hint that this operation was not a small scale one.

"Does anyone have any ideas?" Gravett asked.

"Destroy everything down there," was Sytner's predictable reply.

"I somehow think that subtlety is not in your vocabulary, Frank," Gravett told him in a dry tone.

Sytner scowled at him but said nothing.

"He may be on to something," MacDougall replied. "If the mine was destroyed and there was no trace of our being there, the Russians would no doubt think the place was unstable and move on from it."

"I like it," Gravett smiled. "I take it back Frank."

"Well, I did tell you. I don't see what the drama is. It is what it is," Sytner said.

The group watched the settlement for a short while, making sure their enemy did not notice them.

"How do you want to do this?" MacDougall asked.

"Let me get this right," Group Captain Spice said to his two officers. All three were in Spice's presence as he thought over the plan. He had not been too shocked at their discovery. The thought of the Russians being in the vicinity had occurred to him but to learn that they were strip mining the place for who knew what was a concern.

A coded message to Northwood had followed but with a three hour turnaround, Soper's recommendation that they take matters in to their own hands seemed the only option.

"You are going to break in to this mine, throw a load of bombs into the place and then get out.

And hope to hell you don't get caught?"

"That's the gist of it. Yes sir." Waters stood to attention. If he was any stiffer he could have been freshly starched. Next to him, MacDougall was a little more casual.

"Let me guess. This amazing plan was dreamed up by Sytner and Plato gave you the go-ahead?"

The younger and older man looked at each other.

"Erm.. yes sir." Waters was nothing but truthful.

Spice tapped the table between him and his two men.

"Well, isn't that just charming! Why are we risking our necks when there are three other choppers with us?"

"Mr. Plato was of the opinion that since we, or rather I realized what the Russians were doing that we have first refusal. He was open to volunteers. Well, we volunteered," MacDougall answered.

Spice harrumphed in disgust.

"I'll be glad to let the air staff know my gratitude. If I've told you once I've told you a thousand times, don't volunteer for anything. Do you realize what this means? If anything goes wrong it'll be my head on the chopping block while Plato gets to wash his hands of it."

"My father told me something similar, sir," Waters smiled.

Spice did not share his jocularity, and instead gave Waters a look that made the young Lieutenant think twice before speaking again. MacDougall elbowed the helmsman in the ribs, subtly so as the captain didn't pick up on it.

"I don't suppose we can't back out now can we?' he sighed. He looked at his officers. 'Alright, get your kit together. When do you have to get down there?"

"We worked out that the best way to approach the mine was under the cover of darkness. Sunset will be in 47 minutes."

The air had grown bitterly cold since the sun had dropped below the horizon. The last glimmers of sunlight created a brilliant flare as the sky grew dark. On the right-hand ridge overlooking the valley, two glimmers of light shimmered behind a rocky outcrop, hiding the arrival of MacDougall and Waters. Once they had arrived on point, the two drew their chunky Browning pistols. MacDougall carried a dark backpack, whose color matched their combat outfits.

Peeping over the outcrop, they found to their relief that they were overlooking the mine. Loud clattering of machinery working filled the air, an ideal disguise to conceal their approach. This should be an easy job, mused MacDougall.

Should be.

They made their way carefully down the hillside. It was rocky underfoot and in places the shale was fine, making a broken ankle a very real possibility. Gingerly, the two managed to get down to level ground.

The mine workings were a couple of hundred meters ahead, haloed in the arc lights illuminating the mine.

The air was scented with what seemed to be syrup and melted sugar. Waters had only ever smelled something like that in a flower or a sweet shop. Keeping a watchful eye, MacDougall led Waters around to the right to get a clearer view of the entrance leading underground. It turned out to be the entrance to a cave, it's yawning mouth opened to inky blackness. To its left a much larger cave mouth, large enough to drive a truck in to was set into the base of the hillside.

Two sentries carrying rifles appeared from behind a storage building to their left. There was no cover for several meters in all directions. No option but to crouch low and pray. The guards moved on talking among themselves and eventually were out of sight.

To their left several loads of poppies lay strewn about, with vast piles of them further on.

"Alright, let's make this fast. The locals don't appear to be friendly," MacDougall said softly. He indicated for Waters to follow him.

Tracing the spoil heaps, which turned out to be millions upon millions of poppy stems piled up awaiting disposal, the two made their way to entrance to the cave. Sounds of machinery working and shouting came from within. Despite lamps being set up in the entrance and beyond the tunnel walls, it was still ominously dark.

The passage narrowed and started to descend into the earth. The further and lower they traveled the hotter it became. The air become sooty and the fine powder immediately clung to their clothing. The ceiling hung down in places where the rock had been blasted, and beams supporting the roof had been put in place, mostly carelessly. It was all Waters could do, despite his average height to avoid hitting his head.

Voices from up ahead gave away that they had reached the main workings. The tunnel opened out into a vast underground amphitheater. Catwalks ringed the outer edges of the chamber.

Peering over the side, MacDougall saw hundreds of people, the local population of the villages around here he guessed sat at long tables pulling the heads from the poppy stems and appearing to grind them down, while others had Bunsen burners and appeared to be cooking in large metal pots. Something in the back of Niall's mind tried to remember something about this kind of setup that he had read or seen from years before. What was it?

Along the far wall, people mixed what looked like chemicals together and poured the contents of the large buckets they were working with into drums ready for transportation. A large group of soldiers armed with rifles walked u and down between the tables and among the workers, checking work and keeping order.

A couple of them were making the most of being unpleasant to the natives.

They routinely beat and flogged the workers if there seemed to be a slacking of the work rate or any sort of conversation.

Waters watched in horror as one young man, about his own age and clearly exhausted was beaten by two guards. The guards then laughed at his plight and moved on to their next victim.

Incensed, Waters was reaching for his pistol.

MacDougall simply shook his head.

"We can't interfere."

Mel holstered his pistol. Then, walking in to view came a small Russian with two others walking just behind him. He carried himself like a weapon; alert, straight backed with piercing eyes. He was talking to his aide about his plans for the rest of the evening, what he would be doing and a recommendation to stay in a hotel. The penthouse suite was as good as it got, apparently. Then he stopped to survey the work being done. Whatever he saw he was apparently not impressed.

He barked commands in a guttural voice while pointing out his findings to his two friends. One of the soldiers who Mel had just seen cruelly beating the worker went to him. The shorter man immediately began shouting at him in a throaty growl. The words wore unintelligible but the intent was obvious. The second man protested and yelled back at him.

The smaller Russian, who was wearing the rank of a Commander drew his gun and promptly shot the man who had dared to backtalk him in the chest. He fell down, apparently dead. A woman screamed and ran to where the man was laying, but she was dragged back to her seat by a guard. Waters and MacDougall looked at each other in astonishment. They had just been witnesses to a cold blooded murder, but the other Russians did not look remotely surprised or shocked. What kind of society was this?

Eventually, the man and his two aides moved on.

MacDougall pointed to the large drums at the far end of the cavern.

"If we placed this so that it destroyed that stuff, it wouldn't injure anyone but it would put an end to this."

They looked around and Waters realized the walkway went all the way around to the other side, so was ideal for what Niall had in mind. He nodded to it.

Glancing down, the workers were still too busy with their work. It was an ideal moment.

MacDougall slowly made his way to the platform above the drums, remembering his combat training. *Make no sudden moves. don't run, to do so will attract attention.*

The walkway was open and set on a rickety metallic gantry. Niall could feel it swaying slightly under his feet as his weight shifted. He made it to where he wanted to be. Beautiful, right above them. The walkway itself was smothered in oil and had clearly been poorly if it all maintained.

The metal was old and scratched with rust building up in places.

For some reason, a set of fuel cans had been placed near the drums, presumably for trucks to come, fuel up quickly and then drive out of the cave. Perfect. Anything such as what he was planning to do next involving the canisters which meant the explosion would quickly destroy the shipment of whatever it was as well. His job done, he withdrew slowly, with the gantry still swaying.

Suddenly there was a metallic cracking as the gantry finally gave way under his body weight.

The walkway bowed as MacDougall clung to it desperately. Waters watched in horror as his superior officer fell 30 feet to the floor below, ten feet from the fuel cans.

There was the sickening sound of bones breaking. MacDougall's legs were bent at an unnatural angle and it was obvious he had been seriously injured. Two of the workers went to help him, but were pushed back by their minders. The stocky Russian and his two friends came into sight from below Waters' vantage point. The Commander knelt beside the stricken British officer.

"So, the west has sent a spy into our midst along with everything else. I suggest for your sake that you talk."

MacDougall spat a large gob of blood up and said something too indistinct for Mel to hear. The Commander turned to one of his aides, who in return handed a large curved blade. The leader Twisted the thing in his hands, showing off its vicious looking pointed ends.

"I doubt you will have heard of me, which is very much to your benefit. If you did then you're Either brave or stupid." The man looked down at his captive. 'I am Ulyenkov, and you are trespassing on my territory. Tell me why you are here, or I promise this will not be pleasant."

He stood over MacDougall, still turning the nasty looking thing and passing them between his Hands.

Again, the RAF man said something indistinct, too weak to speak loudly. Waters guessed that his lungs had been punctured. Ulyenkov raised the curved object and struck MacDougall with it. The noise was horrific, even at a distance.

"Leave him alone!" Waters shouted.

Ulyenkov looked up at where Mel was, the thing in his hand bloody. "Get him! Stop him!"

Then from the back of the cavern, the ground began shaking violently. The explosive had done its job. Cracks in the floor and walls of the cavern appeared and the tables began collapsing. The hot vats of what where revealed to be a honey-like substance turned over as the cave walls crumbled. Clearly, this was an unstable cavern that was an accident waiting to happen. The Russian took his two aides and the guards and quickly left, leaving MacDougall and the workers to their fate. Waters knew that he had to get out or it would be the end of him. He was sprinting back along the tunnel as fast as his legs could carry him. From behind he heard the muffled cries as the cavern collapsed, but he could not afford to let it get to him. His very life depended on his getting out. The tunnel seemed to go on forever, and it felt as if the climb out was a lot steeper than the climb in. He saw light head. The arc lights around the mine.

He burst into open air just as a large cloud of dust erupted behind him from the mouth of the tunnel.

Mel threw himself forward behind one of the spoil heaps. He was stunned and breathing heavily, his person covered in dust. Ulyenkov appeared from above where Waters was laying, filling his vision. He knelt down close to the young officer. He was icy calm.

"It's very co incidental that I find two Royal Air Force officers at the same time as my opium is destroyed. You have cost me a very large amount of money and trouble, and now you will pay."

So that's what it was! Ulyenkov was using the locals to produce heroin. That would explain the poppies and all the cooking equipment. Somehow, he still had the curved weapon in his hand.

He raised it. Waters was sure the next thing he saw would be Saint Peter.

He steeled himself against what he was sure would be about to come. But Ulyenkov lowered the blade as a gunshot rang out from the hill he and Niall had clambered down. Another gunshot just missed the Russian's head and he dove for cover behind a car, which he opened the passenger door of.

"Tell your superiors that we'll be back. And we will not be so merciful next time," he shouted as the car sped away. Waters lay there as the dust began to settle. It was the only thing left to do.

Mel Waters sat in the mess hall, contemplating his cup of coffee. It had long since gone cold. He had been going over and over the events of the past few hours in his head, trying to make sense of it all. He had never been in a situation like this before. He had joined the RAF to see the world, not get involved in combat and certainly not to see close friends be murdered brutally.

Yes, he had known the risks when he signed on but it wasn't what he had expected so soon. The whole thing had been horrific, but the worst part was seeing his direct superior, not to mention a close friend killed in front of him in such a needless and cold way. The final look on MacDougall's face as Ulyenkov had held the blade over him was something that would stay with him for a long time.

"You look like you could do with some company," said a thick accented voice. Mel looked up to see a stocky man wearing an engineering uniform standing close by. He had a cup of his own in his hand. He looked drawn and tired.

"Have a seat sir."

The other man sat down across the table from him. His uniform was grubby, probably from running constant repairs after the air battle, Mel guessed.

"Thanks, I could do with taking the weight off."

"Yes sir."

"You don't have to call me sir, I work for a living. Call me Scotty."

"Fair enough er.. Scotty."

Scotty leaned back in his chair. He was not much older than Waters but had an air of someone of fatherly competence. He took a sip of his drink.

"What happened down there?" Scotty asked.

"There's not much else beyond the official report."

Scotty had sensed that there was more. He was shrewd, this one thought Mel.

"Something is bothering you. Otherwise you wouldn't have stared at that drink for an hour."

He had been watching him for that long? Finally Waters let out a small sigh.

"I've never seen death before. But the Russian seemed to enjoy it. I mean... really enjoyed hurting and killing those people."

"Evil comes in all shapes and sizes, our kid," Scotty said expansively.

"But how can someone... do it and feel good about it, sir?"

The other man looked at Mel with a mixture of pity and mild annoyance.

"I told you, call me Scotty." He folded his arms and looked at Mel. "No one really knows what makes another person tick, just they themselves. All you can do is worry about you and what you're doing is right."

They sat in silence and took a drink. The cold coffee in Waters' cup did not sit well.

"How can we go on, knowing that this sort of bad thing is going on?" he wondered.

"It happens. You accept it and move on, or you dwell on it and it drags you down."

Mel looked at his cup again. If this whole thing was going to get ugly, he had to get ugly to deal with it.

"There's something else, isn't there?" Scotty probed.

Waters set his cup back down and rose from the table. Scotty waited patiently for his answer.

"Just before I was picked up, the Russian told me that he'd be back," Waters admitted. 'Scotty, I didn't tell anyone at the debrief. I could get busted for that."

"Then we will just have to keep our mouths shut and our eyes open," Scotty replied.

SEVENTEEN

"That's how I came to now the Russians so well. My superior officer had to die for me to get to know them and their methods. Ulyenkov's face is not one I'll ever forget. So now you know why I didn't want to talk about it," Mel finished his story and went back to concentrating on piloting the Hip. Jim sat in silence, digesting what he had just learned.

From behind them, Colin handed McCleland an iPad.

"I got together all the information I could find on him," he explained.

Waters did his best to tune out their conversation. Jim began to read. Ulyenkov's history read like a horror novel. The number of deaths and mayhem was wince inducing, and he appeared to have very little in the way of morals. He had broad discretionary powers granted by the Russian government which pretty much meant he could go anywhere, anytime and enforce whatever he wanted, and he appeared to only be accountable to the president himself. Being ex-KGB he was a highly trained undercover operative, trained in weapons and martial arts. With what Mel had just told them, he was also involved with illegal business practices and narcotics, so who knew who else he had in his pocket? Half the drug dealers in Europe, Jim guessed. All of this was something that could prove very useful.

The chopper crossed the border into Turkmenistan away from prying eyes, with Mel skillfully piloting the machine through a deep gorge between two mountain ranges and once safely back in open air, the Hip moved down to the deck to get under radar surveillance. Anyone in the area would have had to duck to avoid being given a haircut, Waters was virtually hugging the ground as he continued westward. As the mountains receded into the horizon behind them, Jim had time to gather his thoughts. If they succeeded, it would be a tremendous coup. If they failed, an extremely grisly fate awaited them.

"Send a message to Wren's Nest. Tell them we're going in," he informed Haltwhistle.

***

Black Jack Cartwright had been taking a nap when Matthews woke him. Since the mission had started he had had little rest and finally was persuaded to take a break after the last message from the team.

He had taken the liberty of ordering the police reports surrounding Berry's death. The thick manila folders had been a slog to get through, but had offered some intriguing information. One statement in particular had caught his eye. A witness account from the dock keeper where Berry's boat had been kept that gave a few details from the evening before the boat's disappearance.

He had taken Harvey and Matthews' advice and had gone to bed. His deep sleep was interrupted and he was now wide awake.

"Rapier is calling on the video link," Matthews told him urgently. Quickly the air vice marshal threw on a uniform and hurried to his office. He sat down at his desk and switched on his monitor. Flt Lieutenant Haltwhistle's boyish features were on his screen. He noticed with satisfaction that the message was being sent on a secure and jammed channel.

"This is Wren's Nest, go ahead Rapier."

"Sir, we've crossed the border. We are going in and will be at Happyville in roughly an hour. Requesting you hold station until further contact, sir." Even when the circumstances were serious, Colin still had a polite air about him.

Cartwright checked his manifests and his wall readouts. They could be in Afghanistan in seven hours and be on their way to support if the orders were given. They had transport ready with just a single call if needed. He made his choice.

"Good luck, Rapier. We are sending support effective immediately."

Haltwhistle's eyes widened at that.

"Wren's Nest out."

He signed off. He had very little time for what he had to do. He sent out a page.

"Group Captain Harvey, report to my office immediately." He looked at Matthews. "Pack your bag, Matthews. We're going on a little journey."

Once the video call ended, Colin turned back to Jim. "He said he's sending support."

Jim gave Mel a confused look and by the pilot's expression, he was equally puzzled.

"How the hell did he rustle up some support that quickly? What's he going to do? Charge into the place and nuke it?" Waters wondered.

"Don't ask me, I thought this AID thing was only recently set up?"

"No mate. Black Jack has been doing covert work for years. Who do you think came up with the Mujaheddin support mission that I flew?" Mel gave Jim an affirmative nod. "Try forgetting that now that I've told you."

The bulky Russian machine glided through the air towards its ultimate destination. In the back seat, Colin checked the heading and the time. Not long until they were in visual range of the settlement that was code named Happyville. In the co-pilot's seat, Jim examined the Tokarev pistol.

"Nice craftsmanship, I have to say."

In the pilot's seat, Mel Waters kept a close eye on his instruments. Any mistake at this low altitude would result in a very sudden and very fatal crash. He was well under the radar horizon but he wanted to keep visual identification at bay until the last possible moment.

"You'd better get the access and password codes ready," Jim told Haltwhistle.

"I've had them ready since we left London," Colin grinned.

Jim allowed himself a smile as well. His smile slipped from his face as out of the curved windscreen he saw a dot coming towards them, a dot which was growing rapidly in size.

"Looks like we've got a welcoming committee whether we like it or not," he said.

The rapidly expanding dot became the shape of something Mel had not wanted to see again.

"Looks like our friends out there have got themselves a Hind," he said gravely. He decided to get off the valley floor and come up to a decent altitude just in case trouble started, so that he could give himself room to maneuver. He could clearly make out the swooping wings and stubby front with its menacing quad barreled machine gun as it closed in on them. The Hip, while it had similar wing mounted weaponry had nothing with which to oppose the overwhelming firepower of the Hind's.

The intercom beeped.

"Message coming in," Colin said predictably.

"Unidentified aircraft, identify yourself and state your business," came a voice that sounded like it had a bad dose of the flu.

McCleland knew this was his time to put his best acting chops on. His performance had better be convincing or this would be over in a matter of seconds. He cleared his throat and leaned back; he always found if he leaned back when sitting, he could project his voice much more effectively. In the confines of the Hip's cockpit, standing was somewhat tricky.

"This is Vladimir Ulyenkov. Requesting permission to approach."

The voice sounded taken aback.

"Sir! We had not expected to see you so soon. You are not traveling aboard your usual -"

"I will not tolerate your questioning, man!" Jim bellowed in his best approximation of the Russian despot's gravelly low pitched tones. "Will you grant our passage or not?"

There was a brief silence before the reply came.

"Transmit your identification codes."

Jim intimated to Colin to do so.

"Well? Are you satisfied?" The note of impatience in Jim's voice was not all acting.

"Permission granted. It is an honor to have you here -"

"Enough of your pretentiousness man! Close channel!" he barked. Once the line had gone silent, he grinned. "That wasn't so bad."

"I do believe you enjoyed that." Haltwhistle was smirking behind his Russian disguise.

"Maybe you were right about me cutting a dash as a Russian psychopath, as disgusting as that is."

"You were certainly convincing in the part."

Jim pursed his lips. "Let's hope I can maintain the performance!" He retook his seat and let out a sigh of relief.

The Hip continued on its way, past the Hind which hovered as if to watch it go, and then continued on its own patrol course. After what seemed like an interminable age, the chopper finally came within visual range of their destination.

"You may want to look at this," said Waters. He sounded wary.

Through the forward view ports, the base looked even more imposing than it had in the surveillance pictures that they had seen in Cartwright's office. The camp was embedded into the base of a rugged outcrop of hills, which as they grew closer gave away vast structures built into the hard stone. Large prefab hangars sat with aircraft of both fighter and bomber types close to hand to them.

Interestingly, they were mostly of older types: MiG 21s and IL-28s with the odd contemporary design poking out from the shelter of a hangar. Jim and Mel could see Russian tanks and trucks being resupplied and buildings under construction as people and equipment swarmed around them. This was clearly a major undertaking that was being put together, but there was something more to it. A lot more. Other smaller buildings which must have been barracks were sited around the hangars and stores which must have housed hundreds, perhaps thousands of troops.

"What the hell is this place?" Waters muttered.

All sorts of questions were going through Jim's mind. All of these aircraft, vehicles and equipment was a lot more than just standard operations. There could only be one answer.

"It looks like they're putting an invasion together," McCleland affirmed.

Colin merely watched the rapidly approaching outpost through the front windows of the Hip.

"I can't think of anything else that would answer why there was such a huge operation like this here, Jim."

"Surely the local government would object? You think they wouldn't be too happy with a shitload of battle happy Russians on their doorstep," Jim thought aloud.

"They probably don't even know this lot is here," said Mel.

McCleland dreaded to think about how many people were stationed here. Thousands. Maybe hundreds of thousands. They truly were about to rush in where angels fear to tread. Above all of the structures jutting out of the rock, a vast lattice of steel formed a communications tower and lookout post which loomed over the base. It looked like a huge, metallic castle overlooking the land that the owner held sway over, not unlike some evil Eiffel Tower. It must be there where Clarkie was being held. There was a certain irony to that if that was the case. Locked up in the tower. Mel spotted a helicopter landing pad that was vacant.

"I'm going to set down here."

Colin checked the systems over while Jim watched out for anything untoward. Then the chopper lurched without warning.

"It's nothing, just wind shear," said Waters.

"Alright. We just play it cool and go along with whatever they say. Clarkie is here somewhere so we have to find him, but now that we know what's here, we need the intel, so learn as much as you can," Jim told Colin.

"Jim, I should warn you that because they believe you are Ulyenkov, there will more than likely have a welcoming committee to meet us."

McCleland had expected that, but didn't know what to say to anyone who accosted him, or how to act appropriately. He remembered how offhand Krasnov had been when he had encountered him, as if he owned the room. To pass himself off successfully, he had to play that up to the next level. He reflected on how arrogant and raw Saddam Hussein's people had been, especially when treating the downed pilots during the first Gulf War – and his own experience. He didn't want to get as extreme as those people but it had to be done for this to work. And it must. An awful lot rode on this.

The Hip was being drawn towards the landing pad on the southern side of the encampment. It was the furthest away from the rest of the encampment, which was lucky. Jim watched as a rocky outcrop seemed to be right underneath the chopper. A collision seemed inevitable and he braced himself for impact but at the last moment, Mel twisted the machine around and the rocks were missed. The helicopter's wheeled undercarriage probed for the dusty ground from beneath the smooth underbelly and it touched down with a reassuring clunk. The familiar noise of the rotors slowing and the engines powering down filled the cabin as Waters shut down the twin powerplants. The warning light changed color indicating a successful landing. A strange buzzing noise hummed faintly in the air. It wasn't quite electrical but it sounded familiar enough to Colin that he could say what it was.

"It sounds like they have radar jammers and the same for radios. that's going to make things bit trickier."

"Could we shut it down?" McCleland asked.

"We would have to find where the system is controlled from and disable it, but that could raise other problems. If we were able to transmit what was going on, so could our friends out there."

After checking all his systems for the final shutdown, Mel got up from the pilot's position. He stretched.

Even though he was not a tall man, being cooped up in a cramped seat at a tight console was still quite constricting.

"Stay with the chopper," Colin informed him. "I think we'll be needing you to get us out of here in a hurry."

"I thought we were going to stick together?" Mel questioned, then he realized that he had not been told everything. His voice dropped and he spoke in a tone that told McCleland he was not about to be put off, regardless of seniority.

"I don't mean any disrespect to either of you gents, but I want to know what the fuck's going on, right now."

"Fair enough. Now that we're here, we can tell you what's really the name of the game."

Colin pulled the thumb drive from his backpack that Cartwright had given to him back in London.

He placed it into the iPad's USB port and ran the tape. On the screen, Cartwright appeared, sat at his desk in his office in the bunker.

"Squadron Leader McCleland, Flight Lieutenant Haltwhistle, if you are seeing this information we can assume that the Royal Air Force and indeed the Ministry of Defence itself is under a grave threat to its security, and that contact with the security services is a limited option. We have reason to believe that there are persons unknown in the upper reaches of the RAF who are actively working to destabilize us. We learned that someone high up is, in fact in the employ of a foreign power, but we cannot identify the person in question at this time.

Your mission is to find out who the people or person within the Royal Air Force is and to contain and neutralize the threat. This video is for your eyes only, and must be destroyed once viewed.

You may use whatever means you feel necessary to accomplish your mission up to and including termination with extreme prejudice. Extra support is available at your request, but this is a last resort measure."

Cartwright leaned forward and clasped his hands. He looked concerned but determined.

"Further communication may not be possible. If you or any member of your crew is caught, you are expendable. Good luck Jim, Colin, and Godspeed. Cartwright out."

"Jesus!" Waters looked aghast. Colin took the USB stick from the iPad and crushed it in his fingers. It crumpled to dust on the cockpit floor.

"It explains why he came to me rather than someone active." Mel sat in the flight engineer's position and regarded his two colleagues. "Just don't leave me hanging."

Jim put a hand on his arm. "No danger of that." He had grown to like and respect Waters hugely over the last few days. He turned to Haltwhistle. "Alright, let's get this show on the road."

They rose and gathered their kit that hung on hangers in the cargo compartment. They both knew that the AK-47s and ammo were hidden in the kit bags, but as a supposed fixer, he was beyond searching by the mere soldier here. Colin handed the metal encased precious stone to McCleland.

"Hopefully we shouldn't be long. A few hours. We'll be back as quick as we can," said Jim.

There was much shoulder clapping but Colin looked thoughtful. Jim regarded him, understanding.

"Col. I know how you feel about this, but it may be necessary..." he indicated to the kit bags and held his waist band where his sidearm was hooked to emphasise the point, but Haltwhistle interrupted.

"I got you. And I knew what I was getting in to when I came on this little soiree," he looked at Jim and Mel. "I knew what I was signing up for when I joined up but if something happens to me..."

"We're going to be fine, mate."

"I'm just saying, if something happens to me, tell Anna that I love her."

Jim nodded. No more words were needed. While McCleland had taken the brunt of the action, Colin as a detective had no doubt seen some pretty nasty things during his service and no doubt had had to injure opponents before in the name of defense.

"I think we need to find a way to make a distraction. It'll make getting out of this place easier for sure. Let me take a sniff around and I'll find something to help," the younger man remarked.

"You got it."

"Good luck," offered Waters. "I'll have us out of here like a racing car off a starting line."

At that, Jim and Colin both turned. At their expressions, Mel smiled.

"Just a figure of speech. Got to love some motor racing action."

"That's funny, we were watching a tape of it a few days ago."

"Really? Great!" Mel was genuinely enthused.

The loading door swung slowly open and the two younger men stepped down into the oppressive heat and dust once more. The whole atmosphere of this place was ugly, and just as Colin had feared they did indeed have a welcome committee, and leading them was Krasnov.

Seventeen Darkness, and a pounding headache. A tingling in his right arm and his shoulder and neck ached. Ulyenkov slowly sat up.

"Gratz? Drash? Are you here?"

There was no sound in reply. Ulyenkov started to get up. His cranium hit something hard and unforgiving. he let out a low groan.

Those two dressed like Russians, and the leader who looked like a mirror image of him. What had happened? He had been about to launch a vicious attack on that one. How dare he challenge him? How dare someone change their appearance to match his? Did they not know who he was?

But there was something. Something about the one who had challenged him that seemed familiar somehow.

He felt around and put his hand on something softer. A low moan.

"Gratz? Is that you?"

"Yes..." the voice sounded pained. "My apologies. I was taken unawares. An officer should never be so unprepared."

Ulyenkov and Gratz clawed around in the darkness until Gratz put his hand on a wall. Moving his fingers around he finally felt a shape. Using his fingers he found it was a handle. He twisted and pulled it but it did not move. Another low groan from behind them told them that Drash was conscious.

"Is anyone there?" came his voice.

"Drash. Come here and help us. We will discuss our conduct at a better time," Ulyenkov commanded.

Drash joined them and after some checking, they discovered the seam of a doorway that the handle connected to. Ulyenkov tried the handle again, but it broke off in his hand. He cursed loudly.

"Is anyone out there? We need some help!" bellowed Gratz. He repeated his call for help a few times.

They waited for anyone to hear them or respond, but after a few moments it became clear that no one was coming.

"Your excellency, I have an idea. If we were to kick against the door, it might open," said Drash.

The three laid down in the restricted space and began kicking out in time. The metal sprung back against their feet, but three sets of strong legs were able to overcome the wood and fiberglass in the door. After a few minutes of pounding, the door gave way and creaked open. The three men tumbled out and found themselves in the bathroom of their suite. Ulyenkov, now a little more energised but still feeling somewhat drowsy looked about them. They had been placed in the lavatory of the bathroom. His anger rose even further.

Ulyenkov saw Gratz's shape in the darkness. "We need to get out of here and find out where we are."

They found the door to the bathroom similarly locked but some well-aimed kicks to the door caused the door frame to break away and they were out and into the suite. It was a mass of busted furniture and smashed ornaments. No matter.

They headed downstairs to the car park where his car, a Mercedes 600S sat. Grabbing the telephone, he made a call to his lead pilot who was still waiting with the helicopters that they had arrived in the previous night.

"Comrade! We have been trying to call you since last night! -"

"I was indisposed," Ulyenkov spat. It wasn't a lie. "We are coming to you, get the helicopters ready."

"We have a problem sir. Our delivery was not made and there is no sign of our contact."

Ulyenkov was furious. First he had been waylaid and now his shipment had not been brought on time. What was wrong today?

"Find him! I want my merchandise!"

The report of a huge explosion in the hills above the city had brought Ulyenkov to a smoldering wreck that had once been a truck. The sickly sweet smell in the air was an instant giveaway of what had happened. Three and half billion rubles, equal to 50 million USD of raw opium had been immolated. His opium. The burned out frame of the truck held the remains of incinerated weaponry and the scorched remnants of someone who had been in the wrong place at the wrong time. Tyre tracks going down the track to his right was a persuasive hint that someone had got away, and three bullet ridden corpses lying on the ground 20 yards from the truck added to the story.

Bending down, Ulyenkov searched the first person. Nothing out of the ordinary. His fury building up he kicked the body over the edge of the plateau and in to the valley below.

"Over here!" called Gratz. He had a wallet in his hand. Going through it's contents, several money bills including a British banknote was in one of the sleeves. Apart from identification, there was a business card for a bar in Termez. 'Juliana's.'

"We're going there."

The Mercedes stopped beside the run down looking bar and Ulyenkov got out. He gestured for his two guys to join him. The place was quiet at this time of the morning and appeared to be closed up. Heading for the door the killer found it to be locked, but simply drew his gun and shot the lock, seemingly uncaring of any authorities being contacted. Kicking the door in, he strode into the building, clearly not in the mood for games. Gratz and Drash stood in the doorway to keep an eye out for any law enforcement to show up. Looking up from the bar where she was cleaning glasses, the owner, a dark haired woman in her late 40's saw what had happened to her door and who was responsible.

"How dare you break in here! I knew you were trouble when I saw you last night! Get out!" she shouted furiously.

Walking up to the bar, Ulyenkov saw her trying to reach for something under it and immediately pointed his pistol at her, indicating for her to retreat.

"Back away."

"Hey, this is my place, I give the orders around here!" She noticed his men. "Those two aren't the same as the ones you were with, are they? Or do you hunt in packs?"

But the formidable Russian was not about to engage in pleasant conversation. He placed his gun down and his hands on the counter and leaned over it.

"I want to know where those three men went. Now."

"You should know, you were one of those who left!" she protested with a laugh.

Ulyenkov's eyes narrowed. He reached over and grabbed her roughly. "I am not in the mood for games, madam."

"Are you mad? Get off me!" she grunted.

He cuffed her across the face. She twisted in his grip and he glowered at her. Blood ripped from her lip.

"Tell me. Or I swear I will kill you were you stand."

"I don't know. They didn't tell me anything. They came in wanting weapons I think." She looked at him.

"You defiled my daughter you bastard! You took her last night and she never came back!"

"I'd say she is at the moment exploring the mysteries of what it feels like to be shashlik," he told her coldly, remembering the remains of the truck. The woman screamed and fought against Ulyenkov's hold.

Before he could get any answers Ulyenkov was interrupted by a large, meaty hand clamping on his shoulder.

"Ulyenkov! You will not get away so easily this time!"

The spy turned, only to be decked by the big man who had caused a commotion in the same bar just a few hours before. He had cuts on his face and bruises forming under his eyes. He had clearly been in a fight a short time earlier.

"You murdered my brother!"

He must have come through a back door as there was no way that Gratz and his partner would have allowed him in. They were now rushing over, but were dissuaded from taking the larger man. They knew it was a lost cause to take on someone who tore a table that had been bolted to the floor from it and threw it at them.

"Stand down. This is between him and me." Ulyenkov needed to get some aggression out.

The larger man was muscular but he was over built and ungainly. He swung for his target with a left hook which the smaller man saw coming and sidestepped. The bigger opponent let out a furious howl as Ulyenkov ducked under him and then let out a terrible gurgling, choke as he smashed the side of his hand into his throat. The killer watched as the man he had hit just once dropped to his knees then fell forward.

Blood and vomit flowed from his mouth as he hit the floor of the bar, dead from a punctured larynx.

The bartender was not much help at all but Ulyenkov was satisfied with her insistence that she did not know what had happened and with her daughter no longer being able to answer any questions, there was nothing more to be gained. The fact she had just seen him kill someone in her bar, and he had had her by the throat was enough to convince him she was truthful.

"I thank you for your honesty, but I prefer a mess to be resolved in a tidy fashion," Ulyenkov told her.

Her transparency had not saved her life though. If there were no witnesses, no one could tell of who and what.

The bodies of the bartender and the upstart who had dared to challenge him had been disposed of and the bar itself destroyed in the usual efficient manner.

Now he had some answers. Whoever they were they must be British agents and were clearly there to recover the RAF officer he had been sent to interrogate. They had been trying to procure weapons and with one of them disguised as himself there could only be one conclusion to draw.

They intended to get to Krasnov first and accomplish their mission, whatever that might be. The destruction of the opium that he was due to hand over must have occurred as the exchange coincided with their deal and matters had gotten out of hand.

Upon arriving at the helicopters, he knew that they had to get to Krasnov as quickly as possible, but with the radio jammed there was no way to contact Krasnov and warn him of what was going on until they themselves reached the base.

Ulyenkov was quietly seething with rage.

"Hear this. We will proceed to our meeting with Comrade Krasnov. We will interrogate this RAF officer, and we will find the people who disgraced us," he informed his aides.

"Do you have a plan after that?" Gratz asked.

Ulyenkov's voice dripped menace and venom.

"I intend to find whoever dishonored us. And then... I will kill them. Slowly."

***

Krasnov stepped forward. He drew his right hand to his temple in a salute virtually identical to their own salutes, Jim thought. He returned the salute and squared up to his adversary.

"Comrade Ulyenkov. Thank you for coming at such short notice."

McCleland was more than taken aback to be confronted with Krasnov. They had met face to face. If he so much as suspected, it would blow this thing out of the water. He stepped forward and scowled at the Russian general he had met two years before.

"Let's get down to business Krasnov. I want to see the prisoner you've got hanging around here."

"All in good time, Comrade. I'm sure you have had a long journey. Perhaps we could sit and partake of a few drinks. There is plenty of time to interrogate the Briton," Krasnov countered.

Jim as Ulyenkov grimaced. "Are you refusing a direct order?"

"Certainly not but here I am the ranking officer and you are a guest of mine, in case you didn't remember. And I am expecting my package from you."

The response was delivered with a smile that hid quiet menace.

Package? He doesn't mean the weapons or drugs we just blew up does he? Oh shit! Jim snorted. "Whatever suits you. Lead on."

Krasnov gave the would-be Russian a questioning look.

"First. Your passkey."

The jewel was handed over and the general examined it closely before handing it back.

"Do you know what this stone is?" It was an almost challenging question from the general.

Jim was instantly on edge. *Chrome... Dropside? Diode? Oh bugger...*

"Chrome Diopside." He hoped like hell that the pronunciation was close enough. Beside him, Colin sighed with relief.

"Of course you do. You were the one who instigated this as a passkey," Krasnov half sneered.

"Very good. Are you not going to introduce me to your aide? And where is the other fellow I have heard about?"

McCleland looked to Colin and back to the Russian. "No, I am not. And where my other subordinate is, is of no concern of yours. Let's go," McCleland put his best growl into his reply.

Krasnov merely shrugged and led Jim and Colin to a Tiger armored car. It was a far cry from the UAZ being extremely spacious inside and almost refined. The driver set off and took them on a tour of the base. There were people everywhere working on vehicles or supplies, and all stopped and saluted. And Jim thought his own military was well drilled!

The buildings were not clustered close together but were well laid out and away from each other, presumably so that if there was an attack, collateral damage would be limited. Clearly this place had been designed by a different architect than in the days of old, and from the smell of the air, it must be new. On both sides of the Tiger there were broad side roads and crosswalks that lead to the large hangars where the aircraft that they had seen before landing were birthed.

Eventually, the driver stopped near the base of the vast antenna mast and Krasnov got out. The driver let Jim and Colin out and the doors at the base of the tower were held open for them.

Either side of the entrance stood two T-80 battle tanks. Krasnov led them inside. The corridors had been blasted out of the rock of the hillside that the mast sat on. They were wide and well lit and seemed to go right back in to the hillside. Krasnov was pointing out various features of what Happyville offered and how well equipped it was, especially for something set up so quickly.

Haltwhistle wondered how they had been able to put this together so well and so quickly until he remembered that it was probably achieved with slave labor. He shuddered inwardly and forced the thought from his mind.

Jim turned to the right to head down another hallway, but Krasnov interrupted.

"That area is off limits," he said curtly.

"Even to me?" McCleland demanded. He assumed Ulyenkov's influence had significant pull, but apparently that wasn't the case.

"Yes, Vladimir, even to you." Jim realized Krasnov was mocking him. He clearly had no love for this murderer either. He had also used Ulyenkov's first name which was a huge no-no in this culture.

Jim looked at Colin with the vaguest of hint. Too subtle for Krasnov to pick up on it, but enough for his friend to know what Jim intended.

"What have you got hidden down there? The local harem girls?"

"You know very well what's there. You were in on every aspect of this operation. Perhaps I should have a test arranged of your memory, if it that poor."

"If your intelligence was as impressive as your sarcasm, I'd begin to be concerned." McCleland was really getting in to the role. "And if you ever call me by my name again I'll have your head on a spike. Is that clear?'

Krasnov half grinned, half grimaced and led them on along the wide thoroughfare to a large silver door which slid open to reveal a metal paneled lift. Everything about this base seemed to have been built as vast as possible. As if the designer had some sort of statement to make about Russian brilliance. It rose at a pace more rapidly than the elevators in a skyscraper and when they stepped out they were staring at view ports which gave a dizzying view out at the desert below.

Far below was the base and McCleland realized they were within the tower above the hangars.

He took in the spectacle appreciatively. The Eiffel Tower and the similar Blackpool tower gave comparable views, but nothing this spectacular. It was almost as if they could reach out and touch the mountains across the plain from them.

For his part Krasnov was regarding Jim and Colin. "This way, gentlemen."

"Comrade General," Colin addressed him. "I would be very interested in taking a tour of this facility."

"All the blueprints are available and your master is very aware of everything here," Krasnov responded. "So why would you want a tour?"

"My family worked on the plans," Colin explained, thinking quickly. "I would be intrigued to know how closely you stuck to them when you built the outpost."

Krasnov beckoned to the guard to come over.

"Fair enough. Guard."

"If you will excuse us." Haltwhistle took his leave, and headed back towards the lift.

McCleland moved along, following Krasnov beyond yet another set of silver doors. A vast, plushly appointed apartment was before them, completely at odds with everything Jim had seen of Russian hospitality so far. Woods from all over the world had been carved ornately into wall covering, ceiling decoration and bookcases, where a huge collection of volumes by different authors, some of them human sat.

Jim moved to examine them, his innate curiosity getting the better of him. Shakespeare, Dickens, Twain and a large collection of poetry by Wordsworth, Keats, Byron and others sat alongside books of philosophy by Russian authors, Tolstoy's *War and Peace* of course. A copy of Sun Tzu's *Art of War*, *The Three Musketeers*, the complete *Sherlock Holmes*.

Paintings by various artists adorned the walls, some human. The Haywain was one Jim recognized, as was The Sunflowers by Van Gogh and what must be a copy of the Mona Lisa.

Krasnov was clearly not a typical mindless thug that the west thought hid behind the former Iron Curtain.

"Interesting General. You have an eclectic selection," he said, looking at the books in turn.

"Thank you, Comrade, I feel that to understand your enemies, you should read their classics and appreciate their artistic output," Krasnov replied. "It gives a unique insight into the psyche of the opponent."

Off to the right of the bookcases were more view ports, giving further impressive views out into surrounding hills. Various alcoholic beverages sat in oddly shaped bottles on a presentation table under the windows. The wooden walls were decorated with the heads of creatures that Jim presumed Krasnov had hunted and then preserved in a manner which he had seen in history books and museums he had visited with his parents as a child. He found that a bit gruesome to be honest.

"Quite a collection, Krasnov. How much did you pay for these?" he asked. He knew by his nature that he had killed them, but he wanted to maintain the act and rile him. Also, he was starting to enjoy rubbing his adversary's nose in it.

For his part, Krasnov folded his arms and looked distinctly unimpressed.

"I never knew you had such a pithy sense of humor. If I didn't know better, I'd say you'd been hanging around with our dear British friends too much."

That caused Jim to take a breath. Had Krasnov rumbled him? He could see a very bloody, messy climax to this encounter. "What are you suggesting?" He tried to inject as much venom as possible into the question.

"Well, everyone knows that you have all of those officers in your pocket."

McCleland squinted hard at Krasnov, intending to look as intimidating as possible. "If I had, what business would that be of the military arm of the Federation?"

"It pays to know things, Krasnov. For instance, we were aware of the movements of a certain McCleland of my acquaintance after he left dear old leafy England. We even knew of his movements once he arrived in Afghanistan but swiftly all contact was lost."

That did bring Jim up short. Colin had been right. Fortunately if all communication was cut then Krasnov and whoever else was looking for them did not know what they were doing. It also meant that they must know that they had a Russian helicopter at their disposal.

It also meant that somewhere out there, the agent inside the RAF was at large, just as Cartwright had suspected. For now, he had to play along.

"Yes I was aware. It is unfortunate but there are more where they came from."

"Perhaps you would like to share your intelligence gathering with me? We could pool our resources. That would provide a great advantage for the Federation, comrade," Krasnov was becoming enthused.

"In time perhaps," Jim replied. Then he realized he had his opponent in the palm of his hand. He could get the information he wanted and his adversary would never suspect.

"Tell me how much you know, and I will see what gaps I can fill in."

"I welcome it. And also to know where my shipment is. I have various parties waiting for their drugs, as disgusting as it is, it is a lucrative business."

EIGHTEEN

The BAE 146 touched down at Camp Bastion and taxied to a stop by the main buildings. The occupants of this grand lady had been patiently holding station awaiting news and when it came, the man in charge wasted no time in taking action. Maintaining radio silence since taking off the only contact the gleaming aircraft had made was the code word sent to notify of landing imminent.

Air Vice Marshal John Cartwright was glad to have his feet back on terra firma. A car was quickly sent out to the 146, which had appeared on the radar with no warning. Fortunately, an advance call had been made to the base commander, Bailey to expect them, and a scrambling of the camp's interceptors was avoided.

Cartwright quickly brought the irritated base commander into an office and had the door guarded. To anyone outside, clearly this was a top secret briefing.

"I'd like to know just what the hell kind of authority you have to just turn up and turn the base upside down!" Bailey virtually exploded at him.

"Ministry of Defence, Airborne Intelligence Division and the Secret Intelligence Service," was the blunt reply. "In short, this is a security matter and is not for anyone's ears. Anything that happens in the next 24 hours is to be buried and not documented. Is that clear?"

Bailey, a Lt. General no less, knew his hands were tied, despite that on paper the air vice marshal was lower down the pecking order than he. He gave a snort of derision and pressed his intercom button.

"Bailey to medical."

"Thompson here."

"I want you to prepare every ward down there. Have all your people ready as there could be a lot of action in the next day or so. Have everyone made ready. Understood?"

"All the wards are ready and I'll have the medical staff prepped, sir," Thompson confirmed. "I just hope that we won't have to use them.

"I hope so too, doctor but we have to be ready for anything. Bailey out."

There was nothing to do but wait. The intercom on Bailey's desk buzzed.

"Go ahead."

"Priority message coming in, for the vice marshal," a pleasant female voice said.

Bailey handed Cartwright the telephone receiver. He listened intently as the person to the other end of the line filled him in on the latest intelligence information. It turned Cartwright even grayer than he actually was. McCleland and Haltwhistle had apparently left a trail of destruction across Uzbekistan and had been involved in a deal which saw a rather large amount of opium being made to go up in flames.

The most worrying thing was that a renowned assassin was now on the loose after them, and there was no way to warn his two young charges, or poor Melvyn Waters of what was now barreling towards them.

"I see. Thank you," he gave the receiver back to Bailey.

Cartwright paced around the office and looked out of the window towards the airfield. Then at Bailey's status information boards.

"How many aircraft and air crews do you have available to go at an hour's notice?" he asked.

Bailey looked at his information. "I'd have to put in some calls. We're in the middle of our maintenance cycle at the moment so not too much I don't think."

Black Jack grimaced. "Get together what you have. I'm going to order a recovery mission take off at 14:00 hours."

"I'll give you as much help as I can but I honestly don't know what I can ready in that time," Bailey said, scratching his head.

He and Bailey walked out of the office and met Matthews and Harvey outside.

"Well gentlemen, we have ourselves a major problem to resolve."

They went out and took an Ocelot over to the hangars, where Chinooks were being worked on. A couple of Apache helicopter gunships belonging to the army attachment were being armed and inspected.

Cartwright and Bailey got out and went to inspect them. The crew chief stood to attention, as did the ground crews working on them.

"At ease, people," Bailey said easily.

He stepped around the gunships. The finest attack helicopter in the world being flown by the finest pilots in the world. They were a plum-ugly thing, that was for sure but looks didn't equal ability. It's blunt front end, stubby wings and square stance didn't change that this thing was deadly in the right hands. The crews clearly took pride in their work; the Apaches were immaculately presented.

"How quickly would these bad boys be ready for action?" Bailey was genuinely pleased to see the work that had gone in to these machines.

"Sir. They'd be ready to go as soon as you said so," the crew chief responded stiffly.

Cartwright smiled. "At ease before you sprain something, son."

The young man relaxed, apparently with relief.

"Have these machines on the field and ready to go in 30 minutes," Bailey ordered.

"Yes sir!"

The two men made their way back to the Ocelot and climbed back in. "A couple of Apaches is good but not enough. We could be looking at a whole army out there," Cartwright said, gesturing toward the north. "What about the Tornadoes and Typhoons?"

"I'll look in to it," Bailey assured him. They drove back to the main administration building.

"What are your orders, sir?" the driver asked. This must be serious for two high ranking officers to be coming all the way out here. He had not expected to see an air Vice-Marshal and the base commander going out trying to get together a group of aircraft.

"We wait for the aircraft to be ready. In the meantime, we are just here to observe," Bailey replied. "No one is to talk about any of this."

"Yes sir."

Cartwright smiled to himself, taking everything in. Once back in Bailey's office, he took a seat.

"Well trained crew, well maintained camp. It's been a while since I was out in the field."

"I pride myself on this base being the best British force in the world," Bailey said. He was clearly proud of his work, and rightly so. He might be a good man to have on board, Cartwright thought.

Bailey got up from his seat and joined Harvey as they looked at options available to them, looking at options to put in play quickly. They began making calls and getting lists together.

Matthews stayed in place, watching. The ground crews outside went about their business of getting the Apaches ready.

Cartwright was impressed by the professionalism on display. If Matthews was, he didn't show it, but then he hadn't said much of anything since touching down.

NINETEEN

Once inside the lift, Haltwhistle had the guard take them back to the lower regions of the outpost.

Taking advantage of the man's back turned to him, a quick blow to the back of the head put him out of commission.

The lift stopped and Colin hoped no one was around to see them. He dragged him to a corner of the compartment where his unconscious form would not be seen from the outside, disabled the lift controls and locked the doors before leaving the lift. He was somewhere close to where they had rode the elevator, he was sure of that by the lighting and the passageway layout. He had to find that restricted area again. He knew he had his disguise to protect him, but he had to work quickly if what he knew Jim had in mind was now in play.

He rounded a corner, which he recognized as where Krasnov had warned them away from. He ventured cautiously down the corridor to the double doors at the end. Instinctively he drew his pistol. Touching the door control panel, it ground open to reveal two guards, each packing an AK-47 rifle. Colin knew that talk was cheap in this situation. Hating what he had to do, Colin dropped them with a couple of shots and passed through the doors. There were rows of cannons, mortars and grenades on one wall, large quantities of various bladed weapons hanging in racks against the far wall and combat uniforms that seemed to stretch for several hundred yards in to the dimly lit recesses of the store.

He took off his backpack and drew two claymore mines. Arming them, Colin placed one among the projectile weapons and one amidst the combat uniforms. He knew the blasts would set off a chain reaction among the explosive shells which would destroy or severely damage the whole stock. He set the timers and made his way back to the door. A quick look outside them showed that there was still no one around. Clearly there was no changing of the guard due yet.

Then a faint green flashing drew his attention. Intrigued, Colin crossed to the source of the flashing. A computer terminal. And it was locked out. No matter, he had the codes. Tapping the keys, the response was negative. A lockout.

Evidently the codes had been changed in the time since the originals had been produced. Shit!

His skills as a hacker were now needed. He had successfully guessed the passwords and codes of countless computers and mobile phones which he had hacked to gain valuable information in the past. Cartwright had been correct about him being suspected of unproven crimes. And now it was again.

Using the old codes as a basis, Colin experimented with the password spelling and number combinations. The most likely change was an upward sequence. He punched the keys again and the computer unlocked. If he could access the main computer memory, perhaps the answers to their questions could be gained. He drew his iPad and patched it in by Bluetooth to what he guessed was the computer's download portal. He pressed a few keys, quickly learning how to access the information he was looking for. Footsteps outside the doors caused him to pause, but the footsteps faded. The pause he had made proved to be beneficial. An entire file with the data he had wanted had become available.

Uploading it to the iPad's memory, he disconnected it and slipped it back into his uniform.

He made his way back down the corridor, being careful not to look suspicious to the large number of Russian soldiers still milling around. He dragged the two bodies into a dark corner and slipped out.

The next problem was how to disable the aircraft stationed here. If they were to escape, an entire squadron of fighter jets giving chase would make their break out impossible. Clearly, he could not hope to destroy each one of them in the time he had and infiltrating each hangar was a task in which the odds of success were pretty much nil. No, there had to be another way. Colin's options seemed be limited.

But then a thought struck him. If the hangar's power was sabotaged, the aircraft couldn't leave and so would not be able to be launched. The obvious answer was to disrupt their power source.

His ability to read the Russian language was good enough to read specific words and phrases.

Checking a wall display, Haltwhistle found that the power generation station was two levels down. A quick glance at a map found an elevator about 300 yards away.

"Halt!" a voice came.

Colin turned to find a guard holding a gun at him. He was a young man, slim and eager but clearly he meant business.

"Are you addressing me, sir?"

"I do not recognize you. Provide your identification," the guard pressed him.

Haltwhistle advanced on him.

"I am Gratz, aide of Vladimir Ulyenkov."

"Provide your identification," the guard repeated.

"I would advise you to go about your business unless you wish to have something unpleasant happen to you." Colin's words were edged with dangerous intent.

The guard turned purple. The gun in his hand wavered. He was hesitating. He clearly knew the reputation of Ulyenkov and his people. But he pressed on.

"I know Gratz. He does not sound like you do. Provide your identification!"

Colin pulled the pass out of his pocket. Hopefully his forgery skills would pass muster.

To anyone else, it would have passed muster, but this guy was more discerning.

"Who are you? This pass is not standard!" He reached for a radio, but Colin used the moment's fumbling to his advantage. He hit the young man across the face with the butt of his pistol, knocking him out cold.

He took the guard's sidearm and clips and slipped it into his belt.

"Apparently something unpleasant happened to you."

There was no one else around who had seen what just happened fortunately. This situation was par for the course, Colin assumed.

Following the direction signs, he headed for the outpost's power core. He found a dozen men waiting for the lift that he had identified.

Of course Haltwhistle would have preferred to be alone but it couldn't be helped. He stepped in with the crowd. It was best to travel with them rather than wait. That would definitely arouse suspicion.

The lift rose and a couple of men left, heading off to wherever their work took them. Then it descended to the outpost's lower regions again. The level readout showed that he was on the right floor. Colin stepped off the elevator. It was quieter on this level. There was still activity but only the occasional engineer carrying tools to attend to a task. The corridor curved around in a large arc, so he was looking for a left turn from his perspective. Haltwhistle came to the inevitable junction and took it, but instead of a set of doors he came to a staircase. It was cut into the rock of the hillside the base was built in to. It looked like he was going into the very center of the range of hills.

The staircase came out on a catwalk with metal railings surrounding a huge translucent octagonal reactor which was reinforced with support beams. Control panels surrounded the apparatus, which was smeared with some sort of oily grime. For a brand new construct, it seemed in a very dirty condition. A few disinterested looking workers looked over their controls and were supervised by a very shouty, aggressive fat man. He ran back and forth, waving tools and berating his workers in guttural Russian dialect.

The reactor rose upwards to a series of distribution conduits which glowed and pulsed with energy. If they was disabled, it would take the entire station offline for hours, perhaps days. The distribution coils were just out of reach but the power conduits were suspended from the ceiling by a system of metallic girders.

Calculating quickly, Colin knew that an accurate throw would place the antimatter mine just above the bracing that supported the conduits. Looking in his backpack he had four claymores left.

Peering over the edge of the catwalk, the workers continued checking their readouts and watching the reactor, not looking up and seeing the intruder checking them out.

Haltwhistle set the timer on each of the mines and with a deft movement, launched the first mine at the metal latticework 15 feet to his right. The magnetic body of the mine latched on to the girder out of sight.

Satisfied, he lobbed the second mine which landed snugly on the welded joint of the metalwork to his upper left. The third mine lodged in the bracing in front of him.

Colin threw the final mine, but it touched just short of where he had intended to place it. It bounced frustratingly but it's magnetic field latched it to the support beam where the reactor joined the power conduit which ran above his head. There was no way to disarm or dislodge it.

When it detonated, the detective knew it would cause an explosion which would lead to the reactor overloading. His intention to stop the invasion force led by a violent, unstable madman would become reality, but it could mean death for them all.

They had thirty minutes to make their escape.

Colin hurriedly made his way back to the elevator which would take him back to Krasnov's apartment. He entered to find Jim and his nemesis deep in conversation.

"Ah Gratz. I hope our facility meets with your approval."

"Most impressive, General," Haltwhistle replied.

Krasnov offered them a glass each with an electric blue liquid in it.

"We managed to get a shipment in from Moscow. It made quite a prize to get something so classy," Krasnov explained. Colin took the drink with good grace, as did Jim. Krasnov moved off to his bookcase to look at something. Haltwhistle leaned closely to Jim's ear.

"Don't drink more than a tiny sip of that stuff," he said softly.

Jim sniffed the drink. It didn't smell out of the ordinary, so he took a sip. It was like a lightning bolt had hit his brain. The beverage, whatever it was, was more potent than anything he had drunk before and the intoxicating effect was almost instantaneous. It felt like he had had several glasses of strong whiskey in one mouthful. No, more than that, it made Glenfiddich 20 Year seem tepid by comparison. He fought the urge to gasp. For his part, Colin merely took a small mouthful that didn't seem to affect him. Krasnov wandered back over from his book collection and grinned.

"Are you enjoying your vodka, Ulyenkov?"

"Very smooth," Jim managed to say without wheezing.

Something is not right, Krasnov thought. *Why is the vodka causing him to gasp, has he become soft?*

"So it would seem."

Krasnov invited them to sit. Jim took a seat across from him, while Colin took a place near the windows.

"Now. About my shipment. Where is it?" The general was insistent.

"It is here with us. I will provide it to you... once I have spoken to the prisoner," McCleland assured him.

"Then let us not waste our time and get about this task." Krasnov clapped his hands together.

"What have you got from the prisoner?" Jim said.

Krasnov shook his head. "Not much, I am afraid to say. Even our interrogation methods have not been able to extract much from the Englishman. It seems he has a mental tolerance to it. He has a tendency for chicanery and a very sharp sense of humor which blunts our attempts to question him."

That was a relief to hear. Hopefully Clarkie would be in not too bad of a shape.

"You did not damage him at all?" Colin looked a touch too concerned behind his severe looking beard, Jim thought.

"I fail to see the point in using physical torture. History has shown it is ineffective in the long term. The victim inevitably builds a tolerance to it," Krasnov replied.

McCleland felt satiated now that he knew that his commanding officer had not been too badly mistreated.

They had spent too long together to not have a mutual respect and admiration. They may have covered all of that up with sarcasm and good natured bickering, but at the end of it all, they had each other's backs.

"Then it's time for a different approach," Jim observed, rubbing his hands together in mock glee.

The Russian general grinned his unpleasant smile.

"That is why I asked you here, disgusting as that may be to both of us."

Jim decided that offense was the best form of attack.

"Krasnov if you have something to say, say it. I'm not in the mood for your snide remarks."

The general looked at Jim squarely.

"I do not like you Ulyenkov. I do not approve of your methods, you have no honor," the Russian said firmly. "I simply wish for you to give me my opium and be on your way."

"Honor has little to do with the security of the Federation. Our enemies must be crushed." The blue vodka or whatever it was must be having an even bigger effect, because Jim felt himself becoming belligerent like.. well, like what he thought a Russian was like.

"Honor has everything to do with it. The man who kills without looking his foe in the eye is a coward."

Krasnov was a traditionalist and he had a real sense of pride. He was almost likable, Jim thought.

Damn, this blue vodka was strong stuff. Despite everything, he was agreeing with this arsehole.

Despite everything, despite their last run in, Krasnov was right in everything he was saying.

"The order of things must be maintained."

"If I didn't know you better, I'd say that those westerners have clouded your judgment to our values," Krasnov snarled.

"Gentlemen," Colin interrupted. "Let us stick to the point. You want the RAF officer interrogated and information gleaned. We are here to provide that service. Let us be about our business." He looked at Jim.

"It should take about twenty five minutes."

McCleland quickly came to the conclusion that something was wrong for such a specific time frame to be mentioned. Twenty five minutes until something happened by which time they needed to be well away from here.

TWENTY

In the cockpit of his leading helicopter, the real Ulyenkov sat grimly in the passenger compartment. His two aides occupied the pilot and co-pilot positions up front. Time was not on their side and unfortunately, with the base's radar and radio jamming equipment working perfectly, all Ulyenkov could do was get there and hope to hell that whatever plan the British had was not yet completed and that they were still there.

He could of course have commandeered a faster aircraft from the airport in Termez, but with his pilots not capable of flying anything else, it would have meant a drawn out and bloody exercise to persuade someone to transport them. That was a waste of time and resources. And as for Krasnov, if he couldn't see through the deception that this infiltration unit had in play then he was as incompetent as he was on all the other times he had come across him and needed to be dealt with.

Any resistance on Krasnov's part would be met with swift, direct action.

The cabin smelled of chemical cleansers and plastic, a typical trait of Kamov aircraft. The Ka-60 had a top speed of 190 miles per hour, they had been getting nowhere fast but at least they were headed in the right direction. It was just an infuriatingly slow journey.

"How long until we are in range?" Ulyenkov demanded.

Gratz checked his instruments.

"Fifteen minutes, sir."

In all of his years of serving Mother Russia, Ulyenkov had never been so infuriated. To be impersonated was bad enough but to be bested in such a demeaning way was not only dishonorable, it was downright criminal. Many years before someone had made the mistake of doubting his abilities and training. He had dissuaded the man from the notion by throttling him to death in front of his family. It was well known that Vladimir Ulyenkov was short on temper and long on ability in regard to interrogating and then dispatching enemies of the state. But this was insidious. To add insult to injury his supply of opium, which he was transferring funds from the sale of to bankroll this ridiculous scheme of Krasnov's, which Ulyenkov knew would never work had been lost. When he pointed out just how foolhardy this entire enterprise was, he had been informed that certain parts of the government were behind the plan and that it would be going ahead.

Unfortunately he had been unable to contact the man he knew could shed some light on what was going on from that end.

Ulyenkov grimaced in disgust. The British. Unpredictable, ill-disciplined and they had a knack of sticking their noses into Russian business with almost inevitable regularity. Too many good men had been lost.

No, they were fools for getting caught. A professional can evade even the most persistent of people, and those idiots who had gotten themselves discovered were not professionals. But this man who had dared to wear his face. He either had nerve, or simply did not know who Ulyenkov was. Perhaps Krasnov could give him some idea as to who he was. Then again, probably not.

As if on cue, Gratz finally made the call they were all waiting for.

"The base is dead ahead, sir."

There it was, laid out like a child's battle fort.

"At last," grunted Ulyenkov. "Set us down."

Krasnov led Jim and Colin back to the elevator. It descended swiftly to a lower level. When they stepped from the lift, they were staring at stark, stone walls, so Haltwhistle guessed they were somewhere in the base of the tower, back in the hillside. The corridors did not match those of the loading docks and storage bays, so this must be a prison level. The three, accompanied by Krasnov's security guard marched down a dark passage lined with heavy metal doors, until they came to the end. The last door had a peep hole, which Krasnov now opened.

"William? You have visitors," he called.

Through the peephole, McCleland could see Clarkie stir. He rolled over on his bunk and slowly sat up. He looked grim, disheveled and clearly hadn't slept in the last few days, judging by the dark lines under his eyes. He needed a shave as a firm midnight shadow hung around his mouth and cheeks.

"Get lost, Krasnov," Old Bill rumbled.

Krasnov indicated for Jim and Colin to wait, and went in to the cell. He advanced on Clarkie.

"William. I have tried to be patient. I have tried to be gentle. I have tried to hold off the more unpleasant side of the Russian security services, but the time has come for you to tell me what I want to know," he said gently but firmly.

Clark raised an eyebrow and shook his head.

"I'm done talking to you Krasnov. Just let me out of here."

"You are not going anywhere William. I can assure you of that. Save yourself the pain and humiliation and tell me what I want to know."

Just you keep thinking that, thought Jim. The vodka's effects were wearing off slightly but it heightened the senses. It was a shame it didn't do the same for reflexes. Krasnov turned on his heel and strode out of the cell. He closed the peephole and looked at his two companions.

"You see what I mean?"

"Let me handle this in my own way. I have not been defeated yet and do not intend to be so by a sniveling weakling," McCleland glowered.

"These British are cleverer and more resourceful than you give them credit for. They have what I believe is called a stiff upper lip and an absolute refusal to give up, even in the face of overwhelming odds.

You should know, having several of them working for you," Krasnov countered.

At that, McCleland knew it was time to play his trump card.

"As I said before, if you have something to say, say it. What British officers are you talking about and what business is it of yours?" he spat.

Krasnov was cold.

"You should know Ulyenkov, everyone knows you bribed the man in question to our side with false promises. No doubt he has a few people in his clutches too."

Jim knew Krasnov was on the right lines. What he had told McCleland in their conversation was shocking. The deep cover agents, the contacts, the people buried in plain sight of Federation interests which could bring about the end of everything. But this could be the biggest revelation of all. He produced a piece of paper with a single name on screen. Showing it to Krasnov, the commander simply looked and gave his confirmation wordlessly. That was all Jim needed to know.

If Colin had been a gambling man, he would not have been able to believe his luck. Krasnov had just confirmed who the top Russian agent within the Ministry of Defence was. What else did he know? He just hoped that Jim could play this pretense to the full and they could get to the full truth. But time was not on their side. From within his cloak he drew his mobile phone and keyed a message to Waters on the helicopter. He just hoped that the jammer did not impede phone signal. They had 20 minutes, and he needed to tell McCleland quickly.

"We will discuss this later, Krasnov. Right now, I want to work on the prisoner."

"Fine, suit yourself. But I will not tolerate murder on my base," the gruff general warned.

"Do not intervene, and wait down the hall."

The security guard unlocked the cell door and opened it. McCleland and Haltwhistle stepped inside. The door was closed but not locked and Krasnov and the guard walked off down the hallway.

"Watch the door," Jim told Colin quietly. His friend acknowledged him and stepped aside, taking care to not look as if he was not keeping watch. The squadron leader crossed to Clarkie and sat down opposite him.

"Who the hell are you?" Old Bill grumbled.

"All your questions will be answered in good time, Wing Commander," Jim replied. He had to admit playing a psycho killer and putting the fear of God in to people was quite fun.

Clark groaned. "Oh God. I assume my torturer has arrived, then."

Jim smiled at that. "Depends how you define torture." He leaned closer and spoke softly. "Clarkie, the cavalry is here."

Clark's eyes widened. "Jim-! Talk about torture!"

McCleland raised a finger to his lips and shushed him. The last thing he needed was this whole masquerade to be shot at the last moment because of Clarkie's big mouth, even if he was a superior officer.

"What the hell kind of costume are you wearing? What in blazes is this?" Clarkie hissed, looking at them both. "You look like you've come straight from the pantomime!"

Jim rolled his eyes. "Yeah, it was *Cinderella* but I'm not Prince Charming." Then he became serious. "What have they done to you?"

Clarkie looked resigned. "Oh, nothing except tried to turn my brains into mashed potato. They keep asking questions about Camp Bastion and the strength of our forces there mostly. Old Krasnov out there was very interested in our battle tactics. I dunno what the bloody hell any of that is, and I keep telling them that but they won't believe me."

Jim and Colin exchanged a glance. The plot was indeed thickening. It would explain the squadrons of aircraft and battalions of tanks and troops stationed here, and who knows how many elsewhere? If the Russians were planning an invasion in to Afghanistan, they had an ideal starting point. They had to warn their own people and fast.

"We've learned a few new ones," Jim assured him.

"Are you well enough to travel, sir?" Colin asked, looking the senior officer over.

Clarkie tried to get up, but he was still shackled.

"Apart from these damned things. Anytime you want to move, be my guest. Just get me out of here. Putting up with Matthews' attitude is like paradise compared to being cooped up here," Clarkie assured him.

"I see that you have not lost your sense of humor," Jim teased him. "Sir."

"You're hilarious, Jim, just get me out of here!"

"He's right. We need to get out of here, right now," Colin said quickly.

"What do you mean?"

"I set the mines but the final one didn't seat properly. We've got about twenty minutes to get out of here before the whole place goes sky high!" he explained. "And if Krasnov is getting punchy about those drugs we destroyed, we'd best head for the hills!"

"Great," Jim grumbled.

"What drugs?" Clark asked.

"We'll tell you at the debrief. If we get out of here!"

And now that they were in a labyrinth of tunnels and corridors deep under the hill, they had to go quickly to have any hope of finding a way out.

"You mean you made a mistake, Col? Wonders will never cease." Despite the situation, Old Bill was chuckling.

Colin was sardonic. "It's a pleasure to see you again as well, sir."

They helped him sit up on the bunk. "What the hell have we got ourselves into, Jim?" Clarkie demanded.

"A whole load of trouble apparently." McCleland pointed his pistol at the shackles on Clark's ankles and fired. They cracked apart almost instantly. "Let's go."

Krasnov was waiting for them as they came out of the cell. He had his gun in his hand and two guards with him.

"So. We meet again, Mister James McCleland!"

TWENTY-ONE

McCleland as Ulyenkov looked on as Krasnov gave him a superior grin. The pistol Krasnov held in his hand was grasped firmly, as was the weapons his two minions were pointing squarely at Jim's person.

For his part McCleland had his own automatic trained at Krasnov's head. It was a standoff. Jim knew that the odds of getting out of this godforsaken hellhole had now been cut drastically, but he felt comfort in knowing Colin and Old Bill were with him. All he could do for now was fall back on what he always did.

Play for time while coming up with an alternate plan.

"Don't make a fool of me Krasnov. You know who I am. Do you want me to prove it?" Jim shot back.

"That won't work anymore, Ulyenkov, or should I say McCleland." The gun was pointed directly at the captain and was not wavering. "Ulyenkov himself contacted me and told me a very interesting story about how someone subdued him and his party at his hotel in Termez.

Then a fascinating account about several billion rubles worth of opium being destroyed. My opium."

Jim took a small breath as Krasnov went on with his explanation.

"I suspected it was you but it wasn't until you struggled to drink the blue vodka. Someone who had really drunk it would not have reacted so badly and would not act like that. And your disregard for our Russian values." The General stepped toward them. "I was tempted to kill you for spouting such nonsense until I realized that you were not what you appear to be."

Krasnov advanced on them, his grin growing wider which more than gave away his satisfaction with their predicament.

"I will give you credit for your valor and your daring, but the game is over, gentlemen. I am the dead man's hand to your busted flush."

Krasnov was almost upon them.

"At this moment, your helicopter is being surrounded, and the other of your friends is being rounded up," he chuckled. "Drop your weapons. I promise you the dear old British government will not be informed of this incident. But the new Airborne Intelligence Division will need a new fast jet pilot. And military investigator, Flight Lieutenant Haltwhistle, not to mention a replacement Group Captain."

Despite his enjoyment, there was no trace of smugness in Krasnov, Jim noted. If it had been Hantuchov facing him, no doubt he would be already gloating over his victory and planning all sorts of unpleasantness. But Krasnov was a different animal. He had a code of ethics, which made him much more formidable. It almost reminded Colin of one of the tragic heroes of literature.

"But tell me, why did you come all this way? Why all this risk?"

McCleland let his gun drop but he did not let it go. He stood just in Colin's line of sight.

"I have respect for you, General. You are indeed a man of principle, but the only thing we wanted to know was who the Russian's spies were. We knew there were spies of course, but not who. So thanks for your hospitality," Jim kept it short but sweet.

Krasnov shook his head in amazement. What an audacious, brilliant scheme. McCleland was indeed a worthy opponent and a man of great intelligence. But it was tinged with regret.

"I am afraid, Squadron Leader that you will never be allowed to act on that information."

Colin's Tokarev answered the Russian with a blast that dropped the light fixture above Krasnov's head onto him, knocking him cold and plunging the corridor into darkness. Jim fired at roughly where he knew the guards to be and grunts of pain answered the sharp crack of his gunfire.

"Thanks, Col."

Then Jim turn his attention to what Krasnov had been saying.

"I thought you said that morphine you gave them would last a good few hours?"

"Apparently all the vodka that Ulyenkov drinks acts as a blocker," came the dry response.

"Well next time, you can be the bird in the cage, and I'll handle the medical side!" Clarkie retorted.

Jim smiled a little. The banter between the two lightened any situation considerably, and just as much as he needed his two closest friends, they needed him and each other equally. The three made their way cautiously along the hallway, but a pattering of feet from somewhere up ahead stopped the dead in their tracks.

"They are closing rapidly. Thirty meters, I'd say," Colin's ability to judge distance was incredible. "There is a stairway through that door." He pointed to the left.

They were over the threshold and pounding down the stone spiral steps as above them the first of the guards came down after them as a klaxon began sounding. Jim whipped out his mobile phone. It rang at once.

"McCleland to Waters, come in."

"Waters here," came the strained reply. "The Russians have locked the chopper down, I managed to hold some of the off but I don't know how long I can keep them at bay."

"Dammit." McCleland and Haltwhistle exchanged a look. Unless they could get out of here, they would be dead men for sure.

"What exactly is going on?" Jim demanded.

"I've sealed the doors and shut myself in here. I think the weapons I've got are making them wary. I don't know how long I can hold out.

They might try to blast their way in, but I fired a couple of rounds at them, which put them off."

Things like to get complicated, don't they, Colin mused.

"We're coming to you," he told Mel. "We'll be as quick as we can. Can you get in to the air?'

"I think so," the voice crackled.

Damn, there was always a spanner to be thrown into the works. Nothing was ever as easy as it should be.

"Just watch for us, and hold them off as best you can. Fly out of there if you have to and come back to pick us up."

"I'll keep an eye out." The line went dead.

Jim kicked the door open at the next landing and they burst out into a well let passageway.

Strangely, the corridor was deserted.

"The crews have been called to duty stations," Colin realised.

"How far to the chopper?"

"It's down two more levels." Colin checked his watch. "We've got ten minutes left before this place goes up."

They ran for the nearest elevator, Haltwhistle holding Old Bill up as the older man struggled to keep up. Jim reached the doors first. The pounding of feet from below them let them in on the fact that there was a squad heading their way.

"Sounds like there's a whole battalion of them down there, waiting for us."

"Shit!"

Their escape had just been made harder, but perhaps they could tip the balance in their favor a little. Jim reached for the backpack. Drawing two grenades, he armed them swiftly. He nodded towards the elevator doors.

With some effort, Colin and Clarkie managed to heave the doors apart just enough for the exuberant squadron leader to drop the grenades into the shaft. From somewhere below there was a clang as the shell of each grenade bounced on to the elevator, followed by the sound of the car beginning it's ascent.

A few seconds later a large column of flame wafted up the elevator shaft as the grenades detonated accompanied by a resounding blast of heat and volume, eliminating the group that was about to emerge from the compartment.

"There must be other elevators close by," was Jim's response to Clarkie's horrified expression.

Then a superheated blast shot past the doctor's head. From ahead, six soldiers had taken up position and were now unleashing a barrage of deadly weapons fire at them. Jim dived for cover as Colin dragged Clark into the same shelter of the arched doorway that McCleland had taken.

"Give me your gun," Jim shouted to Haltwhistle.

"Jim! Be careful!" Clark called.

Colin handed Jim the weapon, but still had one himself. With the Tokarev pistols in each hand, McCleland got himself into position and opened fire. A furious hail of gunfire rattled from his twin pistols that took the Russians by surprise with their ferocity. Two went down, scorched and battered by the intense barrage.

With Colin providing covering fire with an AK-47 from his hiding place, Jim did not let up, laying down fire as another soldier fell to his relentless attack. The three remaining men aimed at McCleland's position but the incoming fire was both blinding and murderous. Haltwhistle's pinpoint hand-eye coordination took another of the attackers out.

"Colin, over there!" Clarkie shouted. From the other end of the hallway, another group of soldiers emerged from a doorway and opened fire on them. Colin picked them off with maddening ease, a quick, clean shot to each of the men, which laid them low.

Frantically, one of the men in front of Jim called for reinforcements while another drew a hand grenade.

He was about to launch it at the British officer still made up like one of them, but he was hit in the chest by the blasts that the disguised human was dealing out. The Russian fell, the grenade rolling out of his hand.

His compatriot saw what was about to happen and looked on in horror as the small ball exploded.

A blinding flash and white hot debris filled the air. The grenade's detonation had taken care of the remaining Russians.

Jim waved his two cohorts over. They retrieved whatever weapons that were still serviceable from the soldier's remains and moved on. Moving quickly they covered the route that was marked on Colin's hastily scribbled map.

"There's a lift about one hundred meters down that corridor," said Colin, apparently unruffled by the violence of the exchange.

They headed down the hallway, but a second group of four more soldiers, the reinforcements the first group had called appeared from beyond the curve in the corridor. Then from behind a third group of five emerged at the corner where the passageway met a three way junction. Just to their left were the elevator doors they had been aiming for, but it was maddeningly just out of reach.

"Drop all weapons and surrender!" a lieutenant shouted.

The RAF men were a prime target with no cover on offer, except for the shelter of the elevator that they were trying to reach. They dropped low and rolled towards the doors. Instead of a comforting squeak as the hydraulic ram drew the doors apart, there was a distinct electronic clunk.

"Don't be foolish. Give up now!" insisted the Russian officer.

Jim responded by opening fire at him with his trusty pistol, which he pulled from his waist band and he knew he had a vastly superior amount of stopping power now available to him. The other gun from the first exchange was still good enough for a few rounds, and that proved useful in laying down combined fire. The Russian lieutenant fell to the ground dead as Jim kept up the rate of fire.

"It looks like the elevator has been locked out. I'll try to bypass," Colin called out. "Sir, you will have to lay down suppression fire."

"I'm not a commando!" Clark protested.

"You are now!" Haltwhistle threw him a spare AK-47 from his kitbag he had apprehended. How Cartwright had ever talked him into this he would never know, but he knew he wouldn't allow himself to be convinced as such again. Clarkie turned it towards the five soldiers in front of him.

"Heaven help me," he whispered as he opened fire. He had never been a killer, and as his father had been a doctor he had taken an oath to do no harm, and had drummed into his son a respect for life. But as a military officer he had been trained to take a life if needed. And the situation required him to do that now. He opened fire, laying a blazing trail of destruction at the five soldiers, who fell to the ground as the rifle's furious blasts hit them in turn.

"Col! We need that lift working, now!" Jim shouted over the cacophony of flying lead.

The Russian's fire had spattered the floor in front of him and the walls behind where they were hunkered down, turning the white walls black with scorched pockmarks. Then a whizzing noise filled the air and a grenade landed just inches from him. Without looking, McCleland scooped it up and threw it back at the four men trying to stop them escaping. The grenade exploded in mid air just above the small group. The blast wave threw them backwards, overwhelming them and laying them low. As the dust and smoke cleared the full extent of the effects of the grenade and the gun battle became clear. Then, the doors of the elevator finally opened.

Jim, Colin and Clark piled in and hit the controls. McCleland swapped his depleted automatic for a fresh one and reloaded his GP100. He took a hiding position just out of eye line while Haltwhistle and Clark did the same as the lift stopped and the doors parted. A frantic hail of gunfire fire blasted into the elevator, scorching and burning the back wall. Colin retrieved a grenade and threw it through the doors. The roar as the grenade detonated caused an eerie silence in the aftermath. Jim peeked around the jam of the door. Three more soldiers lay dead.

He waved with one of his weapons and they left the relative safety of the lift.

"Five minutes left, Jim," Haltwhistle reminded him urgently. "The chopper should be on the opposite side of this level."

At a flat out sprint, the three men pounded down the walkway. There was no time to admire the view from the huge Plexiglas view ports to their right. White hot gun blasts whipped past them from behind as another group of Russians pursued them. Colin turned, and saw the large mob of infantrymen chasing them down. Just to their right, a junction box with some sort of warning symbol sat.

Without wasting time, Colin fired into the metallic cube. Wires and circuitry erupted in a destructive fireball and electrical sparks which sent several Russians sprawling. The ferocity of the explosion meant that none of them would get up to offer any more resistance.

Jim took an AK-47, their last one, turned and peppered the group of soldiers with a burst from the weapon. The Kalashnikov may have been old by this point but it was still formidable. It took care of a couple more men, and caused the others in the posse to drop back.

Colin was still hauling Clark with him, and he could see the shafts of daylight coming from outside which told them that the way out was just ahead. The archway come into view around the final curve of this seemingly never-ending maze of walkways that the base had been designed with. From his left, a door opened and a rifle butt was jammed into his stomach. Despite himself, Haltwhistle went down in a heap with Clarkie falling down in an undignified mess next to him.

The disguise Colin wore slipped and partially came off. The same Russian killer with the piercing eyes that he had encountered in the hotel in Termez leant over and pulled the remains of it off.

"Typical Englishman! I should have known!" Ulyenkov snarled. He raised the rifle at Colin's head, only for it to be blasted from his hands by McCleland's Tokarev.

"Unless you value your life, get away from him, wanker," Jim threatened him. Ulyenkov was joined by his two aides. The taller one kicked Colin repeatedly while the shorter one kept Clark down.

"Drop it, or your friends die now," the inscrutable Russian said roughly.

Jim noticed his pistol was out of ammunition anyway. He let it plop to the floor.

"In case you were not aware, I am Ulyenkov. The man you have been impersonating. And you must be the famous James McCleland who I have heard so much about."

"Guilty," was the light reply.

"You have brought me grave dishonor, McCleland-"

"Please. Spare me the duty and honor bullshit," Jim was in no mood to listen to some speech about Mother Russia's imperial sense of justice, especially with their lives hanging in the balance.

"You have no honor, McCleland. I want your life. Now." Ulyenkov advanced on him darkly.

"I thought you were a killer? They generally just kill, not mouth off," Jim responded.

"I can assure you I am more than capable of murdering you, McCleland. But I take issue with you insulting my name."

"Really? If you're so good at your job, how come no one's after you?"

Clark simply rolled his eyes. "Jim, you don't tell a murderer he's crap at his job when he wants to kill you!"

Ulyenkov lunged furiously at the Englishman with a stubby knife drawn. His attack was ferocious. He beat and lashed out at Jim who weathered the storm of blows and blocked him.

The blade slashed at his arms, but McCleland had taken his cape and wrap it around his arms, giving some protection but the blade cut easily in to the fabric.

The soldiers who had pursued them now stopped to watch the vicious hand to hand brawl take shape. Jim gave Ulyenkov a haymaker to the face and followed up with a side kick to the ribs.

The assassin reeled as Jim followed up with an uppercut, which finally caused the knife to drop from his hand. Blood spurted from Ulyenkov's mouth, which seemed to infuriate him even more.

He crouched and jumped, catching McCleland in the ribs and knocking the wind out of him. He rained blow after blow down before setting on Jim with his bare hands, trying to reach his throat.

"I will kill you!" Ulyenkov was frenzied and furious.

The curve of the passageway hid Colin from view, but the taller of Ulyenkov's aides was in full view of the group of Russian soldiers watching and cheering on the murderer as he continued pummeling Jim.

Momentarily distracted by the pitched fight going on, it was all Colin needed. A swift crack to the back of the head would have taken him out, and it looked as if the white cap would simply crack his opponent over the head, but Colin his fingers dug in to the base of the Russian's neck while taking hold of his face and twisted with as much force as he could muster. He didn't even scream. A sharp snap and the form of the man went limp.

TWENTY-TWO

The smaller one of Ulyenkov's hangers-on was given a roundhouse punch for his trouble.

Haltwhistle heaved Clark up.

"We can't leave Jim!" the older man insisted.

"We aren't."

Then a muffled explosion came. The entire floor shook as if an earthquake had just struck. Colin realized that the claymore mines had detonated in the armory. A second, larger explosion came, and he knew that the weaponry in the armory had also gone up.

The group of soldiers looked about them in confusion. Reaching for the rifle that Jim had shot from Ulyenkov's hand, Haltwhistle blasted them.

McCleland wrestled Ulyenkov off him and gave him a straight punch to the mouth. the killer was on his knees, reaching for the knife.

Jim remembered the knife in his belt Mel had given to him. He drew it and wielded it in a typical knife defense pose.

Then a third, much larger eruption came. It was much louder and much more violent. The powerful explosion against the fusion reactor had caused a catastrophic meeting of energy. For the workers in the power plant, it would have been instantaneous as the crippling fireball expanded outwards, blowing out the whole of the lower regions of the installation. The armories and storage bays in that part of the base, containing vast quantities of weapons and equipment were immolated, causing multiple detonations to destroy anything that had somehow survived the fusion meltdown. Almost instantly the lights went out and the corridor was plunged into darkness. The floor shook much more vigorously. The sheer force of the shaking caused everyone to be thrown around and anything loosely lying around was instantly airborne, the lack of light left everywhere in darkness.

Waters had taken Jim's advice, got the Hip airborne and was circling. He could not believe what he was seeing. Dust and debris from the hillside was being thrown out in all directions from what must be huge underground explosions. Deciding to brave it, he brought the Hip around and drew closer, hoping that at least one of his friends would be there.

The sunlight was being blocked out by the dust thrown up but the brightness of the explosions threw some light back into the corridor, allowing the combatants a brief enough glimpse to continue squaring off. The shaking became more intense as the massive destruction fanned outwards, consuming the lower regions sending rock and debris spiraling outwards in all directions.

Ulyenkov was determined however, despite the base falling apart around him. He lunged with the knife.

In the dim light it was difficult to deflect the blow as it came in but Jim had the knife in his hand and he swung furiously, catching Ulyenkov in the side of his face. A muffled grunt of pain was followed by McCleland bringing the butt of the knife's handle down on the back of Ulyenkov's neck. The small Russian, still clutching his knife fell to the floor. McCleland finished the job. He was sure he saw a look of astonishment on Ulyenkov's face as the long blade found its target and made him realize he had been defeated for the last time.

***

Sprinting outside McCleland, Haltwhistle and Clark found pandemonium. Fires were furiously trying to be extinguished, but with no power to the pumps, people were being reduced to throwing buckets of water at burning debris and inflamed vehicles. One of the T-80 tanks that Jim had spied as they entered the compound sat to hand.

"Come on." He sprinted for the fearsome armored vehicle with its imposing gun protruding from the rounded turret.

"What the fuck, Jim?" Colin demanded, trying to keep up and pulling Clark with him. "You can't steal that bloody tank!"

"Watch me," was his friend's blunt response.

He scrambled up the slab side to the main hatch on top of the hull and wrenched it open, landing a heavy blow to the man waiting inside. McCleland pulled him from the hatch and threw him bodily to ground. It was stiflingly hot inside the turret and the interior echoed to any sound. The driver's position was a basic seat with two control columns, one on either side of the chair. Pedals on the floor must be the brake and throttle. A black button on the dashboard directly in front was pressed. The engine started.

Lowering Clark into the tank, Colin, still thinking that this plan to escape was ridiculous, pulled the hatch shut above his head and dropped in to the gunnery seat. He didn't know how to operate any of the equipment in front of him. The eye pieces in front of him gave a view forward. Off to his left, shells and boxes of ammunition filled the white painted cabin.

"I cannot believe you're doing this," Clark grumbled.

"Do you want to get to the chopper in one piece?" McCleland retorted.

Based on the experience of using a joystick to control a vehicle, Jim pushed forward what he took to be the control stick to his left. The tank lurched to starboard.

"Hellfire mate!" Colin complained.

"Just getting a feel for the girl." He pushed the column on his right, which straightened out the machine. The lumbering bulk of the tank rumbled forward and peering through his view port, Jim aimed for anything that could present a threat to their escape. A jet bomber parked ahead was smashed into, tearing the fuselage apart like confetti.

Turning to his left, the T-80 bore down on a fuel bowser being used to prepare a pair of attack helicopters.

"Is the gun loaded?" Jim shouted.

"How should I know? I dunno how to even fire this thing!" Colin replied.

"Well press all the buttons and find out. You're supposed to be a cop. Find the evidence!"

Disgruntled, Colin began jabbing at the controls. From the outside, the turret began rotating. The gun swayed through 360 degrees. Finally, a trigger was found and Haltwhistle held it down. The tank's interior reverberated from the furious rattle of the 7.62 machine gun. The T-80's surroundings were sprayed with heavy gun fire. Soldiers fell as they tried to open fire on the wayward vehicle. Colin's rounds found the fuel truck which promptly exploded, it's flames spreading to the helicopters were parked next to.

By this point a couple of pursuers in jeeps were now giving chase. Hails of machine gun fire tried to stop them but the rounds ricocheted harmlessly from the armor plating. Jim slewed the machine around a corner and smashed through the wall of a hangar, causing people to leap out of the way, but the pursuers weren't giving up so easily.

The machine gun clicked empty. Colin fumbled around, trying to work out how to reload the weapon and played around with the switches in front of him for anything that could be useful.

His eye fell on another trigger, which he pressed.

The still revolving turret with its gun making anyone who came near wary of what would happen next, were wise to keep their distance.

The huge weapon boomed and spat flame from the end of the barrel. The hangar expanded outwards in flame and debris as it and the aircraft within were atomized. The force of the blast shook the tank but it stayed on course as the remains of the building fell inwards, black smoke billowing skywards. The remains of the two jeeps which had been giving chase slewed to a stop, their forms reduced to sparks.

"Jesus Christ!"

McCleland gunned the T-80 onto an aircraft parking area and skated in an arc around the undercarriage of an ancient looking bomber. The gunfire from the remaining soldiers caused damage to the underside of the bomber and ignited the fuel tanks, consuming the old aircraft and the jeep that was now heading underneath it in a massive fireball.

"Good God!" Clark exclaimed. McCleland, still getting used to how the tank handled pulled the machine sharply to the right. The tracks squealed on the concrete but the team had made it into the open desert beyond the rest of the aircraft, hoping to hell that Mel Waters was out there as he had told him. The Hip to his right now dropping to the desert floor told him so.

Jim brought the tank to a halt and scrambled out of the seat.

"Let's go."

Haltwhistle opened the hatch and the sheer amount of destruction that they had caused became clear. He pulled Clark's weak form up and helped him to disembark.

Safely aboard the helicopter, Jim was exhausted and sagged in to the co-pilot's seat.

"Are you alright Jim?" Colin asked him.

Jim waved him off. "I'm fine. We got what we came for, so let's get the fuck out of here."

Clark looked irritated. "I don't suppose you care if I'm alright then?"

"Clarkie, the fact you are demanding to know that is proof enough that you are indeed in good working order," was the cool response. Jim wasn't in the mood to respect rank and was too tired and pained to care.

"You ingrate-!"

"Can we save this bromance for another time?" Waters interrupted them from the pilot's seat.

"Time for some Formula One, then. Get us out of here," Colin flared.

The retired pilot guided the helicopter away from the conflagration below them. The chopper pitched and rolled as the base continued to destroy itself. Exhausted and battered, Colin watched from between the pilot seats and saw the hill seemingly falling in on itself.

The glinting metallic tower at the head of the installation crumbled, splintered and fell in to the innards of the hillside. Sheets of flame flared from the remains of the underground, while the hangars caught fire.

Aircraft and equipment were blasted apart in the furious inferno. The hillside seemed to be heaved off by some giant unseen crowbar as the ridge of hills appeared to shake like a leaf in strong wind.

Pieces of rock which looked tiny from a distance but in reality dwarfed the chopper began ejecting outwards in all directions. The ridge of hills finally, agonizingly tore themselves apart.

What seemed like sparks and flame spat outwards consuming everything it came in to contact with as the reactor core split, releasing it's now uncontrolled fuel which promptly incinerated.

The chopper rocked as the shock waves from the violent explosions overtook them. Super-hot debris rolled past them as Mel tried to avoid being struck by airborne pieces of rock. The Hip jinked, just missing the larger chunks of flotsam as the smaller pieces fizzled against the hull plating.

Peering out of the starboard view port, Clark dreaded to think how many people had just met their fate. Russians or not, an awful lot of people had just died in an especially violent way.

"You weren't joking when you said you miscalculated, were you?" he said to Haltwhistle softly.

The white cap simply glanced at his commanding officer with a pitying expression.

"Being closely associated with someone like him," Haltwhistle thumbed toward McCleland. "Can lead to... a certain amount of rubbing off."

"What do you mean, you cheeky son of a-!" Jim started.

"Are you two always going to be like this?" Waters interrupted irritably. He was in no mood to listen to bickering. Old Bill merely rolled his eyes.

"If they weren't I'd be worried."

McCleland groaned as Colin inspected his wounds. Mostly superficial, fortunately.

"Thanks for the attention, mate."

"Do we have a medical kit on board this rust bucket?" Colin demanded.

Old Bill looked around and handed Haltwhistle a familiar green pouch. If whatever Ulyenkov had done had harmed him, it wasn't showing in his admittedly limited medical skills. He drew a small amount of morphine and injected Jim with it.

"This should keep you going until we can get you home." Once the injection was administered Jim felt the pain in his face and hands fade noticeably. Colin cleaned and dressed the cuts on his face and hands in reasonably expert fashion.

"Thanks Col." Jim finally, thankfully took his own disguise off. It was in pretty good shape, considering the punishment it and he had just received. But it was nice to feel his own face again.

"Did you get the information you needed?" asked Mel.

McCleland, Clark and Colin looked at each other and shared a knowing look. Clark spoke.

"Yeah. We got it."

They settled back in their seats. The last couple of days had been a grueling experience for them all, especially the oldest man present. Who knew how badly he had been affected by the endless interrogation? The after effects of that could be devastating to a mind, Colin mused grimly. Post traumatic stress was a very real issue Of course with modern medical and counseling techniques, the condition was easily treatable but it didn't stop it from rearing its ugly head days, months, even years after the fact. Clarkie would no doubt deny anything of the sort and attempt to cajole Jim and himself into a drinking session to forget all about it.

Colin intended to keep a close eye on his commanding officer.

Looking around, Clark took in the cramped confines of the Hip.

"Where the hell did you come up with this coal scuttle?" he asked.

A bit of the old sharp wit made Jim smile. To be honest he was beginning to like the rugged helicopter. It may be cramped, too dark and not very comfortable. It may have stunk of rubber, hydraulic fluid and burned gunpowder but it had proved to be a reliable, tough old bird and he was going to miss it.

"Well, we couldn't exactly park a Tonka on Krasnov's doorstep, could we?"

Clarkie's mouth twisted and he made a face.

"If I were you I wouldn't complain about the transportation," Mel commented as lightly as he could. Having set the autopilot, the retired pilot came down the ladder and joined them. Colin did the introductions.

"Ah yes, you're the guy who came up with the throwing the Chinook around the sky trick," Clark commented.

Mel groaned. Wonderful, another fan who knew him for just one thing.

"Yes, that was me," he said simply.

"How did you get roped into this? I hope not in the same way that Jim convinced me!"

"If you mean someone got me drunk to convince me, no nothing like that," said Mel. "The person in question appealed to my sense of adventure."

Before Clark could ask who, the proximity sensors beeped a sharp warning. Waters had had his senses heightened again as the men on active duty went to action stations.

Looking at the radar screen, Colin was filled with dread. "It looks like an attack chopper approaching."

It must have been the same one that had accosted them earlier. Would they be friendly or would they fire? Given what they must have seen had happened to their precious base, it was hard to say. The convex view ports were filled with the predatory shape of the Mi-24 Hind as it loomed toward them.

TWENTY-THREE

The inevitable hail came in.

"Prepare to land and turn yourselves over," came the blunt demand.

The four air force men exchanged a look.

"We are in no need of assistance at this time. We have sustained some damage but are able to continue," Haltwhistle replied.

"You are suspected to be enemy agents. Prepare to surrender or we will destroy you."

McCleland gestured for the line to be cut. He knew a weapons lock would be picked up and they would be atomized, so manual firing was the only option. Despite it's bulkier size, the Hip was outfitted with comparable weaponry to the Hind. In a firefight, they could have a good chance of escaping or out-fighting them. Given the option of spending the rest of their lives in a prison camp or worse, the choice was clear cut.

"Mel, open fire on them," Jim commanded. "Time to deal with this the way Senna dealt with Prost."

The wing-mounted rockets roared as pulses of white hot death shot away and impacted the Hind along it's fuselage and engines. It spun but then turned and returned fire. Waters threw the chopper into an inverted move that flung everyone sideways just for a moment. The Hip swooped along the underside of the Hind, right in its' blind spot. Mel paced the enemy, making it appear as if the larger helicopter had disappeared to the no-doubt bewildered crew of the Hind.

He brought the Hip around, steadied the approach and opened fire again, raking the scout's belly with more rocket blasts.

The Russians responded with bolts of furious fire from the front machine guns, which Waters tried to evade by rocking the oval - shaped chopper from side to side. One just raked the starboard wing which caused the gun ship to buck and begin to spiral, but Mel was in complete control.

Bringing the transport chopper about he opened fire with a merciless barrage of firepower. This time a large explosion erupted from the side of the Hind as it split open like an egg. In a second, the Russian gunship flared and erupted into a yellow fireball of brunt wreckage and debris.

There had been too much death and destruction today. It was not the way things should have happened.

"Set a course for Camp Bastion. Best speed that you can. Try to send a message to the camp and tell them," said Colin.

Jim did so. The Hip had a limited top speed however. Not quick but it was enough to get them where they needed to be in two hours.

The message that Matthews had been waiting eighteen long hours finally came in. He had not left his post and was exhausted.

Turning down the offer of relief from Lt. Gen Bailey, he had stayed in Bailey's office, waiting and watching.

His patience was now rewarded.

"Priority message coming in, sir."

Standing beside Matthews' chair, Cartwright turned towards him. Bailey was out of his seat and heading for the radio station.

Group Captain Harvey however remained impassively sat in his seat, as if this none of this fazed him at all.

"On loudspeakers," Cartwright and Bailey both said simultaneously. They exchanged a wink.

The familiar dulcet tones of Jim McCleland filled the office speakers.

"Rapier calling Wren's Nest. Come in Wren's Nest."

Matthews acknowledged them.

"Request immediate assistance. Our course is 163 mark 2," If Black Jack didn't know better, McCleland sounded strained. Bailey leaned over the back of Matthews' seat as he waved for him to speak.

"Report progress, Rapier," he said.

"Mission successful, goods obtained," Jim's voice responded. The transmission sounded filtered and garbled, almost as if someone was trying to jam the signal. Cartwright let out a breath.

So Clarkie was safe, and so was the information.

"Message understood, Rapier, we are on our way."

The message became increasingly garbled and unintelligible. Whatever was going on, they had to get there fast. He turned to Camp Bastion's base commander.

"General Bailey, get your Apaches airborne and get them heading to meet them immediately."

Bailey sprinted outside and began barking orders at his ground crews. The noise of rotor blades turning filled the air as the three Apaches that had been readied took off in quick succession. The three ominous gunships lifted in to the sky and headed north looking very determined. Cartwright and Bailey watched as the helicopters became distant specks in the sky.

'Did you get through to the old man?'

"I think so, but I dunno if it was received and understood, Col. Something was interfering with our transmission," Jim replied.

Haltwhistle's jaw twitched. That would mean just one thing: someone was still out there listening, possibly pursuing them. How could that be possible if they had just destroyed the largest base in the region? It was a worrying situation. How long would it take Black Jack's rescue party to reach them? No doubt if he wanted to, he could get an accurate answer down to the millisecond, but there was little comfort in that if they were indeed being chased. Clarkie, however asked anyway.

"At the vector of our respective maximum velocities and assuming there are no delays, one hour and 22 minutes, 32 seconds sir," was the calm, rational reply.

"I could have told you that, just from my readout!" Waters chimed in.

But the thought nagged at Jim. "Col is it possible that a gunship could have survived that explosion?"

"Oh probably, if it was far enough away from the explosion and it didn't get too badly damaged. If it was ready to take off then yes, we could have a friend out there somewhere," Haltwhistle told them.

McCleland weighed up his options.

"Can you scan for anything giving chase?"

Colin looked at the radar screen which bathed his angular features in green light. The equipment aboard the Hip was badly lacking compared to what was available on the British side, but a short range sensor sweep would still give a reasonably good idea. The sensor systems bleeped and chirped while the console whirred. It was strangely comforting in an old-fashioned way.

"There is a contact holding steady at about three miles distance, directly behind us," he reported.

"Can you work out what it is?"

"I can't say for sure with this equipment, Jim. The imaging and probing tools are rubbish compared to ours."

"Take your best guess, Col."

The white cap sat back in his chair, in that manner that Jim knew well, suggesting that Colin had heard a silly question but was attempting to respond in a way that wasn't condescending.

McCleland guessed the response but wanted to hear it from someone he trusted implicitly.

"I would say looking at this that it's an attack helicopter."

Three miles aft was just outside of most weapons' range, but more than close enough to keep pace with them. If it was indeed a gunship then it didn't have missiles as those had a range of ten to twenty miles, which as a blessing. Either way, they would not last long in a battle without protection and they had to make the rendezvous, especially with the information they had gained.

In the smoking cockpit of the only remaining helicopter that had survived the cataclysmic destruction of his base, Krasnov sat in the pilot's seat.

He had come around to feel tingling from head to toe, the legacy of having a chandelier dropped on him. Evacuation alarms had been blaring, people running for some sort of escape whether that was aboard an aircraft or by grabbing a vehicle to deliver them to safety and it had been general pandemonium. From what he could gather from the scattered bits of conversation, the British officer had been released by two Russians, who he knew to be McCleland and Haltwhistle and had affected escape after a running firefight in which serious damage had been done to the lower regions of the compound.

Worse still, the primary reactor had somehow been destroyed and the resulting chain reaction would quickly consume the base. It was all he could do to run and hope to hell that he made it before the inevitable explosion came.

He was seething. His headquarters destroyed and some of the Russians most hated - and revered opponents - had infiltrated their encampment, laid waste to the invasion and had ascertained the identities of all the top agents hidden within the British military. Krasnov had planned the invasion, had requested the funding for the base, overseen it's construction and then seen everything literally destroyed. How had any of this happened? It would probably cost him dearly.

To top it all, his prized collection had gone up in smoke.

No. It was too late for recriminations. Action was needed and McCleland and his conspirators must be stopped at all costs. Perhaps the Government would not want his head if he brought them one of the RAF's foremost pilots.

Krasnov had at least had the satisfaction of seeing Ulyenkov fail as miserably as he did. He had been more than a little surprised to receive a furious hail from the killer informing of his party being intercepted.

Clearly an impostor was on the station and the assassin had informed Krasnov that he was going to cut whoever was arrogant enough to pretend to be him into pieces. The supposed foremost hired killer in the Russian Federation had proven to be less than stellar. He had allowed himself to be beaten by McCleland and more than likely killed in the blast. He took some comfort in that.

Although he had managed to get to his chopper and had survived the cataclysmic destruction of the base, the helicopter had taken damage to the engines and rotor blades when it was caught up in the blast when taking off. McCleland's chopper had been detected fleeing but with limited maneuvering capability, catching them was going to be an arduous process.

Fortunately, the weapons that they had still worked and he had set out in pursuit of the Hip that had brought the British team to him.

They had observed the brief battle between the Hip and an unfortunate scout. Krasnov had to admit to admiration for whoever piloted the MI-8. It had given them the chance to catch up, but the engines had been unable to give more than a bare cruising speed. The RAF squad was maddeningly just out of range for an assault. Even with depleted engines and weapons, Krasnov was confident that his gunship was more than a match for the Hip if they got within range.

If they could get within range.

"Increase speed," he barked.

"Engines threatening to overload. We cannot increase speed," the pilot responded glumly.

Krasnov slammed the arm of the throne like seat. This was becoming more maddening by the second. If only there was a way to slow McCleland and Haltwhistle down just a little. He was sure he could apprehend the two wily officers and then have him and his men rounded up and presented to his superiors. They would make a great prize indeed. Severe embarrassment to the British government and save face despite what the last few hours had dealt.

"And you're sure we cannot target them and fire?"

He was giving his pilot officer a look that could kill.

"No. They are out of range. We could fire but it would be a lucky shot."

Krasnov watched the fleeing helicopter through his windscreen. It was merely a fleck of dust at this range but dust could be swept, no matter how inept the sweeper. It was a long shot, quite literally but it was the only shot to salvage something from this whole ridiculous situation.

"Battle alert! Prepare to fight. Ready weapons!"

Aboard the Hip, Colin's readouts changed and an alarm sounded. He rechecked his instruments.

"I've managed to get a readout on that chopper chasing us."

"Go on." Jim instinctively wanted visual information but then he remembered the Hip was not equipped with a high - tech readout like it's British or American equivalents. His fighter pilot's instincts were on high alert.

He snapped his fingers in frustration. "Give me a rundown."

"It's an Mi-24 Hind just outside weapons range. They are pursuing us and assuming an attack posture."

"Oh lovely," Clarkie sighed.

Haltwhistle's withering look shot at him quickly silenced the senior officer on board. Colin was clearly not in the mood for snark. "They are firing at us. Blind pattern," he informed them.

"From that distance? Evasive manouvers."

The chopper darted from side to side as Mel Waters swung the controls this way and that. The wave of tracer fire darted past and harmlessly out into the sky ahead of them. The final shot however came in blinded by one of the passing round of bullets. There was only one place the weapons was going to land.

"Incoming-!" started Waters.

The Hip rocked as the tracer round impacted them on the rear boom just before the aft rotor, which promptly cracked. The oval shape of the helicopter spiraled out of control for several seconds, which for the occupants felt like several hours. The consoles sparked and spat electrical flames as the circuit breakers overloaded. The cockpit and flight deck were plunged into darkness as Waters fought to regain control. The helicopter trailed smoke from its tail boom as it plunged towards the hills below.

TWENTY-FOUR

The chopper seemed to be tumbling end over end in a countless series of rolls. Despite the fact that they were not traveling in a weightless environment, it felt to Waters as if they should be floating around. He clung desperately to the controls and applied some power to his tail rotor. It responded, although sluggishly. The rotor control had been damaged, but not destroyed. Slowly, the Hip righted itself, and he managed to get them going again at a reduced speed.

"What's the damage?" Jim spat a gob of blood up.

Colin rubbed his forehead. The sticky feeling he got told him he had been cut open when his face had found a bulkhead amid the chaos and it added to his list of injuries gained on this mission.

He swore to himself he would not get involved in anything like this again and that he would politely refuse John Cartwright's demand for a second mission, if that came to pass.

McCleland mused to himself that if they got out of this he needed to seriously talk with Cartwright about assigning the more ridiculous and crazy missions to himself and not to do so from now on.

"Gyroscopic stabilizers offline. Engines were overloaded but are alright now," Haltwhistle responded.

"We need full engine power now!" Clark ordered. He knew that whoever it was close by would be on top of them in a matter of seconds unless they got the hell out of there now. Haltwhistle fingered the controls rapidly.

"There is damage to the tail rotor's attitude controls. Automatic override is in place."

"Dammit, Mel, get us out here!" Clark shouted.

"Stow it Clarkie," McCleland cut him off bluntly.

The Flt. Lt.'s controls beeped as he quickly and wordlessly worked his computer inputs. Finally, wonderfully, the sound of the engines powering up filled the dark, cramped cabin.

"We have engine power, but I am still working on stability control," Colin informed them.

"Can we go to maximum cruise speed?" Jim barked.

"We can but I wouldn't recommend it without stable maneuvering controls. We don't know where we would arrive at, or if we'd get there in one piece."

'Fuck it, do it!' Haltwhistle shouted.

Waters needed no second bidding and hit his controls. Instantly the chopper picked up speed and momentum.

"How far behind are our friends?"

"They are within weapons range."

As if on cue, the whistle of the intercom came through the intercom speakers.

"McCleland!" Krasnov's voice echoed. "You cannot escape and we have our weapons locked on you. Surrender or I will personally fire the weapons which will eliminate you."

Jim sat at his own controls. If Krasnov brought them home as prisoners, the Russians' treatment of them would not be gentle. No, they had to get home, no matter what the cost. He opened the channel.

"Go fuck yourself, Krasnov. No deal."

"Don't be foolish McCleland. I could blast you from the sky if I wanted to. Save yourself more anguish and give up now."

"We have a saying in England, Krasnov. And you're full of it."

At his station, Colin was feverishly working on restoring the stabilisers and guidance controls. A sudden jolt pitched the chopper into a nose up position before it settled into a level plane. Even seated, the four were jolted around like rag dolls.

"You appear to be having some difficulties, McCleland." Krasnov was clearly enjoying watching their predicament.

Jim cut the channel off. He managed to stand again but he felt heavy and unsteady on his feet.

"I assume that because my stomach hit the floor that we have guidance control restored. Can we maneuver?"

Waters checked his instruments.

"I can out fly him but I can't outrun him."

A chain of tracer fire skimmed past them on their left.

"Hold on!"

The Hip did not feel as sharp as it had before. To Mel it felt a touch sluggish. Oh well if they were to get out of this, he would have to make up the difference. The Hind was firing on them again. Anticipating the not quite so agile controls, Waters looped the chopper beyond the arc of the incoming fire and responded with a burst of machine gun fire of their own. The tracer rounds arced out and peppered the Hind's armored skin. He brought the Hip under Krasnov's gunship's underside, firing along the length of its slender neck section and flared rear. Krasnov's aft machine gunner spat a series of red flame from his external machine gun, which Waters managed to dodge.

"I want them destroyed, now!" Krasnov bellowed at his gunner.

"They are moving too quickly for me to target properly, Comrade."

Krasnov leveled the Hind and brought the Hip into his gunfights.

"Fire all weapons!"

On the horizon, three Apache helicopter gunships appeared above the ridge of mountains to the two battling helicopters' right.

"Looks the cavalry has arrived," Colin said with relief.

Aboard the Hind, Krasnov, seeing the incoming threat, frantically pulled the cyclic over and adjusted the collective.

"Break, break, break!"

The Hind veered away then came back around, opening fire on the incoming gunships with it's front machine gun blazing. The Hip mercifully, finally passed behind the protective line of the three Apaches and took up position hovering behind them.

In response the three British helicopters fired a volley of rockets and gun fire from their stubby, ugly shapes. The Russian gunship twisted and rolled under the onslaught.

Through his headpiece, Krasnov heard the firm tone of voice of the leader of the formation.

"Russian helicopter. Withdraw and cease fire or we will destroy you," came the filtered demand over the intercom. The windshield of the Hind was full of the imposing dark green machines which hovered one hundred feet from his nose.

"This is Russian airspace! You are the ones who are intruding on our territory! You are the ones who have destroyed our outpost resulting in the loss of thousands of our comrades!" Krasnov objected. "We demand that Sqn. Ldr. McCleland and his party be turned over to us."

"I don't think you are in any position to make demands," said the lead Apache's pilot. "Let us do you a favor and you can get the hell out of here?"

There was a long, furious tirade of words in Russian that no one on board the Apaches quite understood, but it was obvious that Krasnov was not pleased. The battered Hind turned about and limped slowly away as the gunships continued to hold station. Then it turned and came back around at full speed, with its rockets and guns blazing. Krasnov was bent on one last, final, dramatic stand.

A furious hail of rockets and Hellfire missiles reduced the Hind to flaming debris as it floated like confetti to the desert floor below. Krasnov must surely have been one of the fluttering remains now fluttering down for the final demise.

TWENTY-FIVE

The pockmarked, scorched and bullet hole ridden Hip flew in low over the outer fence of Camp Bastion.

Whipping up clouds of dust into the air, the gunship settled to the ground with a faint thud and the turbine engines slowed until they were silent and the great rotor blades spun to a stop.

The loading door swung open and the four occupants, McCleland, Haltwhistle, Waters and Clark emerged from the chopper.

Cartwright, Harvey and Bailey were waiting for them as they stepped down from the battered Hip. The occupants looked disheveled and Clarkie especially had been pretty banged up.

"Gentlemen, welcome home. Well done," Cartwright beamed and shook McCleland's hand. He noticed the cuts and bruises marking the Squadron Leader's face. "It looks like you've been in the wars!"

"And I haven't?" Clark demanded angrily. "I've had my mind turned inside out by that damned interrogation, thanks to your brilliant plan!"

"Harvey," Black Jack ordered briskly. "Get Clark to the medical Centre and have a full physical done on him." He was hoping to prevent an argument before it started. Harvey supported a clearly weak Clark and led him to a waiting Land Rover.

"We have sir. Been in the wars I mean. But we made it." Haltwhistle was weary and needed a long sleep, but that could wait.

Cartwright noticed Waters. He went to his old friend.

"Mel, this would never have succeeded without you being there. Thank you."

But Waters was not feeling charitable. He wearily took Black Jack's outstretched hand.

"I am never going through that again. I told you I was retired and I am staying retired. Next time, get some other poor sod to put himself through the ringer, John," was the blunt comment.

Cartwright had not expected to be brushed off. "I'll bear that in mind."

"Sirs, I hate to seem rude but we're not out of trouble yet," Colin cut in. He turned to his CO.

"You were right, sir. There is a spy."

Cartwright and Bailey looked incredulous as Jim, supported by Colin's thumb drive with the information he had downloaded from the outpost's computer told the story.

Jim, Bailey, Cartwright and Colin stood in the base commander's office in grim silence. After what they had just shown the Air Vice Marshal, no one was looking forward to their next action.

Waters had been dismissed and allowed to rest. A crisp knock on the door got their attention.

"Come in," Bailey commanded.

An eager young man dressed in medical garb came in and stood to attention.

"Sorry to trouble you, sir, but the CMO thought you should see this."

He held a small metal pin out. Bailey took it from him and took a close look at it.

"It looks like a homing device,' the base commander said. He handed it to Haltwhistle and turned back to the medic.

Colin examined it closely with a magnifying glass. Squinting, he turned it over to make an inspection of the back of the pin.

"Fascinating."

"Go on Haltwhistle, piss or get off the pot." Black Jack pressed for more.

"The tracker's active, sir. I think you can guess what that means." Colin replied. "What are your orders?"

Jim knew all too well. If Krasnov had got people positioned and they knew that were present on the base, they could have a lot of company very quickly especially as when the darkness came and the place was lit up, it would make a very tempting target. Too many people had already lost their lives keeping the peace in this country. None of them wanted to add their names to the list.

But it also meant that an order for General Quarters would alert the spy that they knew to be on the camp that they were on to him before they could get the drop on him.

"Destroy it Colin. We'll handle things from here," Cartwright ordered.

"What about the information we found, sir?"

"I thought you'd never ask, Haltwhistle." Cartwright looked at his two subordinates.

Darkness was falling. The base's giant floodlights illuminated the gloomy sand strewn landscape. The dunes and rocks dotted around the perimeter of the huge camp made perfect hiding places for anyone who was willing to mount an assault.

Cartwright was about to accuse a high-ranking officer of treason. Five minutes back on front line duty and he was already in the thick of things. As much as he loved his work, he could do with sitting with a good book and enjoying some down time. Apparently, that would not happen anytime soon.

Black Jack nodded to Haltwhistle and McCleland. Their target was watching the crew going about their duty from his set on the port side of the bridge. It was time.

"Wing Commander Matthews, record and make a copy of the next fifteen minutes and transmit to the Ministry of Defence on a live channel," Cartwright ordered.

The four AID officers and the base commander strode through Camp Bastion's corridors towards the medical center, the soles of their boots squeaking on the highly polished hallway floors.

Openly telling a decorated man of such a heinous crime did not sit with Jim, but during the whole of the landing phase of the Hip, the person had not made a move to give himself away.

Either he was a very good actor or he simply thought he was above suspicion. In any case, that person's illusions were about to be shattered.

Arriving in the main ward, Cartwright was relieved that aside from the doctor and nurse overseeing Clark, the room was empty. Group Captain Harvey looked on, grateful that Clarkie was in one piece.

"How is he bearing up?" Black Jack asked the medical staff.

"Well aside from being cooped up and having my brains scrambled, I'm just wonderful!" Clark responded.

Despite what he now had to do, Cartwright smiled, but the cheerful expression soon faded.

"Doctor, you and the nurse can go. Thank you."

The confused looks from the surgeon and his assistant gave way to duty and they trooped out of the ward.

"Group Captain Harvey. You are relieved of duty and placed under arrest," Cartwright told him.

Harvey started. "What? What's the meaning of this?"

"You're under arrest under Section 36 of the Crime and Disorder Act 1998. Treason, espionage and collusion with an enemy power. You can throw in the murders of Air Marshal Berry and Commander Phelps as well."

He produced a small clear bag with a pin inside. An RAF rondel.

"I found it on the towpath near the remains of Berry's boat. Your fingerprints were all over it and the lock keeper was very helpful in identifying you." Cartwright went on. "I have to say I lost a bet with myself. I thought it was Matthews, not you."

Casey Matthews gave his commanding officer a look that was a mixture of shock and anger.

"What? What do you mean you thought it was me?"

"Because you're an arsehole and you always were," Black Jack told him . "And now we know that you also keep terrible company as well."

Cartwright was referring to the friendship between Matthews and Harvey, and the intimation stung his chief of staff's pride.

"Well thanks a lot, sir," Casey looked and sounded genuinely hurt.

"This is absolute madness!" Harvey protested. "I'm a proud and loyal officer! You know that! I commanded a flight and later a base for fifteen years!" The Group Captain was on his feet, his face turning the color of the red alert status lights. His barrel-chested physique made him intimidating and his usually jolly demeanor had given way to pure anger. Now he was pointing fingers at his accusers and loudly protesting his innocence.

Cartwright produced a witness statement from the dock where Berry's boat had been kept. "It makes for interesting reading." He read the section most relevant. " 'I saw a burly man dressed in dark clothing venturing on to the boat the evening before.' " The physical description matched Harvey. "What did you do? Plant a bomb on the engine?"

"I have served my country for twenty-five years!"

"Yeah. Served the Russians apparently," Haltwhistle replied.

"How dare you speak to me out of turn, Flight Lieutenant!' The Group Captain rounded on Colin.

"He has every right!" Cartwright blasted, his voice growing louder and angrier. "What did you do? Read up on Geoffrey Prime and decide you wanted a piece of the action? How many people have died because of you? How much damage have you done to the country you took an oath to protect?"

"This is crazy! I'll have the lot of you brought up on charges! Where's your proof?"

Haltwhistle brought up the information on an iPad and showed Harvey the photos and listings.

"For the records, Flight Lieutenant Haltwhistle is showing the accused information that has been verified as accurate and correct," McCleland said.

"What you are seeing, sir is information retrieved from the GRU's main database and the Russian Military Intelligence database. It was gained by myself, Squadron Leader McCleland and Squadron Leader Waters," Haltwhistle explained calmly.

Images of RAF officers, their ranks, positions and their security level was displayed. Mostly it was crewmen stationed on airbases dotted around the British Isles. One of the faces shown was Sutton, the young engineer who had been aboard before the Globemaster shortly before it departed from Brize Norton.

"You were right about that toerag," Jim murmured.

"This is preposterous! The Russians keep files on almost all the British military officers and installations! We do exactly the same," Harvey complained.

"There's a difference between intelligence information and a list of agents operating throughout the service."

Cartwright's expression was stone faced, but the anger was clearly shown in his eyes. The images kept coming: high ranking officers within the Ministry of Defence, Intelligence and Security services. It was galling. But the final image was of Harvey himself, taken at a conference somewhere in Eastern Europe, Colin guessed from the background. Beside the picture, the information displayed his position, his clearance level and his statistics. The picture itself showed Harvey talking to a Russian officer.

Ulyenkov.

"I think we've seen enough, Mr. Haltwhistle," Cartwright said somberly. It was all the evidence required.

Harvey visibly blanched and turned pale. Black Jack indicated for his officers to take Harvey into custody.

But the Group Captain punched the unfortunate Matthews in the mouth at full force and grabbed his pistol.

"You are not taking me anywhere! I'll kill you all before you take me in!" He bolted for the door, shooting blindly as he fled. The swing doors closed behind him before Jim or Colin could jump him. Two guards moved to stop the wild – eyed fugitive, but the pistol he had stolen came in handy. Both fell afoul of the weapon's bullets.

"Security alert! Priority one! All staff go to high alert!" Bailey ordered.

A klaxon blared; it's shrill, urgent tone cutting through the gathering gloom. The hammering of running feet and the rapid deployment of personnel as Camp Bastion mobilized was a sight to behold. All the military assets, aircraft, tanks, helicopters were instantly placed under armed guard, as was the more sensitive parts of the base.

"Begin a full manhunt search. All personnel to action stations," Bailey commanded.

"I hope it's enough," Cartwright said. "This is a small town, not just a base."

"Maybe we could narrow things down a bit," Haltwhistle offered. "Harvey will make a break for it. So if we target the aircraft and jeeps, tanks and whatnot, it'd seem a good way to go."

"It's worth a try, but there's no reason to not look everywhere," said Matthews.

Jim and Colin made for the vast vehicle compound. Rows of Land Rovers and tanks were parked in columns by their type. They made an impressive display, and now the dusty collection was thronged by armed soldiers guarding them and searching for their quarry.

McCleland was thinking quickly. "We need to bring this prick to us, not for him to lead us on some merry chase."

"I'm open to bright ideas, mate," Haltwhistle said, straining to keep up with his friend's thought processes.

For his part, Jim had an evil gleam in his eye. "I might have one."

In a few seconds, McCleland outlined his idea. The looks and murmurs of consternation in the office meant that his plans were not universally embraced.

"Are you sure about this, McCleland?" Cartwright was a little incredulous. "You were able to pull it off once, but doing it twice? That's asking to push your luck."

"It's worth a try, sir."

What Jim had proposed was foolhardy but to draw Harvey to them, it seemed a practical solution.

Haltwhistle was secretly annoyed with himself that he hadn't come up with it. Mel Waters, who had been settling down to sleep had not been best pleased to have his peace interrupted.

"We'll need a chopper again for this to work properly," Colin said to Waters, who gaped in disbelief.

"Is it being patched up?" Jim asked.

"It barely got you back, man! It's not airworthy!" Bailey protested. "It had the shit shot out of it!"

"That wouldn't work anyway. Harvey saw the state of the Hip, he'd twig instantly," said Colin.

Not for the first time, Waters felt completely ill at ease in this company.

"What about a jeep, or anything the locals would use? Anything that wouldn't look out of place?" McCleland asked.

Bailey stopped at that. "Yeah, there's a couple of trucks over in the vehicle compound. The engineers use them to show how to render a car safe and experiment with bomb disposal and stuff like that."

McCleland's confidence, however, was growing. Haltwhistle may have come up with the idea originally, but he was now going to use it to its full potential. Hopefully.

"At my signal sir, I want you to issue an alert. Something like the Russians Inbound and all of that stuff." Jim grinned.

Bailey looked uncertain. "Now that is asking for trouble! If I send out that kind of message, we'll have to launch jets and start getting tanks ready."

"That'd be the perfect cover to get a jeep started and away, sir," pointed out Colin.

"I hope you realize how much of a risk this is," Cartwright told them both. "I'm pretty sure we can apprehend Harvey without taking these nonsensical decisions."

"There is method to the madness, sir," Jim replied. "What damage is he doing to this place right now? If we can limit that as much as we can, it'll be a risk worth taking."

In the medical bay, the doctor and nurse had returned to treat Clark. He was suffering from dehydration and physically exhausted but otherwise was not in bad shape, all things considered.

It could have been much worse. Unfortunately, Clarkie was the worst kind of patient, the type who thought he knew what was wrong and was trying to tell the medical professionals their job.

Along with his general being ill at ease, the events of the last few days were not sitting well with the veteran officer.

And with the klaxon now sounding and having seen what Harvey was actually capable of, his unease had reached a heightened level.

"What the hell is going on out there? It feels like we're at war all over again!" he grumbled.

"Easy, doctor, just relax and lay down," the nurse said soothingly.

"Sure, relax she says. How can I relax when the place is tearing itself apart?"

If the doctor could have, he would have knocked Clark out by any which way he could.

Harvey flung himself from the cover of the curved hangars where the Tornados were maintained and skirted around the back of them towards the perimeter fence. He found himself on the north side of the camp. He had evaded capture so far and had enjoyed the good natured but rather incompetent search that was currently under way for him.

Off to his right, Harvey saw a guard tower that reached forty feet above the ground, giving a good view of the mountains to the north. He considered his options. He could make for the helicopter that had returned. While he was more than qualified to pilot the machine, it was questionable if the thing would ever fly again. No, that was out. The other option was to commandeer a vehicle and escape the base, but with the entire complement of Camp Bastian now mobilized that wasn't an option either. He would be pursued and destroyed with ease.

He would have to wait for the cover of night. Harvey slipped back into the narrow gap between the hangars, crouching down. His desert fatigues would help to disguise him somewhat.

He was beginning to feel confident when he saw what appeared to be a squaddie marching towards the guard tower from his left. Figuring that it was changeover time for those on watch, Harvey saw that once the man walking was under the tower itself, he would be out of sight of the man standing guard.

Harvey waited for his moment, came up behind the unfortunate crew member and clubbed him in to unconsciousness. He took the man's jacket and helmet, which he put on and lowered the sun visor.

Casually, he walked up the steps to the platform.

"You're relieved."

Glad to have his tedious evening done with, the other man quickly departed. Harvey smiled and waited for his chance. For now, he was content to wait out what remained of the daylight.

"This is strange," Bailey said.

"What is it?"

"Williams, the man on the northern guard tower was supposed to be relieved about twenty minutes ago, but his sergeant hasn't signed him back in and no-one's seen him."

Cartwright's senses were tingling. He picked up his radio. "Wrens Nest to Rapier 1 and 2."

Haltwhistle answered the call. "Go ahead, sir."

Black Jack smiled. "I'm making the call now. Make your way to the area of the northern guard tower as discussed."

Just as Cartwright's order for security alert was broadcast. Harvey slipped himself down from the cover of the guard tower. and made his way down the steps back to the ground. He sprinted along the perimeter fence looking for a hole, a gap, anything to slip out and head away. If his comrades were indeed coming, he could link up with them and bring in some high level targets of his own. Cartwright's grand plan would backfire and he would be the victor.

Looking around, Harvey was heading towards another guard tower. In the gathering gloom of dusk, the searchlights were switched on, but pointed towards the surrounding desert. The fugitive slowed to a casual walk and approached slowly. To his left, the seemingly endless collection of hangars and workshops continued in a curve.

"Stay where you are!" a voice shouted from his left. Harvey turned to see a sergeant with an assault rifle pointed at him.

Instinctively, Harvey kicked up the dust and for an instant he was obscured by the airborne sand.

He fired at the sergeant and when the view had cleared the man in his combat fatigues lay dead.

He was illuminated by the spotlight from the guard tower.

Gunfire came from its elevated confines. Harvey returned fire, aiming for the bloom of the gunfire. A yelp answered his stream of lead. He mounted the steps to the viewing platform and pulled the form of the dead man to one side.

Watching the ground from the safety of the lookout post, Harvey knew that his position had been reported. All he could do was wait and hope that his salvation would come quickly.

The vast edifice of the main hangar where the Globemasters were serviced and stored was just across from where he was now positioned. The huge tanks which contained AVTUR sat close at hand to their right, protected from attack by a reinforced concrete wall, but the domed tops could easily be made out from his vantage point.

"Harvey seen in region of the main hangar buildings," intoned the camp intercom speaker.

"We're on our way," Cartwright's voice filtered back.

Harvey smiled grimly. It appeared as if he was going to face off against Black Jack in person.

He'd often thought about what that would be like.

Krasnov had informed him of the tracker in Clark's arm. It had been placed there just in case someone tried to break the officer out. He could be tracked and whoever and wherever he had been taken to could then be destroyed, but it was beyond his reach and was now useless.

Harvey knew of the devastation that McCleland, Haltwhistle and their team had wrought on their base camp. He wondered if he could gain some sort of revenge for the destruction and deaths of thousands of his adopted countrymen. If he could hold out for a just a few minutes then his escape was assured. He knew the forces were coming. And if by some chance that he couldn't effect his defection, then he would inflict as much damage as he could before he was taken dead or alive. Cartwright's finest hour ending in fiery defeat.

How ironic, Harvey thought.

An Ocelot approached. Black Jack himself and Bailey emerged from it with Matthews at their side.

Harvey watched them from above as they searched around ineffectively. He used their time spent searching to take the dead man's machine pistol, an MP5.

"We have to find him before he has a chance to do whatever it is he's planning," Bailey said.

"He was seen in this area so he can't have gone too far," Cartwright replied. "He's around here somewhere."

"He could be anywhere," Matthews said plaintively. "Camp Bastion is full of hidey holes."

"Fan out, look around, but do it really quietly," Cartwright said in a low voice.

Harvey made his move at that moment.

"I'm right here, gentlemen," he called down from above them. He had the MP5 trained on them.

Realizing where Harvey was, Black Jack was grim. He should have guessed that Harvey would have gone for the height advantage.

"Get down from there, Harvey. It's over."

"Oh, I think not, Cartwright.' The traitor beamed. 'If you try to come up here, I'll destroy the fuel tanks and that, as you well know, will in turn, destroy everything in a pretty big distance."

Matthews could hear the conversation, but he had disappeared from Harvey's line of sight. If he could order an emergency shunting of the fuel to alternative pipes and storage tanks, perhaps he could prevent Harvey from going through with his threat.

"I want a car brought to me, and I want it right now," Harvey told them. "Those brothers in arms out there will be with us shortly, and then I'll meet up with them and leave. With you, McCleland, Haltwhistle and Waters with me. You are all guilty of sabotage. I should imagine my government and the GRU will not be too lenient with you."

"You know as well as I do, we don't negotiate with terrorists, Harvey," Cartwright responded.

Harvey pointed his sub machine gun at the giant kerosene tanks that were used to fuel the various aircraft stationed here. One shot and a spark and the effects would be catastrophic. There was no way that Matthews could have had them drained so quickly.

"You will do exactly as I say. If you don't, I'll reduce this entire encampment to ashes."

"Keep him talking," Bailey muttered to the RAF man. He knew once Jim and Colin were in position and headed in their direction they would have their man, but it would take a few minutes.

"Harvey, I'm sure we can work something out," the Air Vice Marshal played along.

"Yes, we can. You can answer my demands. You have sixty seconds to get McCleland, Waters and Haltwhistle here. I want the helicopter and the jeep that was used as well. On top of illegal intelligence, using stolen enemy equipment and impersonating other forces' officers is a serious breach of the Geneva Convention. It's a capital offence, Cartwright."

"So is treason," Black Jack countered.

Harvey shook his head. "One man's traitor is another man's hero."

Cartwright had to buy some time for his men to get in to position. "Aren't you interested in how we found out about you?"

Harvey's eyes narrowed. "You are playing for time, Cartwright. You now have thirty seconds."

He gripped the machine pistol tighter, his aim at the computer not wavering.

"We suspected you for some time. We knew classified information was going out of the section and worthless details were coming back. You were in charge of that section, so the finger pointed at you," Cartwright explained. "We knew you had to have help, but we didn't know who they were so once we had access to the Hip helicopter, Clark and myself came up with this plan to draw you out and well, here you are. Your little friend Sutton was most helpful, but the intelligence that Haltwhistle gathered was the final nail in your coffin."

At the mention of Sutton, Harvey froze for a second.

"What did you do to him?" he demanded.

"Oh nothing as dramatic as your Russian friends would pull off. He didn't know too much but he did say where his orders were coming from. He just couldn't identify who was passing them on," Black Jack smiled thinly. "All a bit cloak and dagger."

An engine clattering and the familiar shape of a UAZ pulling up on the other side of the high fence got Harvey's attention and the clattering vehicle stopped under the shadows of the guard tower.

"Come on! Now!" the harsh voice rasped.

Harvey looked at his way to freedom and weighed it up against his not bringing his enemies with him. He decided his own life was more important than personal glory. Leaping from the watch tower twenty five feet to the sandy ground below, he dropped and rolled, then was heading for the vehicle. He turned and took aim at the kerosene tanks but realized that the concrete wall shielding now blocked any direct shot.

He was too close to them and would be immolated if he opened fire anyway.

With a self-satisfied expression, the former RAF officer climbed in to the 4x4. He pointed ahead.

"Take me home."

"With pleasure," a cut glass English accent he recognized as Colin Haltwhistle replied from the driver's seat. Harvey felt the unmistakable muzzle of a large caliber gun barrel at the back of his head.

He turned to see Jim McCleland had peeled off the disguise and the remains of Ulyenkov were placed on to the seat next to the pilot.

"You wanted us, here we are," Colin explained.

"Consider it a hearty salute to Glasnost, arsehole."

The UAZ took off and headed for the main gates of the camp. In the front passenger seat, Harvey let out an impassioned scream of defeat that was as shocking as it was loud.

Cartwright, Bailey and Matthews were waiting for them as they stopped at the base's entrance.

"Dammit!" Harvey cursed as he saw that the game was finally up. He was dragged from the car.

"You're finished, Harvey," Cartwright said firmly. Harvey was about to respond but was met with a punch in the jaw from McCleland, who had removed himself from the cramped rear of the Soviet machine. He and his partner forced Harvey through the gates, where Bailey and Matthews were waiting to escort the disgraced officer away.

"Take him to the brig."

Harvey gave them all a scowl.

"This isn't over. Not by a long shot, you'll see."

"Not for long. We have all the names and details," Colin assured him. "I'm sure the maximum security cells in Wormwood Scrubs have more than enough space in them for you."

Harvey lunged at Haltwhistle, but was manhandled to the deck by four security guards. Once they had him restrained, he was hauled off by the four men, all pointing their Glock 17s at him.

The intercom whistled.

"Control to General Bailey," a male voice came.

The base commander thumbed the intercom button in the gate house. "Bailey here," he answered with a relieved smile.

"Radar reports there is no inbound activity. There is no sign of threat, I repeat no sign of a threat."

There was relief in the radar technician's voice.

"Very good Mr. Burton. The base is to go back to normal procedures. All personnel are ordered to stand down. Attack is not, I say again not imminent." He looked at the AID men who had prevailed. "Bailey out."

Colin put his hands in his pockets, and felt a small metal disk. He took hold of it and in his hand, the chief's dog tags and rank patch. It weighed heavily on his mind. Cartwright looked at them.

"I'd like this man to receive an award, sir. He didn't ask to go with us and he sure didn't ask to be killed." He handed the items to his CO. "Without him, we couldn't have done what we have."

"I'll take care of it." Black Jack considered the pieces for a second.

EPILOGUE

The Globemaster touched down at Brize Norton and was approached by the RAF ground crews as the huge aircraft rolled to a stop. Jim and Colin stepped down into the bright English sunshine with Harvey under lock and key and Cartwright bringing up the rear with Clark in tow.

"Welcome home," was the warm reception from "Hello Steve," Cartwright replied. "Take Group Captain Harvey into custody. He is not to be saluted or given any privileges of rank."

Williams was taken aback by that. "Understood sir. Were there any problems?"

Jim and Colin looked at each other "Nothing that we couldn't handle. Have a security team standing by."

"Yes sir."

Cartwright led his men into an office and sat down with them. Producing a bottle of whiskey and Three glasses, Black Jack poured a finger into each glass for each of them.

"What did you find out about why Harvey turned?" Jim asked.

"It looks like Group Captain Harvey did not like the way that the incident back in 1988 was handled. He felt that the British government was in the wrong for the way we were helping the Mujahideen. In the aftermath he expressed pro-Russian sentiments among his crew and a chance encounter while on an exchange tour led him to be introduced to Krasnov. From there it was a simple case of indoctrination," Colin explained.

Jim shook his head and took a swig of his whiskey.

"Why didn't we pick up on it at his promotion screening?" Cartwright wondered.

"The vetting process was not as tight twenty years ago as it is now. He slipped through the cracks. So you don't have any reason to feel guilty, sir," Colin assured him.

"And we didn't know that we had a Russian spy high in the Air Staff for the best part of two decades," Cartwright filled in the rest. He shook his head. "Can you imagine the secrets he let out? Intelligence will need a top to tail review after this."

"I should imagine that the Russians will be pretty pissed off with what we did as well, sir,"

Haltwhistle said stiffly.

"I doubt it," countered McCleland. "That guy was funded by them but he was outside of his remit, and the Russians won't want to kick up a stink after they found out that two of their best went rogue."

"You were a little heavy handed with how you handled it," Cartwright said. The fact that they had destroyed millions of rubles worth of equipment, had a direct hand in the deaths of hundreds of military personnel and removed three of Moscow's top intelligence officers meant that his comment was a gross understatement.

"There will probably be squeals and letters to the Prime Minister. But that's the price we have to pay to keep the status quo and stop things like the invasion you prevented and people like Harvey from existing." Cartwright drained his shot glass. "And I should imagine that their yelling will fall on deaf ears this time considering the information we now have."

"That seems reasonable," Colin smiled.

Cartwright looked at his two officers and smiled to himself. They made a formidable team.

"Well gentlemen. I'm pleased to tell you that after the success of this mission, I've received some news," the AVM began.

"I'm not sure that I'm ready to hear this, but go on sir," Jim said slowly.

"I can tell you officially that the Airborne Intelligence Division is as of 4pm today, active. While we're not part of the RAF anymore, we do have access to any equipment and resources that the service has on line.'

Colin and Jim looked at each other. "What does that mean for us, sir?" Haltwhistle asked.

Black Jack poured them another finger of whiskey each.

"As of right now, Haltwhistle, you are both transferred to the department permanently. It'll be a tough job, but I have a feeling that you can both hack it."

Jim was grinning broadly while Colin looked shocked. "Sir. I'm not a spy."

"No one is asking you to be, Colin. Just to help keep this island safe and as free as we can make it from people who would threaten it's shores."

Black Jack went over the remit of the division and how it could take over any crime scene and investigate any matter no matter how trivial. Made up of past and current air force personnel, it was ambitious and with Cartwright at the helm, well organized.

A small, specialized unit that had access to all the RAF's and by extension the MoD's vast resources, including equipment, vehicles and aircraft was a formidable proposition and would be an effective deterrent to aerial threats to the United Kingdom.

"Don't get any ideas. This won't be easy. We're a deliberately small team of only 20 people but we have the advantage of being under the radar, if you'll pardon the expression which gives us a lot of leeway," Cartwright explained. "I need both of you to give me your very best for this to work."

Jim downed his whiskey. "I'm in, sir."

Despite his earlier misgivings, Colin finished his own drink and set the glass down. "Me too, sir."

Outside, Harvey was put in the back of an armored van, clearly being taken off to wherever it was he was to be held awaiting trial. His hands were in handcuffs. He was subdued but clearly seething. Security placed him in the vehicle and the door was slammed shut on his glowering countenance.

"Good riddance to bad rubbish," Colin said with disdain as he watched out of the window.

The van pulled away and was out of sight. Cartwright sat back. He wanted Clark and Waters to be here to share in the mission's success. Then there was a tap at the office door.

Speak of the devil, Black Jack thought as Clark entered the room accompanied by Mel Waters.

"Clarkie. Are you ready for a drink?"

"As long as it's not the same stuff that landed me in that damned prison," the Brummie twang in his voice was stronger and more sure than when they had returned from the mission. "Next time, I'll take my leave somewhere where no one can find me, thanks very much. And don't get any ideas, I want no part of this little club you've put together!'

"Waddo awaits for you, Clarkie!" Cartwright was relieved to have his friend back in more or less one piece. On top of that, he had asked Waters to take time out from a well-earned retirement and inadvertently placed him in more danger than he had realized. If he had known about the risk, and the two younger men's plan of action, there was no way Black Jack would have drafted the veteran in.

"Do you have time for a drink, Mel?" Jim asked.

"I thought you'd never ask!" Waters replied. "Where would a man be without a beer or two down his neck?"

"It'll just be a quick one for me. I've got a date," McCleland grinned.

Haltwhistle rolled his eyes. He suspected that this behavior was something that he would have to get used to if he and Jim were working together now.

"Why doesn't that surprise me? Who's the lucky girl?"

Jim grinned. "The lass back at the bunker I was chatting up the other day."

The five sat around the desk and thought about what they had achieved. It had been a hard fought and occasionally painful victory but they had pulled it off in the end.

"Cheers," Cartwright raised his glass to them all.

It was just the beginning of the story.

THE END

ABOUT THE AUTHOR

Barrie Taylor was born in the UK in 1982. Raised in a military environment, he emigrated to the USA in 2016. Enjoying writing from childhood, Barrie progressed from short stories to full length manuscripts. He lives with his family in Missouri. Hard Pursuit is his first novel.

NOTE FROM BARRIE TAYLOR

Word-of-mouth is crucial for any author to succeed. If you enjoyed *Hard Pursuit*, please leave a review online—anywhere you are able. Even if it's just a sentence or two. It would make all the difference and would be very much appreciated.

Thanks!
Barrie Taylor

We hope you enjoyed reading this title from:

www.blackrosewriting.com

Subscribe to our mailing list – *The Rosevine* – and receive **FREE** books, daily
deals, and stay current with news about upcoming
releases and our hottest authors.
Scan the QR code below to sign up.

Already a subscriber? Please accept a sincere thank you for being a fan of
Black Rose Writing authors.

View other Black Rose Writing titles at
www.blackrosewriting.com/books and use promo code **PRINT** to
receive a **20% discount** when purchasing.